THE END OF THE STRAIGHT AND NARROW

THE END

OF THE STRAIGHT AND NARROW

STORIES BY DAVID McGLYNN

Southern Methodist University Press

Dallas

This collection of stories is a work of fiction. Names, characters, places, and incidents are either the product of the author's imagination or are used fictitiously.

Requests for permission to reproduce material from this work should be sent to:
    Rights and Permissions
    Southern Methodist University Press
    PO Box 750415
    Dallas, Texas 75275-0415

Cover photo: "The End of the Road" by Kenny Braun
Jacket and text design by David Timmons

Library of Congress Cataloging-in-Publication Data

McGlynn, David, 1976–
    The end of the straight and narrow : stories / by David McGlynn. — 1st ed.
      p.   cm.
    ISBN-13: 978-0-87074-550-8 (alk. paper)
    ISBN-10: 0-87074-550-6 (alk. paper)
    I. Title.
    PS3613.C485E53 2008
    813'.6—dc22   2008024272

Printed in the United States of America on acid-free paper

10   9   8   7   6   5   4   3   2

For my parents

Christians talk about the horror of sin, but they have overlooked something. They keep talking as if everyone is a great sinner, when the truth is that nowadays one is hardly up to it. There is very little sin in the depths of the malaise. The highest moment of a malaisian's life can be that moment when he manages to sin like a proper human. . . .

WALKER PERCY, *The Moviegoer*

CONTENTS

PART I

MOONLAND ON FIRE

HE WAITS BY THE TRUNK while Rhonda shares Christ with the skycaps. The skycaps wear pressed white shirts and black caps. There are two of them. They peer over Rhonda's shoulders at the yellow booklet squeezed between her thumbs. *Four Steps to Salvation.* "There is a gulf between God and Man," she says. Her voice is garbled some by the traffic and the plane passing overhead. Gary hopes it is Nolan's plane. Gary has circled LAX twice and doesn't want to go around again. Two years since he's seen his son, and he's thinking of everything that could go wrong at the last minute. Traffic could jam up and Nolan could grow tired of waiting, figure himself forgotten. The landing gear could break, a rogue wind shear could sweep across the runway from the Pacific, someone could have a gun stashed in a seat pocket. Just yesterday he saw a news report about a saw blade flying off the back of a truck and slicing through a windshield. Rhonda says he can expect a lot worse: when the Rapture comes, planes will fall from the sky. A gust of heat blasts his face and neck. Beside him a woman holds her hair in place with her hands. Cars emerge suddenly through the rippling haze. He hides his hands in his pockets and listens for the sirens, the explosions.

Rhonda's booklet is three-by-eight and has only four pages. She's on the second. "As far as the east is from the west," she says. She spreads her arms to illustrate the distance. Her breasts stretch the buttons of her rayon blouse. The booklet flaps at the end of her hand. "Farther than this," she says. "Much farther." The skycaps nod, their octagonal caps bobbing, visors glinting in the sun. "If you died today, do you know what would happen?" She has a way of saying that word, *know*, that leaves everything in doubt. The man on her right is sweating. He removes his cap and wipes his shaved head with his palm. Gary watches Rhonda wet her teeth with her tongue. Her teeth cant outward along the top row, and her upper lip always looks slightly pursed. She flips to the end and asks the skycaps, "What's stopping you from giving your life to Jesus?"

Gary wants her to hurry up. Nolan has met Rhonda only once, a disaster Gary would rather not repeat. Nolan and his sisters met Gary and Rhonda at a Mexican restaurant in Richardson, just north of Dallas. The restaurant was a storefront converted from a karate studio, the walls dressed up with colored rugs and sombreros, pralines wrapped in wax paper buried in the chips. Neutral territory. The divorce had been final for a little more than a week; he and Rhonda were leaving for California in three days. After the waiters walked away with the menus, Rhonda spread the *Four Steps* booklet on the table and said, "This could change your life forever." Nicole, seventeen, spat back, "I think you've done that already," and stormed out without waiting for her lunch. Natalie, eleven, went with her, her bottom lip pushed up into her mouth, her chin clenched like a fist. Gary didn't chase after them. He tried to send back their food, but the waiter said he couldn't. Nolan ate both his own plate and Natalie's—shoveling big spoonfuls of rice and refried beans to keep from talking—and took Nicole's home in a box.

As the baggage-claim doors hiss open and shut, it scares Gary to think that he might not recognize his son. Nolan might walk right past him and he wouldn't know it. Gary turns his mouth toward his shoulder to pray, but stops when he catches a little girl staring at him. Then he sees Nolan pass through the doors, an enlarged version of the child he left behind: sixteen now and a good three inches taller, his arms long and wiry, his jawline speckled with patchy stubble. He wonders how his daughters look, how much weight, if any, Nicole has gained her first two years of college and whether or not Natalie has begun to wear makeup, if Sharon allowed her to pierce her ears. Such little things make us into different people. He thinks of Sharon, too, the point of her nose and the pouty upper lip she passed along to Nolan—how many men she has dated, how many she has slept with, how many have awakened to the sound of his children among the other noises in the house.

Nolan carries a backpack and an army-issue duffle bag, a green tube packed tight as a bomb. He shifts the duffle from his right to his left and extends his hand. He squeezes hard. "Hey, Dad."

"How was the flight?"

"Okay. They showed a movie."

"Anything good?"

Nolan shakes his head. "It passed the time."

"You made it," Rhonda says, suddenly beside him. Gary flinches, and when he turns he sees that her cheeks and neck are flushed. The gospel does this to her. One of the skycaps stands with his arms crossed over his chest, the other with his hands in his pockets. They both look a little dazed. Rhonda says, "The Company of Heaven just got a little more crowded." Gary feels Nolan stiffen beside him; a vein emerges on the underside of the arm holding the duffle. Gary is almost thankful to see the airport police two cars back, the officer's tongue extended to the tip of his pen. Gary reaches for Nolan's bag and says, "Let's go before I get a ticket."

. . .

Four freeways take them south and west to the Pacific Coast Highway. The highway crosses through the state park, bronzed hills above the road, and a rocky beach below it. Gary takes the first left and turns onto a street filled with cottages built in the fifties, but renovated to include rooftop balconies and backyard guesthouses and small squares of groomed lawns. Among them, Gary's house looks out of place. It looks like the house in a movie where children go in but do not come out. The wood shingles over the roof and walls are rotted and splintered, the white paint weathered yellow-gray. The front yard is a pit of weeds and cracked dirt, and brown skeletons of sun-murdered ivy snake up the walls to the crumbling chimney. Several panes in the diamond-light front windows are broken, black holes scattered against the glare.

Nolan shields his eyes and turns his head. Gary is embarrassed by the house. He can't believe he ever thought of bringing his daughters here. It's all he and Rhonda can afford, and even it is a stretch. Rhonda works at a church on the inland side of the state park. Her job pays very little, and Gary's still got lawyer bills and Sharon's credit cards from before the divorce and Nicole's college tuition, all on top of the 18 percent of his paycheck deducted each month by the Texas Child Support Division.

Next door, an orange-haired woman paces behind the glass walls of a porch overlooking the driveway. Rhonda climbs out of the backseat and waves. "That's Aggie," Gary tells Nolan. "She's been here since the street was built. Nothing gets by her." Aggie's house isn't renovated. Gas heaters have been added to the porch, and security lights installed on her front walk, but the shutters and clapboard siding are original, clean, and well kept. Her fig tree is manicured to keep the overripe fruits from landing on the hood of her car. Her car is a Mercedes, typical of the street, only an old one, a diesel.

. . .

Clouds sock in the coastline the next morning. Nolan can see a stripe of blue over the hills of the state park, but overhead is gray and colorless. He spends the morning cutting branches from the oleander, the thorny stems pricking his neck and arms. He sits on a pile of bricks beneath the avocado tree, elbows propped on his knees, while he chows down a ham sandwich and an orange and a handful of Ruffles. Chewing, he looks up and studies the small black fruits dangling above him and the discolored lemons hanging over the fence. No one has fruit trees in Dallas. After lunch he climbs into the avocado tree and cuts away the dead limbs. He makes a pile of branches near the top of the driveway. Trash pickup is the next morning. "Wait until the neighbors set out their cans," his father told him. "Then find the ones with room left to fill."

His lungs burn, and at the end of the day he coughs deeply. "It's the pollution," his father says, "though out here we just call it smog." And fire. As Nolan works his way from the backyard to the front, the air smells always like burning wood. The air is clouded with it, but he isn't sure if it's the smell of smog or of something else. He's thankful when the yards are cleared and he can move inside to begin ripping up the carpet and the linoleum. Beneath the floor, he finds nails buried in the wood and pulls them out with a hammer claw. It is dirty, hot work, on his hands and knees, the hammer rusted and loose on the handle, the paint scraper he uses to chisel off old adhesive buckled in the center. He cannot say exactly what he expected for the summer, but he knows it was different from this. He had imagined himself doing something closer to construction, rebuilding an old house one room at a time, a craftsman unbothered by solitude. Instead he feels lonely, anonymous. Neighbors passing by the house don't notice him, or else they glance quickly then look away. Aggie moves naked through her house, from her kitchen window to her glass porch, unconcerned about being seen. His father kisses Rhonda in front of him, presses his lips to her neck and circles her waist with his arms and whispers in her ear while she's standing at the sink, as though Nolan isn't in the room. His father and mother were never like that, and as strange as it may have been to watch his parents kiss, it is worse to watch one parent kiss a stranger. Worse still is watching his father and Rhonda, his lips on her lips, her ear turned to his chest. Such a small movement, but it is the root of everything—the reason his father left Texas, and the reason he is here.

There's a queen-size bed in the master bedroom, the bottom half of a bunk bed for him in another room, a square table and a line of chairs set down in a ragged crescent across the living room's wooden floor. No TV, no stereo, not even a couch. Nolan remembers his father leaving Texas with his clothes stuffed into three Hefty bags, his business suits laid across the backseat of his car, but he expected they would have bought a few things. When he asked why they didn't have more, Rhonda said, "You shouldn't put new wine into old wineskins." He knew that was from the Bible, and it kept him from asking more.

• • •

She shares Christ during her lunch break at one of the fast-food joints crowded together near the freeway: Arby's, Burger King, Carl's Jr., Del Taco—she likes to go alphabetically. She's careful not to draw too much attention. She can't afford to get thrown out. The church where she works is just a mile up the street. Before she was with Gary, she didn't care about such things; she was happy to get thrown out of a restaurant, even arrested, for Jesus. She approached people in lines at the movie theater and the supermarket, rode the bus through some of Dallas's worst neighborhoods just so she could talk to people on their way home. It was a particular kind of rush, the last deep breath before speaking, the strange fear in the eyes that turned to look at her, the words that seemed to come from a point outside herself, as though listening to herself on tape. When it came to bringing people to Christ, there was nothing she wouldn't sacrifice—her pride, principles, even her body. One time, on a bus through South Dallas, she approached a man with a gun sticking out of his jacket, an empty space where his top row of teeth used to be. The way he swept his hand across his lips and chin reminded her of Kirk Dunham, and that was enough to convince her.

Kirk Dunham was her high school boyfriend. He ran track fast enough that North Texas offered him a scholarship, but he wanted to fly helicopters. He wrote to her once a week from Fort Rucker, at first all about the machines and what he was learning to do in them, and some of his letters arrived with words, even entire lines, blacked out. Later he wrote to her about his weekend visits to Pensacola and the things he dug out of the ground outside the barracks: a sand dollar, a three-legged starfish, two bottle caps joined with wire. "I am standing on what was once the ocean," he wrote. "Every day I feel farther away."

After Alabama it was Hawaii, and this time Rhonda went with him. Before he took her to quarters, he took her to the chapel at Ala Moana. The pastor asked for a marriage license, and when Kirk said he didn't have it, the pastor said to get one and come back. In his dress greens still stiff after three flights and eighteen hours, his hair neatly shaved beneath his cap, Kirk produced a roll of twenties and said, "Marry us before God. We'll get the license and bring it back next week." Five dollars more bought them leis made from real orchids, wet, perfumed petals that clung to Rhonda's neck and the skin beneath her jaw. The pastor's secretary lent her two hair clips to fix her bangs, then stood as her maiden of honor. The breeze flapped the hem of Rhonda's skirt against her calves and pressed her blouse tight against her belly. They said their vows on the beach, her sandals set beside Kirk's shoes on the edge of the sidewalk. She worked her toes down into the sand until they disappeared. She never let go of Kirk's hand.

With a ring on her finger and an apartment in the junior officers' quarters, the piece of paper from the state seemed less necessary. She was Rhonda Dunham, and everywhere she went, she wrote it: at the commissary and the post office, into the fogged mirror when she stepped from the shower, into a plate of ketchup. In bed, she scrawled her initials into Kirk's stomach with her fingernail until his skin turned red and raised. "What's that?" he asked.

"My initials," she said. "RD."

"RD's a helicopter maneuver. Rapid Deceleration. You use it in emergencies. Pull back hard and flare the nose, slows you right down." He laughed, rolled to an elbow. "Sounds like what happens in bed. Rapid Deceleration. I never thought of it that way until now."

"What are the others?" she said. "Your maneuvers. I want to know them all."

He told her about slope and running takeoffs, steep approaches, hovering autorotation, runaway clutches, and ditching. Ditching was a last resort; helicopters fly lower than planes, which leaves less time to get out. She remembered the word when the major came to her door. Kirk's helicopter had gone down in an area called Penguin's Bank, off of Molokai. "Training run," the major said, "we're still not sure what happened."

"Could he have ditched?"

The major lifted his eyebrows. "I'm impressed you know what that is." He told her the cutter found the wreckage with the bodies of the crew still strapped into their seats. The rotor blade had curled through the windshield. It should have pinned Kirk inside or else cut him in two. But it didn't. He wasn't there.

They were married for eight days, though not in the eyes of the army. Kirk's uniform, the folded American flag, even the certificate that declared him dead were shipped back to his parents. Rhonda took a commercial flight home. She landed in Dallas just ahead of a thunderstorm, the air charged and thick, the horizon burning, strange in its own way but familiar enough that it left her uncertain about whether or not she had ever left. There was her bedroom as it had been, her hair still netted into the bristles of her brush, her prom corsage pressed flat and brown. At night she replayed all that had happened—the major's knock on her door, his big hands cupping her shoulders, the way he folded Kirk's T-shirts into rectangles and his pants into squares—but in the morning her eye caught a single blade of the ceiling fan, watched it spin around, and she wondered if she'd dreamed everything. Maybe she missed him hard enough to conjure him home from Fort Rucker. Maybe he never existed at all.

• • •

Gary dreams of Sharon hovering in the dark above him, her face visible, but not her hands, though he can feel her pressing against his chest and belly, his thighs and balls, his fingers and toes. Every touch leaves a red mark, a handprint, his skin red-hot. He dreams of Sharon sometimes, dismantled like this, and of his daughters separated from him by missing staircases or rooms without doors, their voices growing distant as they recede into the house. He wakes up drenched with sweat, desert air pressing back against the coastal fog. Through the open porthole windows along the ceiling he can hear the ocean, the faint crash and swish. Rhonda is asleep beside him, her crooked teeth chattering *ratt-tatt-tatt, ratt-tatt-tatt.*

In the bathroom he washes his hands and face. He sees a yellow Post-it stuck to the mirror, Rhonda's slanted writing, and the verse—he doesn't know where in the Bible it comes from—*Train a child in the way he should go.* She's been leaving notes for him all summer, in his wallet and shoes, wrapped around his car keys. She means, *Talk to Nolan.* He promised he would be the one to share Christ with Nolan, but he hasn't yet worked up the courage. He knows Nolan has heard an earful from his mother about how Gary's been brainwashed, and that's enough to make him nervous. He doesn't like the idea of pleading his sanity to his son. Though it is not why he hasn't done it yet.

From the time Nicole was seven until the year before he left, Gary ran four nights a week with Bucky Freeman, a computer consultant who lived three houses up. His girls were practically the same age as Gary's. Sharon played tennis on Tuesday nights with Bucky's wife. A jogging trail followed the greenbelt alongside the floodplain, skirted the pines, and then curved back to the country club, a six-mile loop. With a water break, it took about an hour. One night they hit the clubhouse striding and Bucky waved off a stop at the water cooler. They headed out along the golf cart paths where water sprayed in Vs over the fairways and tees. It was the farthest, and hardest, they'd ever gone, and when they stopped to stretch at the far corner of the course, Bucky stood humped over with his hands on his knees, breathing hard, sweat dripping from his chin and nose. Gary breathed through his teeth.

Bucky put his hands on his hips and walked in a circle. "You know anybody in actuarials?" he asked.

"Sure," Gary said. "I know folks."

"Heard of any openings? I think I'd be good at that."

"You thinking of a change?"

"More than thinking."

"And actuarial is your idea? You're doing better with what you've got going."

"I need something different," Bucky said. "Soon. Like tomorrow morning." He was breathing hard, high and shallow. Gary couldn't tell whether or not it was from the run.

Gary leaned his hands against a pine to stretch his calf. He looked at the thorns snagged in his laces rather than face Bucky. "I'm not so sure computer consulting translates all that well. Actuarial is more than computer work."

"That's not my only experience," Bucky said. He told Gary computer consulting was a sham. His real business was computer stealing. He stole from stores and businesses, from office parks, even from schools. If a job had a safe inside, he'd take it home and blowtorch it open in his garage. "I'm actually really good at getting them open." He'd wanted to quit for years, but his family was used to the lifestyle. "Look around," he said, pointing to the houses across the fairway, turquoise swimming pools glowing. "I don't have to tell you this don't come cheap." Gary agreed—some months it was all he could do. "I'd make a sharp actuarial if I could just get started," he said. "Since I know the ins and outs."

Gary asked how much he took in on a job. When Bucky said, "Up to thirty g's if I get lucky," Gary said, "I know a place."

He'd sold a policy to a customer-service call center on the outskirts of McKinney. The call center was the only business in a squat row of stucco buildings all alone at the end of a brand-new road. "The street doesn't even have lights yet," Gary said. "And everything inside is state-of-the-art." He drove Bucky out to see it, and Bucky agreed it looked good. He told Gary to wear a light shirt and jeans ("two guys in all-black draw too much attention"); he knew which phone lines connected to the alarms, and to circle the block to see if cutting the wires had summoned the police. They cleaned out the place in half an hour. Gary waited in a Denny's while Bucky took the haul to the fence, and two hours later, just past three in the morning, Gary arrived home with five thousand dollars in his pocket, fifty one-hundred-dollar bills he counted in his garage, and then in his bathroom, and then in his closet where he stuffed the cash into the toe of a shoe. Naked in the tight space between his slacks and suit jackets, a narrow rectangle of light crawling across the carpet to Sharon's sleeping back, he thought of the day Natalie had stolen a doll from the Wal-Mart, how he had marched her back to the store and stood with his arms crossed while, sobbing and rubbing her eyes, she confessed to the manager. He had hated watching her cry and had wanted to pick her up, but he didn't. She needed to learn. Now he had not only undone his own teaching, but had gambled his entire life for what amounted to a twentieth of his annual income. All the rationalizations that had allowed him to get into the van and into the office, and out again, trip after trip, bottomed out. *I'm doing this for my family* was a line spoken in the face of regret, no different from *I killed my husband for my lover*, or *I went to war for my country*, or *I quit school for my children*. No one did anything for anyone, not really.

His crime colored everything. He quit running, gained twenty pounds, and was plagued by strange, pulsing pains that started in the arch of his foot and traveled up his hamstring to his groin. He cupped himself in the shower and winced. He was too nervous to sleep and too afraid to sit in the living room, and instead lay in bed listening to his bedroom walls echo the distant howls of sirens traveling over the country roads beyond the neighborhood, certain they were growing louder and closer. The newspaper's slap against the front door shocked him awake. Sharon's eyes were full of vague contempt, as though she knew, somehow. He brushed his teeth with the lights off and tied his neckties in the car with the rearview mirror angled downward so he could only see his hands working the knot.

And everything that had once seemed impossible was no longer. He'd had coffee with Rhonda before and had never once considered it anything other than business. She sold office supplies; he ran an insurance agency. Now he listened to her talk about Jesus while tracing the lines in her upturned palm with his middle finger, studying the gold cross that plunged into the crease of her blouse. It wasn't until they were in bed that he found himself trying, but failing, to confess. He told her *I've broken every commandment* and *My life's in a ditch* as he sobbed against her stomach, but he never could say exactly what he'd done. Running her fingers through the back of his hair, she asked him if he wanted to pray. He said okay and repeated after her, word for word, one sentence at a time. When she said "Amen," he said "Amen," and then she kissed him one more time, harder than before, hard enough their teeth touched and their chins pressed together, hard enough for him to know he'd done an awful thing.

. . .

He finds Nolan up early, drinking coffee in a chair on the back patio. The sun casts a freckled shadow through the oleander and the towels hanging on the line. Nolan asks, "What are you up to today?" He knows Gary goes to church. Rhonda has told him not to miss the opportunities the Lord presents, so Gary says, "Come with me. Just check it out. We'll go to brunch after."

Nolan nods. "Okay."

The Church Without Walls overlooks the highway and the east side of the park. The building is square and made entirely of glass with thin strips of steel between the panes. Gary tells Nolan the pastor wants people driving by to see inside. Night services are held three nights a week, all the lights on, the church glowing above the highway. Above the entrance a banner reads, "I AM NOT ASHAMED OF THE GOSPEL." The floors are wooden and scuffed. Black streaks go in every direction. Rhonda sits on the stage in a white high-backed chair shaped like a throne. She lifts her eyebrows when she sees them, and smiles. Gary leads Nolan to the front row of chairs. They sit beside Amelia, a young woman with very straight, very long, very black hair. She's married to the pastor, the young man standing on the stage in a pink shirt, fitting a microphone clip over a button. To the left, the band is warming up, a drum set, a guitar, a piano, three women in matching blue dresses with tambourines resting against their hips. Nolan says, "What does she do here again?"

"She's the children's pastor."

"Without kids of her own? How does she know what to do?"

"She teaches them how to share Christ. She's got kids as young as four years old doing it in their preschools."

"Isn't that illegal? Separation of church and state?"

"Not in preschool."

Nolan folds his arms across his chest and waits, quiet. Gary watches him watch a balding man in a burgundy shirt pick up the guitar, study his hands as he positions them on the fret bar, and then stroke out an electric wail. The congregation leaps to its feet and the glass windows begin to vibrate. "Whoa," Nolan says. "Is this church or a concert?" A screen descends from the ceiling, displaying the words of the song in blue letters: *I waited for the Lord on High . . . I waited and He heard my cry.* The singers bounce the tambourines against their hips, and some in the congregation have tambourines too, with gold-and-silver streamers that ripple through the air. Amelia unfurls a length of purple ribbon from a glittered wand, waves the tip around her black hair and dances inside the coil, one foot over the other, shoulders and hips liquid. Rhonda dances beneath the glowing words, her skirt sweeping across the floor, her arms folded against her ribs. Gary doesn't dance, not with Nolan there. He says, "This is only at the beginning and the end. Bear with it, I know it's different." It's different for Gary, too: after two years he hasn't caught on to the rhythms of this music, to the grown men crying behind him, to the teenagers with their hands clasped together as they jump up and down, to the shouts of *Yes, Jesus!* that come from nowhere and everywhere.

Rhonda says, *God blesses those who praise His name.* But he can't quite bring himself to do it.

A hand brushes his arm. When he turns his head, Amelia seizes his wrist and pulls him into the aisle, spins him twice around, leading him. He shuffles his feet, stomps, tells himself, *I am not ashamed,* but telling himself he isn't only shows him that he is. He looks back and sees Nolan's eyes upon him, narrowed, judging everything he sees. Gary wants to stop, but he can't. Amelia has him and will not let go.

• • •

Lightning sparks fire in the mountains to the north and east, the flames fanned by the Santa Ana winds. The air is crisp-dry and hot, trapped beneath a diffused copper haze, unrelenting. The smell of smoke is everywhere, falling steadily, the sun glowing red. "See?" Rhonda tells Nolan. "This is how it starts."

"What?"

"The End Times. *It will be revealed with fire, and the fire will test the quality of each man's work.*"

Nolan doesn't ask another question, but he can feel Rhonda's eyes upon him, waiting. He doesn't want to hear about the fires of Hell, or about Jesus, either. But later, he thinks the winds here feel different than in Dallas. They're hotter for one thing, and weighted in an odd way, as though the heat itself has a mass. Neighbors drag their trash cans to the street with their necks bent. His tools feel a few ounces heavier, as do the kitchen tiles, which he unpacks from the cardboard and organizes in stacks of four and six.

He spends a week tiling the kitchen floor and countertop, his hands crusted white, his knees callused. Nolan's father showed him how to mix and trowel the thinset and how to work the wet saw. He has a *Time-Life Complete Home Repair Manual* checked out from the library to figure out the rest. Each day is like the one before it and the one after, measuring and cutting, voices chittering on the radio, hot wind stirring the trees. One of these days is his seventeenth birthday. He checks the phone. It's working but doesn't ring. The mailman brings only junk and a catalogue for children's Bible songs. He's both surprised and not that his father doesn't remember. He walks to the Circle K and buys himself a Coors, a tallboy, sets three ones on the counter and waits for the change. "Find everything?" the clerk asks. "All I need," he says. The clerk doesn't ask for ID.

Nolan drinks the beer on the front steps, proud of himself for not reminding anyone of his birthday, for not dropping hints. He watches Aggie saunter naked through her kitchen door onto her glass porch. He studies her slack breasts and soft belly, the graying hair between her legs, her puckered ass when she turns her back. When she sees him staring she lifts an eyebrow and sets a hand on her hip, as if to say, "See anything you like?" Nolan lifts his can and goes back inside.

He's proud of what he has accomplished. The floor is level, each tile twice measured and squarely set, hardly a botched cut. He can't imagine any of his friends doing this kind of work. He can't even imagine his high school, the noise, the number of bodies.

That afternoon, in spite of himself, he calls his sister Nicole in Pennsylvania. He has never been to her school, but the pictures show clusters of ivy-covered buildings bathed in tree-softened sunlight, circles of sun on the lawns and the library's wide stone steps. Nicole lives in a house with three girls and four boys, with a couch on the front porch. Nolan considers hanging up before he presses the last number. Nicole picks up on the third ring.

"Well if it isn't Nolan," she says. "Mr. Benedict Arnold himself."

"Nice to hear your voice."

"Oh relax." Her voice sounds too twangy, laid on too thick. Her college is a place where a Texas girl could be loved for her accent and her blond ponytail and her fascination with snow. "So how is it in The Neighborhood of Make Believe?"

"Good." He hesitates. "A little lonely sometimes."

"Guess you should have thought of that. Think of how Mom feels."

"I wouldn't know. She hasn't called."

"Phones work two ways, Nolo." He hears a voice in the background and a can popping open. "Anyway, it serves you right. I hope it sucks there. I hope it's the worst summer ever."

"What's up your ass?"

"You called me. What did you expect?" Nolan doesn't have an answer. He should have known what his sister would say. She's been on their mother's side of the divorce since the beginning. Her boyfriend in high school had cheated on her not long after their father started up with Rhonda, and in Nicole's eyes there are criminals and there are victims, the two as separate from each other as earth from sky. Since his father left, his

mother has dated two men, both of whom Natalie has claimed were her
real father returned home from the army. Nolan has never known quite
where to stand. There have been days when he felt angry; others, night-
time most often, when sadness flooded in waves; still others when he felt
relieved, even happy, everything was over. No one sleeping on the couch,
no muffled sobs through the bedroom door. He watched television late
into the night and no one said a word.

"So," Nicole says, "any bumps on your head from her Bible?"

He thinks about his father dancing at church, his butt wiggling and his
eyes closed. Nicole wouldn't understand. "They haven't pressured me to
join anything, if that's what you're asking."

"Well don't get sucked in," she says. "Really, I can't believe you're even
there at all."

And why is he there? He is surprised she doesn't know. When his father
called in April to tell his mother he'd finally bought a place and wanted
Nolan and his sisters to fly out for a few weeks, his mother had said, simply, *No*, as businesslike as if she were ducking a telemarketer. Nicole was
staying in Pennsylvania, Nolan had a job lined up, Natalie had tennis
camp, and then softball camp, and then cheerleading camp, hardly a
weekend's break in between. "You want to see them, you fly here for a
weekend," she said. His mother stood with her back to him, the phone
squeezed between her jaw and shoulder, but Nolan could hear the echo of
his father's voice, pitched and desperate, loud for the first time in years.
"If Nicole has any plans of staying at her sweater-vest college," his father
said, "she'd better get her ass out here." His mother had shouted "Asshole!" and hung up the phone. An hour later, Nolan called his father himself and said he'd come for the entire summer if the girls could stay where
they were.

"You're going back, right?" Nicole says, backing down, her voice tinged
with worry, like his mother's on the way to the airport: *Don't forget where
you come from.* "Senior year is the best. You don't want to miss it."

"I think so," he says. "I'm pretty sure."

· · ·

She sees him everywhere. A man reading a newspaper at a bus stop will
crinkle his nose; a woman pushing a shopping cart will crack her knuckles by pulling her fingers forward from their sockets—she'll remember
Kirk did that to keep his hands nimble. At times it is as simple as the way

someone turns his head. This is where Kirk lives now, scattered among the bodies of strangers, and sharing Christ, she touches that lost part of him. She's never seen Kirk in Gary; two years of watching Gary dress and eat, two years of touching him, Kirk has never once shown up. Kirk's absence makes it possible to love Gary. Nolan is a different story. He wears Old Spice and uses Ivory soap. There have been days when she has come home to the smell of both wafting through the paint and dust so overwhelmingly she thinks she's fallen asleep in the car and reentered an old dream. Nolan's slight, soft drawl, his one eyebrow rising, the hunch of his shoulders when he sits in a folding chair and rests his elbows on his knees.

Ten weeks have passed and she can wait no longer. She leaves for lunch and doesn't come back. She arrives home resolved. The house smells of paint and plastic, and she hears a woman's voice talking quickly, then sighing, then talking again. She wants to call out Kirk's name. She's almost certain he would call back, *I'm here*. She walks from the kitchen to the living room to the hallway to the master bedroom, her bedroom, where she finds Nolan on a stepladder, his wrist flexed as he drags the brush in a precise line along the seam between the wall and the ceiling. The radio sits on the floor, turned loud enough to spit back static. "Hi!" she shouts, louder than she intends. Most people say her voice is too soft. Nolan jumps, smudges burgundy paint onto the ceiling. He presses both hands against the wall to keep from falling. "Jesus!" he says.

"Sorry," she says. "I didn't mean to scare you."

"I just wasn't expecting it." He holds up both palms. "You caught me red-handed."

She laughs, "Boy, it's hot!" Then, "I'll be right back." She removes her pantyhose in the bathroom and when she comes out, she drapes them over the end of the bed, still covered by a plastic tarp. Nolan's standing beside the ladder, the radio off. "Sorry I had it up so loud."

"It's okay." She hands him a can of soda. "Here, have a drink."

She watches his Adam's apple slide up and down. "Hits the spot," he says.

She opens the door to the patio. "Let's sit outside." Nolan shrugs, follows. She pulls two chairs together, one facing the other. Nolan sits, clicks his teeth on the rim of the soda can, and licks the sugar from his teeth. A spider climbs the air just behind his head toward the slats of the patio roof. Through the open doors Rhonda sees the legs of her pantyhose lift and settle in the dusty breeze. She says, "I've been meaning to ask you something."

"About Jesus?"

"That's right. Have you heard about what He did?"

"I'm from Texas."

"So then, what do you think?"

"It's a good story . . . especially the soldiers rolling dice. It's like watching TV when a tornado's chewing up the house next door."

"So you believe it? The crucifixion happened?"

"Sure, I guess. It happened."

She feels her hand shaking. She sets the soda on the ground and squeezes her fingers with her other hand. "If you died, do you know what would happen?"

"Hopefully that's a long ways off."

"You never know. Jesus will come like a thief in the night." Nolan hunches forward, nods. Rhonda feels his long exhale against her bare knee and thinks of Kirk's breath against her neck. She feels Kirk around her— his voice, his heat—she feels him reaching. *I'm here.* She is desperate to hear Nolan say *Jesus.* She says, "*Behold, I stand at the door and knock. All you have to say is 'Yes.'*"

Nolan shrugs. "Okay. Yes."

She takes his hand and squeezes, presses her fingers into the center of his palm. She digs in her purse for the booklet and quickly flips it to the prayer at the back. "Just read this aloud." Nolan holds the booklet between his thumbs and reads the entire paragraph in one monotone breath. But they are the right words, God the Father at the beginning, God the Son at the end. She stands, and when Nolan stands, she spreads her arms. Nolan steps forward cautiously. "Don't tell your dad about this," she says into his ear. "Let it be our secret."

• • •

Smoke drifts through the sliding door. Nolan's rolling paint onto the living room walls. The wooden floors are refinished, the ceilings scraped clean, the walls repaired. Nothing left to do but buy furniture. He sees the smoke drift through the oleander and the avocado tree, thin and gauzy, like stretched cotton. Flakes of ash land in the paint tray, gray-white floating on yellow. Beyond the fence, a cloud rises from the hills. In the distance he hears a siren, long and groaning as it climbs. Nolan watches ash fall against the wet wall, soak into the new paint. He waves a newspaper. Outside someone is yelling. He slides the door closed.

• • •

A highway patrolman turns Gary around at the northern entrance of the park, tells him to go back and wait. He can see lights up ahead, firefighters carrying axes in yellow coats and hats. He can see smoke rising. He tells the patrolman he lives on the other side and that his son is at home, but the patrolman says Gary can't get through. The police will evacuate when it's time.

He parks his car at an Albertson's and slips down an alleyway, which leads him to the beach on the north side of the park, a short crescent of sand to the rocks at the base of the cliffs. He can see a narrow trail through the boulders, foot-worn from fishermen, splotched with algae and barnacles. Five miles of this separate him from the pathway to his house, and he doesn't know the whole trail. Halfway in he could run into a point that juts into the water, impossible to walk around and too dangerous to swim. He's wearing khakis and loafers. He imagines the fire crews reaching his street and looking upon his still-dilapidated house as the one they can let burn. He imagines the firefighters drawing the flames toward it, telling one another it's abandoned, Nolan somewhere inside.

When the sand ends he must move on all fours. The descents are steep and he must sit and slide down on his pants. Cracks are filled with speckled anemone and purple urchins, which prick and sting his fingers. He is taking too long, moving too slowly; his house is probably already lost. Everything is already lost. By the time he rebuilds, or finds another house he can afford, by the time he has walls and a roof and space for his family, too much time will have passed for his daughters to remember him, let alone think of coming to him. They will recall only fragments, his rubber boots in the garage, his peanut butter jars filled with nails and screws, the smell of his coffee on the Christmas morning when they circled one another in the cul-de-sac on polished new bicycles—Nolan swooping with a foot extended to kick his sisters' front tires, Natalie squealing, Nicole reaching to slap him, Gary standing on the lawn and shouting, *Be careful!* All fleeting things. Each Christmas will erase the one before it—

new presents, new clothes, new men sitting cross-legged on the living room floor doling out gifts. Gary will evaporate from their lives like the fog on the lawns that balmy year, which like everything else, no one will remember.

The last wisps of pink in the sky have blackened and the clouds have grown thicker. Flakes of ash fall from the smoke, covering the rocks and waves and the crown of Gary's head with a gray pall. Gasping, Gary finds a smooth outcropping of rock near a tide pool, places himself belly first against it so that his lips are inches from the water. The air is cool, fresh. His face ripples in the mirrored surface, his hair gray around his temples, his cheeks sunken. He's thirsty, but the water around him is salted and sour. His back is throbbing, his clothes ruined, and he's shivering as one wave after another crashes and sprays his back and neck and head. His faith is failing, if it was ever there, if what he claimed was faith was ever anything more than the echoes of regret and shame. His forehead touches the water, the wave his body makes lapping back against his skin. He coughs to disrupt his reflection. He doesn't want to watch himself cry.

• • •

Nolan watches the black clouds move across the sky, bottom-lit by the flames he cannot yet see. The windows of the houses on the hill glow copper. Small streams of water disappear into the billowing smoke. His neighbors watch the hills as they dart between their houses and their cars. They pack their trunks and backseats, strap surfboards to roofs, and then drive away. He's worried about his father, that he'll do something crazy like try to walk through the flames, or worse, turn and walk away and leave him alone in this mess. He wonders how long he should wait. If the fire makes it down this far, he figures he'll head for the beach, though he has avoided going in the ocean for most of the summer, frightened by the rocks hidden beneath the cold, black water, the thought of kelp tentacles climbing up from the deeps to tangle around his ankles. It scares him to think of entering the water, his last resort against the burning hills. A weak swimmer could get swept out and no one would notice.

Aggie raps against her porch windows, her orange head glowing in the firelight. "This is bad." She's almost yelling. "We used to get canyon fires in the sixties, but there weren't so many houses then. Now everybody and their great aunt want to live here . . . for the scenery." She looks Nolan up and down, then the house. "You come jump in my pool if it gets dangerous."

"I'm going to the beach if it comes to that."

"Good idea. Don't try to be heroic. It's just a house."

"It's not even mine."

She turns her head to the doorway. "CNN's made it. Come have a look."

"Are you dressed up there? All the way?"

"Please." She peers over the rim of her glasses. "I've been naked with the best. Don't think all I've done is hang around this house."

But inside, it looks as though she has. Every corner is filled with furniture, bowls of avocados and lemons, oak shelves that take up an entire wall, filled with colored bottles, a tarnished tuba on its side near the seaward window. "You play?"

"Not like I used to." She wiggles her hips and bounces her hair as she moves from the cupboard to the freezer, her white shorts high on her waist. She drops ice into two glasses. "The tuba belonged to a friend. He was in the theater. I had a lot of friends in the theater. He's gone now, so I keep it. The cat sleeps in the bell." Nolan imagines her Siamese sliding through the narrowing pipes, lubricated by the residue of saliva, folding back its ears and narrowing its shoulders to crawl deeper inside.

Aggie turns up the TV in the kitchen, pours gin over the ice, and then vermouth, which spreads downward through the glass. Nolan can see his father's house through the window, still dilapidated and weathered, a lot of work left. Aggie hands him a glass. "For courage. Don't rat me out."

"Don't worry." He clinks his glass against hers.

She glances at the TV, says, "Look at this. It's just up the hill."

Flames consume the center of the screen, growing out of the windows and skylights of the house. A woman stands in the street with her arms clutched across her chest, while firefighters in yellow coats drag hoses across the pavement. "She may not have had much time," Aggie says. "These things can move fast. Say 'fire' and you're dead." The camera focuses on the roof in time to see a skylight pop, a muted *oh shit* from the firefighter standing with his back to the camera. The camera shakes as the reporter runs back, and then the feed cuts to the anchor in Atlanta, bleached hair, green collar upturned. "Jesus," Nolan says.

"That's right," Aggie says. "These sorts of things can make you see God in a hurry. Better come clean while you can."

This is, he realizes, the first conversation he's had with someone outside his family since he left Texas. He gulps from the glass and thinks of telling her how he studied her body, but he doesn't know how to say it, so instead he says, "I told Rhonda I accepted Jesus, but I didn't. I prayed with her, but I kept my fingers crossed. The whole thing just seems crazy." He pauses long enough to watch Aggie's cat leap up onto the table, look toward him, and then look away. "Also, I think my older sister is a bitch."

"Fair enough," Aggie says. "Most older sisters are." She jangles the bracelets on her wrist. "My turn. I was with a married man for thirty years. Everyone knows that now. What I don't tell anyone is that I bled him dry. I promised to call his wife if he didn't keep me happy. He bought me my jewelry, two cars, my china set, even this house. His children didn't have money for college. When I die, this house is going to them." She rolls her bottom lip between her teeth. "You think that's the right thing to do? I don't want his kids to think less of him. We weren't married, but in a way, we were."

He thinks of Nicole telling stories at her college, the words *father* and *adulterer* in the same sentence, in every sentence, the girl or boy seated across from her nodding in sympathetic disbelief. *She doesn't know anything,* Nolan thinks. "They'll be glad to have it," he says. "It could turn their lives around."

"Looks like your dad made it home," Aggie says. Nolan follows her eyes to the street. His father stands beneath the streetlamp, the halo of light snowy with ash.

Nolan stands on his toes and to peer over the glass walls that surround Aggie's porch. "What happened to you? Where's the car?"

"North side of the state park," Gary says. "I walked the beaches from there."

"I haven't heard from Rhonda."

"She's probably still out at the church. All the roads are closed. She's better off." Nolan looks down the street. A few dark shadows stand in the road; a few others scurry back and forth. The sky over the hills is throbbing. Burning embers of shingles and siding drift through the air, glowing with heat. Nolan sees a flicker, a pulse, and then the flames appear, a yellow line behind the houses. It's bright enough to light the driveway and the tip of his father's nose. "Hurry down here," his father says. "Pick up everything not attached to the house and put it inside."

"I did that."

"Everything else then."

"I did that, too."

"Just hurry down."

Gary runs to the garage and comes out with a bandana tied over his mouth and nose, his pant legs tucked inside black rubber boots. He climbs up the trellis to the sidewall and onto the roof, then calls down for Nolan to hand him the hose. Nolan turns it on full, but the pressure is weak and only a trickle leaves the spout. "Too much water on," Gary says. He paces back and forth, wetting down the shingles and spreading the water with the sole of his boot. A sheet of newspaper floats overhead, rippling in the air as it passes over the avocado tree. The tree lists in the wind and releases its unripened fruits, small black grenades that bounce and roll over the driveway. An ember lands in a palm tree and the whole thing goes up in a whoosh. A branch breaks off and whips in the wind. "Better go inside," Gary says. Nolan paces the driveway below, looking up.

"I can help."

"It's not safe." Gary hunches his shoulders and coughs. "You've got to pack up a few things. One box for each of us, and make sure they're light." Nolan turns his foot and his sole sticks to the blacktop. He sees his father press his thumb over the mouth of the hose to force more pressure through the nozzle, and lean back on his heels. He remembers his father standing in this old, relaxed pose to water his mother's zinnia beds. His father squats near the chimney and lets the water run and spread across the shingles and down the walls to the driveway. It hisses as it steams. He watches his father's lips move against the wind as flakes of ash land on his eyebrows and the crown of his head. He watches his father pace and slap at his chest and yell at the flames and wind. His old father, the father who read *Architectural Digest* and *Forbes* in the supermarket, and arranged his ties by color on a revolving rack, is now gone. Nolan knows it. He watches the fire catch the power line above the oleander at the back of the yard and climb up the wooden pole. The wire sparks and the streetlights flash dark, and a house one street above them starts to burn, the summit of its roof spewing smoke and oil, flakes of insulation floating upward and disappearing. Aggie's windows are black. Nolan goes inside.

With the lights out and the table and chairs piled in the center of the living room, the house feels emptier than ever, as though his summer of work and sweat and solitude has come to nothing. He stuffs his clothes in a backpack, scoops shorts and T-shirts and golf shirts into another bag for his father, and then sets two cardboard boxes in the center of the living room floor. He isn't sure of what to save. There is a clock, a frame without a photograph, an award plaque from his father's previous job. He slides open Rhonda's dresser drawer and grabs a fistful of underwear, trying not to look and folds them inside a pair of jeans, and a pink blouse from her closet. He can hear his father's boots pacing back and forth above him. Water trickles down the windows, then slows, and then stops. He goes into the bathroom, wets his hair in the toilet, pulls off his shirt and dunks it in the water and puts it back on with the collar over his mouth and nose. He sits down in the bathtub and waits for his father to climb down from the roof, to come find him, to call out, *Now Nolan, run.*

· · ·

They watch from inside the sanctuary, kneeling shoulder to shoulder in a line near the windows. They light candles, touching wick to flame and passing it down the line, fire a barrier against fire. Rhonda, at the far end, watches the light swim up every neck and chin, more than a dozen in all, the tip of every nose glowing as it leans over the flame. They sing together, *Silently I stand before the Lord . . . Waiting for Him to rescue me,* the song's usually slow rhythm hurried now by the helicopters chopping across the blackened sky. A light shines through the glass and sweeps away. The man beside her sings out of rhythm. Rhonda touches the window. The glass is hot against her palm.

They sing one song after another, and in between, they pray. The pastor, at the head of the line, asks for the Lord's protection, for His hand to stretch across the sky and bring rain, for the fires to draw back up the hillside. Amelia asks for the church to be left standing when the fires at last die out, for people to see that Jesus and only Jesus has the power to save. There are no instruments. When the prayer ends, a voice begins to sing and the others join in. Some keep their eyes closed the entire time, but for most the singing is a time to watch the windows. The wind shifts harder west and keeps the fire from traveling farther down the hillside. Rhonda hears long exhales down the line; she is the only one who lives on the other side of the park.

The man beside her prays, "May we make Your will our desire," and the line of voices answers, "Your will be done."

All through the next song, she thinks of Gary and Nolan, the two of them inside the house as it burns. She thinks of the house, of the breezes across the kitchen tile and her bare feet in the mornings, and of the afternoons when she's returned home to find entire rooms suddenly colored and new, and of the little town that has by accident become her home, where bearded men watercolor in the park and cars roar up and down her street and shops sell paintings too decadent for her to hang inside her house and bathing suits too skimpy for her to wear, and when the song ends and it's her turn to pray, she presses her forehead to the floor and asks God to save it all. "Save the men who dye their hair and the women who inject collagen into their lips and silicone into their breasts and have the flesh You gave them sucked from their hips and thighs. Save the rich who still believe they can carry their gold through the eye of the needle. Save the alcoholics sleeping on the beaches and the junkies shooting up beneath the boardwalk. Save the sodomites kissing beneath the café umbrellas and holding hands as they walk down the street. Save the activists marching with banners and pickets, who throw stones and blood at the construction crews for widening the canyon road. Save the Hare Krishnas in their pink robes and shaved heads, leaping and drumming until all hours, calling out to false gods and graven idols. Save Aggie who crossed her index fingers when I tried to share the Gospel with her. Save those who pass out condoms in schools and maps to abortion clinics, who want to eradicate every mention of Your name unless it is profane. Save the haughty and the tan. Save the evil, save the promiscuous, save the murderous. Just save my house."

"Rhonda," the pastor says, his voice sheathed in darkness. "Are you okay?"

She feels the blood pool in her forehead and cheeks, and the heat from the glass spread from the tip of her head to the back of her neck and down her spine to her legs. She is tired of praying. Her back and her knees are sore, and she feels her exhaustion throb down her spine. And she is tired of the illusion that this life is an illusion, that the vacuous hole in her chest she calls a soul is somehow more real than clothes and food and warm beds and other bodies, and she's tired of supplicating a God who allowed her only eight days of illegal marriage and who has now brought fire to the door of her house. If this is how it ends—if this is The End—she wants no part of it. "I've praised Your name long enough," she says to the floor. "I've brought enough people to Your feet. Save my house or it is over between You and me."

"Rhonda," the pastor says. "*Rhonda.*" The man beside her touches her elbow. But she doesn't feel it. She's inside her house now, moving from room to room, spreading her arms to block each wall. "Burn not this one, nor this one, nor this one . . ."

• • •

The beach is already crowded when Gary and Nolan arrive, and loud with excitement. There are more people than Nolan expects, neighbors from the street he thought had left hours ago. Where were they in the smoke? Most are clustered along the railings of the lookout point above the cliff, the ocean churning over the rocks, the little town spread along the coastline to the south. The flames have moved toward downtown and the canyon road, once-safe hills now on fire, the once-imperiled street now quiet. Nolan watches a single light—a motorcycle headlight, maybe, or a flashlight, it's hard to tell from this distance—descend out of the smoke, and cross the highway, and disappear. Nolan thinks of the other people in other houses staring up into the flaming sky, running inside to throw together boxes of photographs and letters and mantel clocks, soaking their clothes in their toilets. All around him his father's neighbors shake hands and embrace in hearty, backslapping hugs. A man and a woman kiss with the woman's back bent over the rail, her arm slung around the man's neck. Nolan thinks of A&M football games after a touchdown—the cannon, the smoke, the mass kissing. It's one of the things he'll miss about Texas. One man, whom he had seen driving a silver Maserati up and down the street, whose name he doesn't know, punches his shoulder and says, "I knew after all that work you'd done on that house, we'd make it through. It just wouldn't have been right for it to burn."

Nolan shakes his head, "No, it wouldn't have been right." The man laughs, but Nolan doesn't. His father leans back against the railing with his arms crossed on top of his head, both armpits stained dark. His father drops his arms to his waist and turns around, faces the fire. "It was close," Nolan says.

Gary nods. "Yes, it was." He drops his head and says, "I gave it all up.

On the roof. I told God he could take the house and he could take Rhonda and"—he looks at Nolan sideways and bites his lip—"you, too. I turned off the hose and I waited. The oleander went up fast and so did the telephone pole, but then the winds shifted and the fire drew back." He looks at Nolan as though searching for the right word, or, as though afraid of the word he has already found. "It was *something*."

It doesn't come out quite right, but in the coming weeks and months he'll search for better words. He'll tell his story to the men who deliver the furniture, and to the man who installs the cable, and to his daughters when they fly out to visit. "Right to our door," he'll say, "and then it stopped." He'll show Natalie the ashes embedded in the crevices of the windowsills and in the grooves of the floorboards, and the faint black rings pressed into the cupboard paint. "We were saved," he'll tell her.

"No joke," Nolan will say, corroborating. "My freakin' shoes melted."

Natalie won't believe her father yet, and Nicole will roll her eyes, but it won't matter. Gary will touch the sky and feel the hot air and believe. Late summer will come, lightning will flash in the inland hills, and for an hour, for a night, the sky will smell of fire. They'll be eating dinner on the back patio when smoke drifts through the oleander. A napkin will flutter, a broomstick will slide and fall, a candle will hush itself out as though afraid of its larger, more ferocious self. Rhonda will stand up, turn her nose to the hills, and watch the lower sky grow orange and shadowed. Nolan and Gary will climb the trellis to the roof to look, the girls staring up from the table. "See anything?" Nicole will ask, and Nolan will only shrug. They won't see flames, or even smoke. Just that low humming horizon, the Santa Ana winds blowing hot out of the desert, Aggie lying naked beside her swimming pool—the entire world close to bursting.

LANDSLIDE

THE EARTH MOVED ON A NARROW BEND in the Pacific Coast Highway, about a half hour north of Cayucos State Beach. It was the kind of place I had seen only in coffee-table books on *America's Great Scenic Drives.* Cypress trees leaned sideways over the cliffs' edges, which alone amazed me, and dark bushes of chaparral speckled with yellow and purple carpeted the hills. Driving home that way after playing golf had been Greg's idea, and when the traffic backed up I had no idea what we were in for. It was an El Niño year and a deluge of rain had saturated the soil and overfilled the runoff channels. Down in Los Angeles, the concrete riverbeds ran full for the first time I could remember. A small earthquake, maybe 2.5 on the Richter, too small to feel, was all it took to send who-knows-how-many tons of mud and rocks tumbling down the gully, wiping out the road, and pouring over the side of the cliff to the little rocky beach a hundred feet below. I have said, in the countless times I've told this story, the road was higher than that, more like a thousand feet, but it was a hundred. I'm trying to stay true to the facts. Debris piled up on the highway, sloping toward the edge of the road in line with the hillside. A blond graft was missing from the otherwise brown hill above. How anyone could have survived getting buried beneath it is something I can only explain as the grace of God.

However, people did survive, at least for a while, and somehow managed to call for help. This is one aspect of the story that seems improbable, and I am not quite clear on the details. It was what I heard at the time, and being awestruck by the mound of earth I had walked nearly a mile from our parked car to see, I didn't think to question it. Greg and I arrived to see people already digging, one man with a short-handled shovel and the rest, maybe a dozen others, using tire irons and buckets to pound and scoop away the dirt. A woman was bent forward with her hair in her face, scooping between her legs with her hands while a man in a green cap stood beside the open door of his Dodge Ram talking into the square receiver of a CB, the coil stretched completely out of the cord. I could see other people standing on the other side of the slide, a crowd mirroring ours, but I couldn't hear their voices. The slide was a massive, consuming wave of tree roots and earth and rock that had crashed over the roadway, and all that lay beyond it seemed like a different country.

We were there for two minutes before the highway patrol arrived, a single car driven by a single officer with close-cropped hair and a yellow windbreaker over his beige uniform. When he stepped up to the edge of the road and looked down at the beach, his sleeves flapped in the wind and pressed against his arms and torso, revealing the bulk of the bullet-proof vest beneath his shirt. He appeared worried, which is an easy emotion to spot from far away; he rubbed his jaw with the heel of his palm and looked back and forth between the slide and the edge. He couldn't have been much older than I was at the time, but it was his responsibility to take control of the situation. He returned to his cruiser and sat down in the front seat and then spoke to us over the PA, kindly asking everyone to get back. He even said *Please.* Composing himself, he explained that the slide wasn't stable and that a simple shift could send more earth cascading down. He asked the people in the crowd to go back and wait at their cars. Those digging ignored him and kept right on with what they were doing. Greg and I wanted to help; it seemed better than just standing around. But despite every Good Samaritan impulse within us, every urge to sacrifice ourselves for the sake of strangers, neither of us was about to disobey the police.

A line of cars ahead of us tried to turn around and head back, but it wasn't long before a second officer rode by on a motorcycle and announced that the lane needed to stay open so emergency crews could get through. The road we were on was now closed and an officer was posted at the turnoff; anyone caught trying to go back before we were directed to would be ticketed. At that point, people surrendered to the wait, and though I was impatient to get home, I prayed I would surrender, too. People unfolded chairs and blankets and set out food, intent on picnicking. It wasn't the worst spot for such things. I heard eight different radios tuned to eight different stations, at least two in Spanish. A few hundred yards ahead of us in line, four young boys stood shoulder to shoulder throwing rocks over the water, doing all they could to outthrow each other.

This gave Greg the idea to hit a few balls. He popped the trunk and unsheathed his three-iron and got out his grocery sack filled with chipped-up balls from the driving range where he'd worked the previous summer. The balls were going to be thrown out; he never would have taken them without permission. The back of our dorm faced a grassy slope, too steep to build on, which bottomed out at a junior-high soccer field. Greg drove balls from the hill whenever he was bored or had a problem he couldn't figure out, one of the many things about him I never fully understood. That morning I'd played my first full round of golf at a tiny public course outside Pasa Robles, about a hundred miles west of Bakersfield, where we'd attended a wedding the night before. Golf was a sport I never had much talent for, and on that day especially I found it required much greater patience and concentration than I'd been prepared to give. But the Book of James instructs us to consider it joy when we encounter various trials, so I committed myself to learning, at least for the day.

I played with an old set of clubs borrowed from Greg's uncle. Greg taught me to grip the club with my thumbs down, to square my shoulders with my hips, my hips with the ball, and to go through this routine each time I stepped up to hit. One deviation and the ball went into the water or the trees, or into the grape vineyard beyond the course's perimeter. We took a break at the turn to eat lunch, two gigantic cheeseburgers spilling with lettuce and shredded carrots, and potato chips, and a dill spear that stained the paper plate green. When we were finished, Greg leaned back in his chair and closed his eyes, his spiked shoes crossed one over the other, his fingers interlaced across the stomach of his powder-blue golf shirt. I'd seen him sleep this way in the library and in the Basilica, our study commons, and seated at his desk in our dorm room. His sleep, even at night, appeared like a brief interlude between two greater, more consequential thoughts. I putted on the practice green while I waited for him to wake up.

• • •

The shoulder beside the car was six feet wide, and covered in weedy grass. Greg chopped at it with the head of his club in high strokes like a reaper until he cleared a small patch of dirt. He dropped two balls in the grass and pulled one back toward himself with his club head, then squared up, dug his shoes into the dirt, and did that thing that always made me laugh, no matter how many times I saw it: the little waggle of his butt that made him look like a duck. "Quack, quack," I said.

"Quiet." He kept his eyes fixed on the ball, then wound back and crushed it. The ball swam upward in the mist and carried forward against the stretched blue horizon, a white speck I lost for a moment in the sun and found again in time to watch it splash. The water near the shore was green-blue and full of rocks, fallen chunks of the cliff deposited by earlier landslides. I wondered how many God had placed there Himself when He created the earth, and on which day, and it gave me pause to think of the care God took with each minuscule detail. Greg's ball landed in the dark blue. "Nice shot," I said.

"See the spot you want to hit before you even swing. Make the ball go where you tell it." He pushed the second ball my way. "Let's see what you've got."

"Haven't I seen this in a movie? Two guys hitting golf balls into the ocean?"

"It's a beer commercial," he said. "The guys are in business suits, playing hooky from work, or something like that. 'One more for old times' is the slogan." He lifted an invisible beer and I did the same. We mimed the clink and swig. Then I tried to mime what I'd seen him do only a minute before, the grip, the stance, the waggle. I kept my head down and swung. The club nicked the top of the ball and sent it bouncing over the edge of the cliff. Greg fished another ball out of the sack and tossed it to me. Without scorn or sarcasm, he said, "Take a mulligan. That one never happened."

The mulligan was my favorite thing about golf. It was the perfect example of the first two verses of Psalm 32: "Blessed is he whose transgressions are forgiven, whose sins are covered. Blessed is the man whose sin the Lord does not count against him." Greg and I were seniors at Southland Pacific University, a Christian college perched on a hill on the south side of Los Angeles. Southland Pacific was an innocuous name for a conspicuous place. There wasn't a corner of the campus that lacked Christian intent or import. A wealthy judge had donated the land seventy years before to establish a school that would be "a light to the world"; our chapel was, in fact, shaped like a lighthouse. We joked that the water fountains were clean enough for baptism, and we had a thousand meanings for the initials SPU: Student Pastors' University, Sowing and Planting University, Savior's Pride University, Start Packing University (as almost every student spent time in the mission field). We never ran out of names, though most of us just called it SPEW, for more than math, which was Greg's major, or history, which was mine, or any other discipline, we were taught the Gospel, how to memorize whole New Testament books verse by verse, mnemonic exercises to help us quote them on command, ways to link the fifty major messianic Old Testament prophecies to Jesus, techniques for sharing Jesus with everyone we met. Professor Tulliver ended each Pagan Psychology class with the admonition: "Love your neighbor, share your faith." While other college kids went to Santa Monica or to Tijuana to drink and score, we went to witness. Our scores were measured not in phone numbers or drinks, but in souls, the tally of those I saved recorded on a sheet of paper taped to my closet door. One of my best lines was, "Heaven is like a party. God hands out invitations years in advance, and all you have to do is RSVP." It worked more times than you might think. I had a way with analogies and anecdotes, though back then I didn't call them anecdotes. Back then I called them parables.

I practiced my parables on the youth at Fisher's Church, just down the hill from SPEW, where I interned my senior year. The name came from Pastor Dale Fisher, who founded the church in his living room, but also from Mark 1:17, when Jesus tells Simon and Andrew, "Come, follow me, and I will make you fishers of men." Fisher's was a church for the unchurched, an antidote to the hymn-bloated, wood-pew, fire-and-brimstone services most pagans associated with religion. As Pastor Dale said, and which I've said many times myself, we weren't religious, we were relational. We came to church to be with Jesus. We didn't sing hymns; we sang praise songs, led by a band instead of a choir. Fisher's was already one of the largest churches in California, though in my lifetime I would see it become one of the largest in the country, and the complex that seemed so expansive to me then would become too small for Sundays.

Youth activities took place in a series of trailers on the northeast side of the church property, a square encampment that included several classrooms, an all-purpose room filled with sagging secondhand sofas and out-of-date movie posters, and a worship room where we held something of a pseudo-service during the second hour. I was focused and enthusiastic.

Each week I regaled the youth with stories of God's presence revealed in daily life. I told the story of my neighbor in Escondido who scraped and saved to afford a hot tub so he could relax after work, and when it at last arrived, he gave it to his aunt who'd recently had hip surgery. It wasn't exactly true—my neighbor had plenty of money and in fact owned the house his aunt lived in—but as a story, it worked. Kids could be so consumed with themselves, with their hair and shoes and that month's brand of blue jeans, that a little airbrushing of the details could be justified if it led them to sacrifice for others as Christ sacrificed for us. Everyone understands that the parables of Jesus were intended for this purpose, not as a record of historical facts, as is true with the rest of the Bible. I spent the entire year looking for stories I could shape into parables, watching the sun rise and set from the edge of SPEW Hill, watching students talk outside the library, watching hour after hour of television reruns for some plot line, some scene that would strike a relevant chord. I wrote everything down in a five-subject spiral notebook.

My internship ended with the completion of my degree, and as a graduation gift, Pastor Dale had asked me to preach that Sunday at the ten o'clock service. Maybe it comes from living just south of Hollywood, but I felt that tomorrow would be my big break as a preacher, a giant leap in my pastoral career. I could feel the Holy Spirit pointing me down my triumphant path.

• • •

I told Greg I should find a way to work this into my sermon.

"What's that?" He kept his eyes on the ball. The wind lifted the hair from his forehead.

"This," I said. "All of this." I waved the club handle at the sky and the sea, like Moses extending his staff. "Sometimes God blocks our paths to force us to wait on Him. Usually it means we have a lesson to learn, and until we learn it, we can't go forward. Sometimes that lesson is patience itself. If you hadn't taken that catnap at lunch, we could have been one more mile down the road. We should give thanks and praise for God's perfect timing."

"Sounds good," he said. He blinked, lost his concentration, and straightened his back. "Do you know why golf balls are dimpled?"

I shrugged. "So they'll sit on the tee?"

"They create Magnus lift, which keeps the ball aloft during the initial part of its flight." He picked up the ball. "Driven balls have backspin. Magnus force relates to the drag on the top and bottom parts of the ball."

"Balls have tops and bottoms?" I said, playing along. Greg was full of stuff like this. "They're round."

"At any one point in time, there's a top and a bottom. The top moves slowly and produces less drag. The bottom moves fast and produces more. This force creates lift. You've seen a golf ball fly upward, or slice to the side? That's Magnus."

"Something new every day," I said, and spread my arms. "Our blemishes propel us toward God. Perfect." Unaware of anything I just said, he drew the iron up and over his head and swung hard, turning his hips when he made contact with the ball. A tuft of grass and earth flew up and disappeared off the side of the road, and Greg tapped the grass around the divot with the clubhead.

· · ·

Greg was the only person I knew at SPEW who studied mathematics. I mean, the college had all the science majors, including chemistry, physics, biology, and several brands of engineering, but the majority who took those degrees did so to work in the mission field—either as teachers at missionary schools or else as missionary doctors. Karl Beckman studied biology in order to prove "evolution a crock," and spent most of his time reading books that declared Darwin an apostate. Greg studied math for math's sake, for the love of numbers and equations, neither of which fit SPEW's mission. Everything is for God's glory, we were told, not man's. What's more, the Math Department was joined with the Physics Department, and even though our professors were Christians, everyone knew most physicists were atheists. Greg said Einstein believed in a divine being, but Einstein was no Christian. Anyone could look at the starry sky and feel the echo of creation, but no one comes to the Father except through the Son. Worse was the fact that Greg studied abstract, difficult subjects that seemed to lead nowhere near Jesus, and worse, led no one else *to* Jesus. Students, in my time at SPEW, were known to shout out, "What does this have to do with Jesus?" in the middle of a lecture, and to tell one another before going out on weekend nights, "Think of Jesus." This was before those purple bracelets and bumper stickers became so popular, and we thought ourselves both original and righteous, holding one another to a higher standard.

Greg's textbooks had queer titles like *First Course in Modular Forms, Calculus of Variation and Homogenization, Methods for Structural Optimization, Applied Complex Variables and Methods.* I remember the titles because I remember leafing through the books, page after page filled with an alien typography. I know math is pure logic to those who practice it, but without the presence of a number, I failed to see the sense in any of it. Even stranger was watching Greg do his homework. He worked out problems on graph paper, his writing geometrical in its movements, boxy and square, but illegible on the whole, the kind of writing practiced by government code breakers and spies, at least in the way I imagine both. Ethan Prufer, one of the guys in our small-group Bible study, saw a sheet of Greg's on his desk and said it looked demonic. I said I thought it looked more like Aramaic and told Ethan to be careful about accusing other Christians of demonism. Ethan apologized. He's not a bad guy.

More than one of our friends, and more than one of Greg's professors, suggested he would have been better suited for an institution like Caltech. But like many of us, he'd only attended Christian schools and his parents insisted he remain close to the body of Christ when he went to college. They understood that college was a dangerous stop for any Christian pilgrim. We all had friends who had lost their faith at the public schools. And Greg didn't dislike SPEW; in fact, just the opposite was true. His senior year he rarely left campus. He did almost all of his coursework by independent study; he checked in with his professors once a week and spent the rest of his time in the Basilica. I always knew where to find him, and when I saw him there he'd be surrounded by pencil shavings and eraser bits, his hands sweaty and often in his hair, pages of graph paper stacked just beyond the bend of his right elbow, always in the same spot. He also began to write on himself, his skin merging with his paper as he moved across the page, just as one form of mathematics merged with another. There were nights when he came back to the dorm with bloody hands and knuckles, crimson rings in the cuticles of his fingernails and pink streaks on his forehead and in his hair, which in the right light had a translucent quality. I used to joke that math gave him stigmata, which neither he nor I believed in. I saw the marks on his skin merely as the passion of a mathematician, a passion I've seen elsewhere only among missionaries who, in their resolve to reach the world for Christ, bought one-way passages abroad and took their coffins with them. Had Greg desired the missionary life, he probably would have had a lot more dates. Many women at SPEW were eager to marry, and to become, missionaries.

SPEW made it easy to set your thoughts on the noble, the right, the pure, and the lovely, as Paul tells us to do in Philippians. Stumble in your faith, someone was there to pick you up. Sin, and you had your Bible study to hold you accountable. No women in the men's dorms, no R-rated movies, no *Rolling Stone* or *GQ* or *Cosmopolitan* magazines with their lustful advertisements and perverted sex quizzes. Virginity is not so hard to keep if everyone agrees to it going in. We signed an honor code the first day of freshman year, agreeing, among other things, to abide by 1 Thessalonians 4:3, to control our bodies in a way both holy and honorable. Love was a serious, grave matter and we knew not to fool with it. If two people were in love, it was best to get married, lest one begins to act improperly toward the other. That's Paul again, in 1 Corinthians, though I am paraphrasing a bit.

We all knew we couldn't stay at SPEW forever. We knew we'd have to descend the hill for good and live among the pagans, which nobody wanted to do alone. Senior year felt a little like the last call at a bar, when people scramble to pair up, wincing and dazed as the lights come back on and the jukebox shuts off. I saw this in a movie; I myself have never shut down a bar. There were a lot of engagements senior year, women hugging and crying after chapel, guys staying up late to talk about what it would be like to finally "get some." It was, as I have already said, a wedding that brought us to the landslide: Josh Rapenburg and Crystal McKnutt, whom everyone called McNuts, which made us all laugh, every time. Crystal didn't want to graduate an unmarried woman. She wanted her diploma printed with her married name, which she would be known by for the rest of her life—not an unreasonable desire. The wedding took place two days after classes ended, three days before finals week was to begin, at a flat-roofed, un-air-conditioned church in Bakersfield. Crystal's sister sang while her brother played the guitar, both off key. Greg and I wore jackets and ties, but not tuxedos, and stood arranged by height on the steps leading from the floor to the pulpit. The ceremony included a sermon about Jesus's power to save; it lasted forty-five minutes and ended in an altar call. I stood the entire time, thinking about Kenna Stites.

Kenna sang in the praise band at Fisher's Church and helped out some Sundays with the children. Though she was only nineteen and in school part-time, she seemed to me more mature than the other girls her age. She wasn't ashamed to sit with the children in the miniature chairs in the Sunday School classrooms while she worked the tiny, dull-bladed scissors through sheets of construction paper. I liked her broad shoulders and her soft chin, though my favorite thing was watching her sing. Her voice was true and clear and seemed to rise with the music. When a song like "Lover of My Soul" or "There Is None Like You" would get to its high point, she would close her eyes and point her chin and lift one hand to the ceiling, palm flat and open. I'd watch the vocal cords vibrate in her throat, the quiver in the hand that held the microphone, the soft underside of her arm, which appeared to turn pinker and more flushed as the song built. It sounds like a small thing, and it was, but at twenty-one, it was enough to drive me crazy.

Rather than ask Kenna out on a date, I drove out to her parents' house in Whittier and spoke with her father. I arrived while he was mowing the lawn, and I waited in the dining room while he washed his hands and changed his shirt. I sat next to the head of the table and imagined the years to come and the seat that would become mine, and when Mr. Stites came into the room in a flowered Tommy Bahama shirt, his thinning hair slicked back over his ears, I stood up and without any other small talk told him I had feelings for his daughter. I said I believed she was a right, upstanding Christian woman who would serve a family as she served Jesus, and in due time I wanted to make her my wife. I didn't want to date, I said, as dating was practice for divorce. Instead, I was there to ask his permission to court Kenna. Courting was the big thing at SPEW. I told him I would pursue Kenna in group activities that included both her friends and mine, and I planned to ask her to attend a couples' Bible study with me. He asked if I'd shared any of this with Kenna, and I said I hadn't yet. I wanted his permission first. Then I promised not to kiss her until the wedding day. I wanted him to be the only man she'd ever kissed before she kissed her husband. I said it just like that, to the man's face—I felt righteous in my intentions and spoke without fear. Mr. Stites hiked up his belt and touched the hairless spot on the back of his head, and stuck out his hand. When I shook it he said, "I appreciate you coming, son," which I took to mean I'd done the right thing. I've often told this story as an example for how other young people and couples should conduct themselves in relationships. I've even told it on television. To this day I'm thankful I was able to behave rightly toward women and put first things first in matters of love and marriage.

. . .

The arrival of the equipment summoned us back to the landslide, about forty-five minutes after we'd returned to the car. An orange front-end loader came first down the road, followed by a yellow backhoe with a shovel attached to a long hinged arm. Because of the narrowness of the road, both were driven in, rather than towed in on trailers. A Caltrans crew in orange vests and white hardhats followed behind in the back of a pickup. The backhoe had to work the corners, backing up, inching forward, rolling a tread up on the side of the cliff. We practically walked alongside it. I whistled "Onward Christian Soldiers." The highway patrol had taped off the landslide and the area around it. Across the mound I could see the flashing lights of an ambulance, the bay doors already open, a fire truck behind it. A team of paramedics waited on our side with a gurney, a tackle box, and an oxygen bottle. The highway patrolman spoke with the backhoe driver; the driver nodded and pulled the levers in front of him, and the backhoe began to scoop, in its lurching way, shovelfuls of earth from the slide. After each scoop, it backed up and swung its arm to the edge of the road and emptied the shovel over the side. Then the front loader pushed in and took away its own haul. It wasn't long before the rear fender and taillights of a white Volkswagen Rabbit appeared, like an egg buried in the dirt. At that point the backhoe reversed and the crew moved in, working frantically to knife away the dirt around the car. Greg, with his arms crossed, leaned close to my ear and said, "No way, not a chance." It took a few minutes more before I saw that the Volkswagen was rocked up on its right side. Greg looked at the hills above us, and then at the debris spread over the road, and then at the car. How the slide, with all its sudden force and gravity did not sweep that little car right off the edge of the road was a mystery. "It's not possible," Greg said. "This thing would have taken a building over the side. I don't see how it didn't toss that car."

"Well, there it is," I said. I hadn't thought to question it. "Look and be amazed, for I am doing things in your own lifetime that you must see to believe." That's from Habakkuk 1:5, the Living Bible translation, one of many verses I kept scribbled in my notebook.

Greg put his hands on his hips, then crossed them back over his chest. "Whatever. Call it a miracle, then."

I did. I trusted Greg completely when it came to matters of math and physics, and if this little car had defied the laws of physics, then a miracle was the only explanation. Not every miracle turns water into wine or fills the sea with frogs. I half expected the dirt to be brushed away and the doors to be opened and for the people inside simply to step out, blink in the sharp sunlight, fill their lungs with sea-blown air, and wave to the crowd. I prayed I would have the courage to shout out *"Praise Jesus!"*

Of course, it didn't happen quite like that. When the slide buried the car, it crushed the hood and windshield and the front of the roof, and when the jaws of life at last managed to tear away the door and side paneling, and the crews were able to shovel out the earth, the man and the woman inside were both dead. No one told us; the highway patrolman never turned and announced it, but everyone could tell. The Caltrans workers removed their hardhats. People groaned and I could feel the air exit every mouth around me. Beside me a mother shielded her daughter's face, then closed her own eyes and kissed the top of the girl's head. The woman in the passenger seat was extricated first and laid on the gurney and covered with a white sheet.

But then something happened that has kept me talking about the landslide ever since. The jaws of life winched away the passenger seat and fender, and a crewman put his hardhat into the backseat. He yelled something, I couldn't hear what it was, and then he backed out of the car carrying a car seat, the bucket kind, the baby inside it still alive. The roll bar in the roof of the Volkswagen had survived intact; it provided enough space, and with the parents dead, enough air, for the baby to fill its tiny lungs until help arrived. It came out of the car filthy, a long scratch on its forehead, and within a second the paramedics were upon it, papoose board, intubation tube, needles. The crowds on both sides of the slide went crazy. Some people cheered, but others sobbed and covered their mouths in fear, which is the right attitude when a miracle is witnessed, for the power of the Lord's intervening hand, His puncturing of the fabric of time and space, is filled with terror, with lightning and thunder, and death to those without the reverence to fall to their knees and touch their lips to the dirt.

Which I did not do. I stayed on my feet and did my best to memorize every last detail I could see, the waffled tractor treads in the dirt, the broken taillights on the Rabbit, the yellow tape flapping in the breeze, even the ropy outseam of the woman's jeans I saw when the wind flapped the sheet up an inch. I turned and looked at Greg. His jaw was clenched and his eyes narrowed into slits, his eyebrows knit together at the top of his nose, and he held his scabbed hands together in an odd way, the flattened fingers of his left hand pressed between the flattened fingers and thumb of his right. He had a strange look on his face. I slapped his shoulder, pumped my hand around the knob of the bone, and said, "I praise you, Father, Lord of heaven and earth, because you have hidden these things from the wise and the learned, and revealed them to little children."

Without turning to look at me, he said, "Sure. Right." He gritted his teeth. I heard them grind back and forth.

I didn't know it then, but this was the last day of our friendship. Although we talked some on the way home, mostly we were silent, looking long out the windows at the setting sun and the lights of Los Angeles when we came down into the valley. When we parked in front of the dorm, I went straight to the Basilica to rewrite my sermon, this time telling the story of what I had just witnessed, working in Isaiah 25 and Ephesians 2 and the story of Jesus raising Lazarus from the dead. The next day I preached with fire, God's voice on my lips, and after the service Pastor Dale shook my hand and said, "I didn't know you had it in you." Kenna's father invited me to lunch, where I retold the story of the landslide with Kenna's fingers interlaced with mine beneath the table, and afterward Kenna hugged me for the first time and whispered that she thought I had a gift. The smell of her shampoo and the bacon from her BLT, the warmth of her cheek and her breasts pressed against my chest stayed with me all through finals week and made it hard to concentrate on my papers and exams. Greg sequestered himself in the Basilica for the entire week, his bed undisturbed for five straight nights, his neck bent over his graph paper and books as though he didn't want to look up and find the week had ended. The next time we were face to face, we were donning caps and gowns and Greg was rubbing Neosporin and Vaseline on his hands. We moved out of the dorms that afternoon; I went just down the hill to an apartment with another Fisher's intern, he to his aunt and uncle's house in Pasadena.

I saw him one last time at my wedding. Before the ceremony I helped him with his cufflinks and saw that his hands were worse than ever, scabbed with crisscrossing lines and dark spots where ink and pencil graphite had imbedded beneath his skin. The marks disappeared up both sleeves, on both sides of his arms, like prison tattoos. He'd told me he was working at an engineering firm, but I didn't know which one and I didn't press him to tell me. The chairs beyond the door were full of my relatives, I was on the verge of kissing Kenna for the first time and the entire boundless frontier of marriage, and I didn't want to think of anything unpleasant.

· · ·

Then life got between us. Fisher's hired me on full-time, and by Christmas Kenna was pregnant. Pastor Dale asked me to preach one Sunday a month, and then every other week, and when he retired, he tapped me as his successor. I saturated my life with God's Word as chocolate syrup saturates a glass of milk, and weekly encouraged my congregation to see the world the same way, to *open your eyes and look at the fields*, as Jesus tells the disciples in John. I was a good storyteller, as any effective speaker must be, and became known as the preacher who could see God in a ladybug crawling across a leaf, or in a dog at the end of a leash. Eventually my notebooks of parables and file drawer of sermons would get typed up and published in a book, *God Is Everywhere*, my half-factual autobiography told through a rosy lens, the climax of which was, of course, the landslide. "You, too, can emerge from disaster," I wrote, "you, too, can come out of your own grave and live again. Believe and God shall raise you up." It's a story I can tell when I am nervous or ill-prepared or needing to dazzle. I can thread it to any Bible verse, adapt it to every situation. For a long time, I believed God had shown it to me to do His will and to make disciples of all nations.

The only problem is that Greg isn't in it. I tried at first to include him and the larger parts of that day, the cypress trees leaning sideways from the cliffs, his closed eyes at the turn of the golf course, his lessons about flight and lift. But space was limited—"Don't make people read too much at one time," my editor told me—and all I knew of what had become of him I knew by hearsay, rumors filtered to me by an old SPEW acquaintance whose mother went to church with his aunt, or a friend of a friend in Salinas, where he grew up. I heard he was married, but isn't any longer, that he'd had a daughter who moved out of state with her mother, that he'd bounced around between jobs, his talents never quite matched with his employers' needs. I didn't know how to make any of that fit. I thought of his stacks of graph paper, and what Ethan Prufer said about them, and I imagined him in a sparsely furnished room in a shabby hotel rented by the week, unbuttoning his shirt at the end of his bed, his biceps and shoulders and chest and stomach inked black with a language no one else could read, and I deleted half of what I had written.

· · ·

I could have tracked him down, found his parents, or his aunt, gotten hold of a number. I didn't have the courage. Instead, Greg found me. He called me deep in the early morning. This alone didn't surprise me; many people have my number and I am used to the phone summoning me from sleep. In a church the size of Fisher's, people leave and come into the world at every hour of the day. It wasn't until after I had said "hello" and "hold on a sec" and moved from my bed to my study and sat down behind my desk—that week's sermon drafted on four sheets of legal paper—that I realized who was on the phone. His voice was far-off and graveled, a faint whistle through the line, wind blowing in the background. "Hello from Miami," he said. "I saw you on TV. You look good."

"Miami," I said. "How'd you get all the way out there?"

"I just did."

"Greg," I said. I hadn't said his name in years. "What's going on?"

"I'm in trouble."

"Trouble?" I said. "With the police?"

"No, nothing like that." I could hear a tapping on his end. "Things just aren't right." I wrote "not right" on the legal pad, out of habit. I circled it twice. "I can't make heads or tails."

At first I thought he was just in a tough spot, confused and defeated, but then I thought about his hands again. I'd seen enough sadness to know the difference. I said, "You need to get some help. Go to the Emergency Room if you have to. Write this number down." I scrolled through my file for the number of a pastor I knew in Miami. Then I took his number down, and his address, and I said I'd call someone on his behalf. I said, "Let's pray," and I rattled off Jeremiah 29:11–14, and prayed for God to grant him peace in times of calamity. I did everything a pastor should have done. I called the prayer chain, I mobilized resources, I set my elbows on the desk and my knees on the floor and prayed for him. But I didn't put on my pants and brush my teeth and get on a plane. I didn't go to him. Instead I went back to bed and told Kenna nothing was wrong as I stroked the broad plane of her back and fell asleep. The next morning I dialed the number he gave me more than a dozen times, and each time listened to a woman's voice, half-southern, half-computer, tell me it was disconnected.

Ethan Prufer explained it this way, shaking his head: "He never was good at the basics. Plain speech, conversation, paperwork, the little ins and outs. I'm surprised he figured out how to dial in the first place. I wouldn't make too much of it." My phone calls to Miami had yielded nothing; the pastor I knew there had tried to visit, but couldn't find him. Ethan and I see each other every few months to barbecue—it surprises me sometimes that of all my friends from SPEW, I have remained closest to him. We talked about Greg while we stood beside the grill, turning over the burgers and waving away the smoke. "A merry heart is a good medicine," he said. "His problem is he never had a merry heart." I nodded because it is a good phrase, even though I knew that wasn't it. That's not the way I remember him.

I remember the paramedics disappearing over the landslide and the ambulance-bay doors closing, and the rig driving away, lights and sirens spinning, and the crowd dispersing back to their cars and the long wait that lay ahead. The highway patrolman shouted traffic would be diverted to a service road that would take us back toward San Luis Obispo and the 101. When I told Greg I was heading back to the car, he gripped my wrist and said, "Let's go back to the golf course." His hand was shaking and hot against my skin. "We'll play one more round and spend the night in a motel. Eat steaks. I'll buy. I don't want to be on the road anymore."

But no way was I going to miss my shot at preaching. "Relax," I said. "Be not afraid." He pressed his lips together and looked down. The backhoe roared up behind us, spewing out a black puff of exhaust before digging its shovel into the earth. I slapped Greg's arm and told him the backhoe had the faith of a mustard seed—it could move the mountain from here to there. I couldn't fathom anyone would see it otherwise.

DEEP IN THE HEART

LET'S SAY WE'RE IN AUSTIN, TEXAS, close to winter when the weather is shifting and unsteady, in a house bordering woods, whose neighbors are only visible when it's cold, and fires are lit, and gray smoke rises in the gray morning, the trail from the chimney to the sky dissolving as it ascends.

There is a tall, athletic father; an attractive mother; a short-haired son, who, before he contracted cancer at age nine, had never felt pain or oppression, used to play in the woods behind his house, and knew the statistics of athletes who first played professionally the year he was born.

Now Wesley Proudeaux is dying of osteosarcoma, common enough among children that its tragedy cannot quite usurp its banality. Call it an accident, a stroke of chance. Children like him live in every town. In this town, the child is Wesley. And he is not the only one, not by a long shot.

The neighborhood does what it can to help. Mothers talk about Wesley with the telephone cord wrapped around their fingers as they stand in the kitchen. Children younger than Wesley accompany their mothers to his house, carry in casseroles, place cookies in Wesley's lap. Some of them understand that being sick means more than missing school. Some do not.

What seems unimportant now will become essential later. These casserole-carrying children will remember Wesley and the house where he died years from now, in college, when the very word "suburban" sounds made of plastic. Wesley's cancer will reassure them that they too have touched a larger world, that their own neighborhood was not immune from struggle. One boy will talk of Wesley at parties to persuade girls to climb into his car. In their writing classes, they will write about him until everyone is nauseous.

Nausea will consume them.

. . .

Wesley is nauseous. He is home, sweating out the chemotherapy. He is throwing up. His mother and father walk the house in thick socks to keep the floors from creaking. No one makes any sudden moves that might jolt him from sleep. Even the boyfriend of the girl across the street knows not to honk his horn outside her house. Wesley will die within a year. His house will appear on the news, then disappear, then reappear. The insurance will run out, debt will overwhelm the equity, and it will be sold at an auction. Then the house will be forgotten.

. . .

Turn out the lights in the kitchen and sit quietly by the window. Deer run into the backyard from the woods. They come out when it's cold. They feel safest in the dark. They nibble the shrubs. They circle tentatively around the salt lick, now pointed and angular from the deer's autumn feeding. Their eyes glow beyond the kitchen windows, floating weightlessly in the dark, their bodies invisible. Everywhere Andre looks, bodies are losing their weight.

Andre put the salt lick there himself. In a city of hunters, the capital of a state of hunters, Andre does not hunt. The house has no guns. There is nothing to shoot. IV drips, needles, plastic brown bottles with white caps—these are the instruments of death. The time of year makes little difference. Connecting cancer to a season is useless. There's no metaphor to contain it. In Austin, some days are cold, others hot. Children bundled up for Halloween, wearing coats and hats over their costumes while they roamed house to house. The following week, the candy melted in their lunch bags and everyone wore shorts to school.

For Wesley, the outside temperature matters even less. He spent the Fourth of July buried beneath a stack of blankets, shivering, feverish. Now he kicks the comforter from his bed, his damp pajamas clinging to his belly and Hannah rubs his chest with Vicks.

. . .

Hannah sits upstairs in a T-shirt, cross-legged on the floor of the room next to her son's. The laptop is on the floor, lid open, on. It is one in the morning. She belongs to a listserv for parents of terminally ill children. She had wanted to join a support group, but hoped she and her husband would join together. "I'm not going to be a Ronald McDonald House parent,"

Andre told her. She subscribed to the listserv and the chat room. The listserv told Hannah what to expect before she brought Wesley home from the hospital: the vomiting, the loss of appetite, the acute sensitivity to sound. The list falls apart after that. There are no common threads beyond the basics. Everyone goes a little differently. Nothing is really helpful about it, save taking her mind off Wesley in the next room. But the cancer has now consumed even her distraction. She can think of little else.

She finds solace in the parents worse off than she. A couple in Milwaukee had two daughters, eighteen months apart, both with advanced Duchenne muscular dystrophy and little chance for survival. Another mother lost three sons to the same unpronounceable neurodegenerative disease, the name of which she typed over and over in her emails. Her repetition of the name did not suck out its power to kill. Words did not revive her sons. They are still dead.

Hannah reads vague references to former members, those who have dropped off the list. They were once words connected to voices connected to people connected to sadness. Now their silence pronounces the death of their children.

When Wesley dies, Hannah will watch the videos of herself and Andre and Wesley together until the tapes warp and break. Wesley's voice will be lost and Hannah will forget the sound of him calling out for help.

The list mentions the Make-A-Wish Foundation, which gives children a final experience, a memory they can carry with them into death. The idea of a last hurrah bothers her. Andre says, "They should make children work in a landfill for a day so they can see the dump they are leaving." He is not making light of his son's illness. He is not trying to be funny.

. . .

Andre is barrel-chested and thinly bearded. He works downtown, walking distance from the capitol and the job Hannah has given up. Three nights a week, he stays awake with his son, who now requires almost constant attention. Hannah sleeps these nights with a towel wedged beneath the door to block out the sound. She trusts Andre to take care of Wesley when he wakes up screaming, his pajamas soaked in vomit. The other nights Andre spends at another woman's house. Hannah does not think her marriage will outlive her son.

Wesley is Andre's only son. He has accelerated the progression of their relationship to include the stories he would tell on the nights that will never occur: Two years as a minor league baseball player, ski trips to Canada, the first girl he slept with his sophomore year in college, the night he walked the check at a Denny's in Newport, Rhode Island, after he lost his friends, missed his ride back home, and ran out of money. Wesley looks up from his bed at his father's groomed face and grimaces. "What's the matter, my man?" Andre asks.

"I'm itchy."

"Itchy where?"

"Here," Wesley says, pointing to the small rise in the center of his NFL sheets.

Andre smiles, and for a minute forgets about Wesley's fever rashes and hair loss. "Sit up, like me." Wesley swings his feet out of the sheets, curls his knees over the side of the bed. "Let me show you how to properly take care of that problem." Andre scratches. "Now you try it." Wesley has been told not to scratch at his rashes. He scratches like he's picking at an ant bite. "Not like that son, you got to use your whole hand, really get up underneath there. Give them a good pull." They do this together, a leg apiece up on the bed, a single hand cupped between their legs. Wesley's over what he will never rightly use; Andre's over what could not, by his estimation, prevent his son from the randomness of disease.

"Know any dirty jokes?" Andre asks.

"A couple."

"Well, let's hear one."

"I'm not sure Mom would like that."

"Your mother isn't here. It's just us men and times like this call for dirty jokes."

"Okay," Wesley says. "Do you know who the first carpenter was?"

"Who?"

"Eve."

"And why is that?'

"Because she made Adam's banana stand." The joke will be Andre's final thought one day, and when he thinks of it, he will not know whether he feels happy or sad. His death will be dark, unobserved, when even the quiet is quiet.

. . .

Wesley's friends still come over. Their mothers worry about them observing the slow march of death, but worry is not enough to keep them away. They burst through Hannah's back door, fingers sticky with pine sap. Hannah reads the newspaper at the kitchen table, a page rolled up in her hand, her socked feet crossed one over the other. A teenage girl battling AIDS completed a marathon. Hannah jumps a little at the sound of the door against the frame. The boys hide frogs in their pockets. "Is Wes here?"

"Upstairs," she says. She doesn't bother to warn them that Wesley is sleeping. He'll be awake and sitting up by the time they arrive at the top of the stairs. She knows keeping them away from her son will do no good. She stands up and heads for the refrigerator.

Hannah hears Wesley's feet hit the floor, the other boys' bottoms hit the floor, their knees across the floorboards as a frog urinates in their hands, is dropped, and leaps beneath the bed. Damon's father is a hunter. When Damon turned ten, he was allowed to accompany his father and his older brothers deep into the woods, to sit covered head to toe in bright orange, in the body of an old Jeep converted into a blind, to wait, to ask no questions. He was told to watch the trees for eyes. He tells his story again and again, the details swelling over time. First, they only thought they heard a mountain lion. Then they actually saw one. Then it clawed its way into the camper, growling and salivating. Damon is steady with the action sequence of his father leaping from the blind to follow the first shot with a second. "The first shot is always followed by a second," Damon says. The height of his father's leap increases with every retelling. The boys believe any version Damon tells. The plurality of truths does not bother them. It makes the story worth hearing again.

"How did it look when your dad shot it?" Wesley asks.

"How did what look?"

"The mountain lion. How did it look?"

"It looked like nothing. We couldn't see it. My dad knew where to aim and he hit it in the neck."

"What about the blood?"

"It sort of squirted for a second and then stopped. Before that all we could see were its eyes."

"What did its eyes look like?" Eliot asks.

"Like marbles, I guess, like eyes. I didn't look at them for long. I wanted to see the body. My dad said if I saw its tail move, I was supposed to tap his arm." The frogs jump back and forth between their feet and knees within the circle the boys have formed on the floor.

"Were you scared?" Wesley asks. He imagines the marbled eyes through the trees, the lion's receded upper lip exposing the row of yellowed incisors, black packing around the gums. Blood staining the fur as it bubbles up from the neck, like the time the water pipe burst in the yard.

"What would I be scared of? We had the guns. Nothing could kill us as long as we saw it first."

"What if something came from behind?" Wesley asks.

"It didn't. We were watching both ways. We were up high. We could see everywhere at once."

"Did your dad let you shoot the gun?" Eliot asks.

"Once, at a couple of cans on a fence post. It's strong. It can knock you over. My dad stood behind me and helped me hold it. I got to take my BB gun and shoot a little bit at squirrels."

"Did you hit any?"

"One, but it ran away. It's probably dead now." This is a lie. Damon never hit anything. But the story will sound better if he did.

They open the window in Wesley's room, pry off the screen. Damon throws his frog out first, legs spinning as it tumbles though the air. It lands in the woods, just beyond the yard. Eliot's windup is a little crooked; the leg of the frog hits the window and it drops into the shrubs below. "Good one," Damon says. He tries to wipe the blood off the glass with his shirt, but leaves behind a long crimson smear in the sunlight that bends into a brown smudge. There's a frog for Wesley, but he doesn't want to throw it. He's afraid it won't go far enough, that he's too weak. Instead he looks down into the bushes, hoping to see Eliot's frog. He wants to see it bleed. He wants to see what death looks like.

The sun sets. The phone rings. Hannah calls upstairs. The boys go home. She watches them run out the back door, their T-shirted backs twisted, the bottoms of their shoes still traced with mud. She will move away soon, once Wesley dies. The boys' mothers will keep up with her, send her Christmas cards and photographs. She will watch, year by year, as the boys step further into the forest of manhood—their jawlines lengthening, their shoulders broadening, the first traces of facial hair, which they will grow into patchy beards and goatees, and finally shave. Over the phone she will hear of their refusals to take out the trash, insignificant car accidents, prom dates. She will visit once in a while, then less, then not at all. When the boys leave for college, the pictures will only include the parents, and she will put them in a drawer she never opens in a room she never uses, unable now to imagine her son.

. . .

Andre and Katherine lie shoulder to shoulder. The ceiling fan spins slowly backward above them, its late-afternoon shadow cast on the wall behind them. It is Tuesday, Hannah's night with Wesley. He has already said he'll work late. Like Hannah, Katherine is tall and rather pretty, was married once a few years ago, and has grown tired enough of being alone that she accepts Andre, and his weight of guilt and sadness, into her nervous bed. Andre talks little of his wife and instead traces a finger up Katherine's side and around her earlobe. He feels a sharp pain in the center of his back. He's carried Wesley up and down the stairs so many times that he slipped a disk.

Katherine found a photograph of Hannah when she went through Andre's wallet one night while he was in the shower. She is not much different than his wife, and Andre is most likely drawn to her in the same way he was drawn to Hannah fourteen years ago.

"Have you thought about one of those foundations?" she asks him, a hand resting on his chest.

"What foundations?"

"For Wesley. So he can ride in the cockpit of an airplane or something. You know, do something really cool before it's . . . time." The room buckles in silence. "I'm sorry."

"I don't think that's such a good idea."

"For him or for you?"

"What's that supposed to mean?"

"Nothing. Just maybe you're afraid it would seem too official, like you're announcing the end."

"There aren't too many people who don't know about that."

"So then why not? Why not let him have some fun, something you can remember doing together?"

"I just think that parading him out onto the fifty-yard line at a football game and saying 'Look everyone, this boy is here because he will die soon' won't do much to make him feel better. I can take him to do fun things myself."

"But those foundations allow him to do things you can't give him."

"I'd rather not talk about this anymore," he says. Katherine knows the conversation is better left unfinished. Andre rolls over and falls asleep. She tries to sleep but cannot. She is a detour and the thought bothers her. Andre's back and shoulder rise steadily in the dark. If he wakes up in the night, he'll rise slowly from bed, dress himself, and slip out her front door. He will slide past Hannah on the floor in the guest bedroom, slide past Wesley's room where his door is cracked and his body lies knotted and deteriorating. Falling asleep means the night is over.

When Katherine hears him rise, she pretends to remain asleep until the latch catches in the lock. Then she gets up, ties her robe around her, and sits down at the kitchen table.

· · ·

The Make-A-Wish Foundation writes to Hannah:

Dear Mr. and Mrs. Proudeaux, We are writing to express our deepest sympathies about your son's battle with osteosarcoma. A friend of yours, who has asked to remain anonymous, wrote to us about the possibility of our helping Wesley fulfill his special dream.

Please submit an official request to us, providing the name of Wesley's doctor. Once we gain medical approval, we will help him carry out his wishes.

We know that our efforts cannot properly assuage your family's grief, but we sincerely hope that we can help you create a special memory that will last forever.

Andre is away when Hannah reads it. She crumples the envelope in her fist as she walks upstairs, where Wesley waits, nauseous.

· · ·

"You don't have to meet a celebrity," Hannah says. "You could just go somewhere. Do something you've never done before." She and Andre sit together at the foot of Wesley's bed. It's Sunday morning. Today is calmer; Wesley doesn't feel so bad. He drinks orange juice through a plastic straw.

"Don't feel like you have to do this," Andre says. "We can take a vacation together." He looks at Hannah. "All three of us. We could go see the Grand Canyon. You talked about seeing it."

This morning is almost enough. Wesley not feeling sick, Andre and Hannah home together on the same day, in the same room. Andre's mention of a trip they might take as a family allows them momentarily to imagine themselves sleeping in hotels and driving in rented cars, snapping photographs by signs and scenic overlooks as they blend in with the other tourists who, like them, have left their lives in other states. The idea of escape is appealing.

Wesley is afraid of dying. He's afraid of doing it alone. And he's afraid of saying what he wants. His father will frown and walk out of his room, or else he'll slap him lightly on the knee and say, "Come on, boy, you don't want that." His mother's mouth will tighten into that same tense line as when she checks his temperature on the mornings that always result in him throwing up the most. She'll cry and fight it, as she does when she's holding his head over the toilet. He can read his parents' faces well enough to know what they'll think, and though he's only ten, he knows time is running out. He understands the immediacy of choice in a way his friends will not comprehend for years.

"Mom, Dad," he says in a voice his friends use when asking for additional allowance, "I want to go hunting. I want to shoot a deer."

· · ·

What most bothers the Animal Rights Coalition is not the prospect of shooting the deer—they understand that animals are and will continue to be shot—but rather the potential publicity of the event. "Make-A-Wish events often collect quite a bit of attention," writes the president of the group. "There will be cameras present for the hunt. A media entourage following your son through the woods in search of a deer will not only rejuvenate interest in hunting, but will certainly harm the animal. We have fought a long and difficult battle for the rights of animals and are aware that, to the public, your son's illness is grave enough to overwhelm any consideration of the deer itself."

"Please do not misread my concern, Mrs. Proudeaux," the letter continues. "I do not mean to deprive your son of his wishes. But you must consider the avalanche of consequences. Media attention like this, in an election year, will make it difficult for the congressional candidates we support to speak out against animal mistreatment because it will make them appear unsympathetic. I am asking you, as someone who values the sanctity of life above all else, to help your son reconsider."

Hannah crumples the letter and throws it away. It is just one sick child and one insignificant deer. It will not cause the frenzy this man fears.

. . .

The NRA comes over to take Wesley's photograph. The local 4-H club signs a petition for the hunt not to happen. Wesley goes back for more chemo. He vomits before he leaves the hospital. Wesley's fourth-grade class sends him a card. Wesley cannot sleep. He hallucinates, feels like he is spinning in space. Hannah mops the floor around his bed, the bathroom. The news vans arrive. A reporter with tall, feathered bangs asks to interview Wesley. Hannah refuses. Andre stays at Katherine's over the weekend. Remington sends a T-shirt and a cap for Wesley to wear when he uses one of their guns for his hunt. A man brings a rifle in a long, dark box, a package of ammunition, and shows Andre how to load and fire. The rifle is small enough for Wesley to handle. A deer runs into the woods.

. . .

The reporters and camera crews eat roast beef sandwiches on the Proudeauxs' lawn. They drink water from bottles. They stand in a half circle on the dead grass. They shoot the house, the lawn, the woods behind it, the neighbors. They shoot cars going and coming down the street. They use up all their tape and send a messenger back for more. There's always more to shoot.

The house is on the news in the evening, then in the paper, then on the morning show the next day. Hannah doesn't give a statement. What else can happen? A lawsuit? A petition? Time and interest are waning.

Wesley sits up on the couch, watching television with a box of juice. The blinds are drawn. The cameras cannot see him; his mother won't let him outside to play or near the windows in the front of the house. Hannah refuses comment. Andre does not come home. The news vans leave. There is nothing more to shoot.

. . .

Katherine rolls over and faces Andre, propping her head on her arm. "I'm afraid for your son."

"He still has some time," Andre says. "There's no need to be afraid yet."

"But it's not long. I know you have it figured down to the day."

"I don't."

"You do. I don't think you want him to die, but I think it's the one event you can count on. When it happens, you'll no longer be a father."

"You think I look forward to that?"

"No, but its certainty makes sense to you. Right now, you don't know what to think of yourself. You come to me because I'm a secret. You have no identity here, if you don't want to."

"Why do you talk to me like this? I didn't come to hear this."

"Because when Wesley goes, so will you. You've already said your marriage will end then. If you stay with me, I'll be where you are." And where Katherine is, so is Andre. She is pregnant with a baby girl. She doesn't know this yet, and Andre never will.

"So you have it all figured out?"

"I want you to stay. I want your son to stay so you'll stay. I don't want you to pretend I was never here. I think it would be better if you left." Andre collects his clothes and walks out. Nothing more is said.

· · ·

Hannah throws a plate. She throws a glass. The first is followed by a second. Andre ducks. They shatter against the cupboard, falling in shards to the floor. She throws a saltshaker. It bounces off his arm.

Hannah has suspected what she now knows is true. Given the circumstances, her husband's infidelity is unimportant. She doesn't care. Given the circumstances, she needs to throw something. She needs to exert force upon Andre's body. She needs to move his body in space while his body still can be moved. She wants to punch him; she doesn't want to touch him. She throws the pepper shaker.

Andre drops behind the island in the center of the kitchen. He covers his head and stands back up. He is barefooted. Hannah throws a mug. "I want you to go," she says. "I want you to leave."

"Not yet. I'm going to stay for as long as Wes is around."

"No you're not." She throws a bottle of olive oil. It breaks and spreads thickly over the cinders of glass. "I'm not going to stay here with television cameras looking in our windows every other day and you hopping back and forth between here and another woman's house." She throws a spatula. "Stay there. Let them know what you're doing. Let them make the connections."

"None of this is relevant. I'm no longer seeing her." His body is tense. He can feel the point where his disk has slipped, one bone grinding into another. He wants to sit down, but knows better than to remain in the same place for too long.

"She did what I should have done long ago."

"This isn't about you. It's about Wes."

"Exactly. And look where you go instead of being with him. Do you think I'm his mother only on my designated nights?"

Andre lowers his head. There's nothing more for him to say.

Hannah stops throwing.

. . .

Andre stands on his back porch, that same night, looking into the woods behind the house. It is quiet. He could sleep out here if it weren't so cold. He has a sleeping bag in the garage. He could wrap himself tight and tuck himself into a chaise lounge. His wife is upstairs sleeping. His son is upstairs sleeping. His girlfriend, pregnant with his daughter, is at her apartment sleeping. The street, the neighborhood, the freeway are sleeping. He is awake, alone in the darkness.

He thinks of cities where he might move once his son is dead. He plans to sign the house and the insurance over to Hannah, take what little money is left in his name, and go. He likes the idea of public transportation, bodies pressed randomly against him throughout the day, conversations without words or gestures. He imagines himself there, a different haircut, his beard shaved. He remakes himself in another life, without Hannah and Katherine or children. Without stop signs, without batting cages, without woods. Without the endless signs of grief.

The wind blows up his jacket sleeves. What usually does not happen in Austin happens. It begins to snow.

He'd like to crawl upstairs, into bed with Hannah, defrost his snowy hands against the oven of her back. He would like to slide beneath Katherine's door, slip his hands around her belly. He would like to cover himself with Wesley's sheets, his son inside his chest, hum himself to sleep with images of baseball, and weight lifting, and fly-fishing. His son's nausea is too acute for him to share his bed. His wife and his lover are both silent to him.

He sits down on the edge of the deck. A deer runs into the yard. Its hooves leave tracks in the thin snow. It licks the salt from the footpaths. The gun is in the house. Andre stands slowly, moves backward toward the door he left ajar. The door is well oiled. It doesn't make a sound. The deer doesn't flinch.

"Wake up, son," he says, hovering over Wesley.

Wesley doesn't move.

"Wake up, son," he says again. He nudges the boy's shoulder.

Wesley is slow to move. "What?" he says, his eyes cloudy with sleep.

"Come on, get up. It's time."

"For what?"

"I'll show you." Wesley drops his feet onto the floor, pulls on his socks. Andre wraps him in a jacket, pulls pants over his legs, shoes on his feet, a hat on his head. Wesley's weight seems to double with the layers. He follows his father down the stairs.

Andre takes the rifle out of the closet. He loads it and pulls back the lever.

"Where'd you get that?" Wesley asks.

"It came in the mail." Andre opens the door leading to the deck. "Quiet now."

The deer is still in the yard, licking his way along the footpath. "Can you see him?"

"Over there," Wesley whispers. "I see him."

"Don't say a word. Be real still."

"I want to do it," Wesley says. "I want to shoot him on my own."

Andre kneels behind Wesley, helps him position the gun in his arms. "Square the sights with his neck. That's where you want to hit him."

"Okay, I got it."

"Be ready, it'll recoil. It'll kick at your shoulder."

"I'm ready." The snow falls thick as leaves. The moonlight is clouded, dull, as if it comes from nowhere. Wesley fires. Hannah sits bolt upright in bed, presses her hand against her heart. The deer runs back into the woods, a thin trail of blood in its footprints.

"You hit him," Andre says. "He won't get far." Andre runs into the woods. He looks in the snow for tracks, for the deer's eyes—two glowing orbs awash in the trees. He listens for the deer's labored breath.

The deer lies down in a patch of leaves, bleeding from the thigh. Andre runs between the trees, in and out of shadow.

Wesley imagines a pair of marbled eyes through the trees. He raises the rifle a second time.

Let's say it happens this way. In Austin, Texas, when the weather is shifting and unsteady. Call it an accident. It is just one sick child and one insignificant deer. The quiet is quiet. No one makes any sudden moves. There are no cameras, but there is more to shoot. Wesley waits, nauseous.

He's afraid of doing it alone. The first shot is followed by a second. Andre feels a sharp pain in the center of his back. He lies down in a patch of leaves. The wind blows up his jacket sleeves. Nausea consumes him. His body is losing its weight. The idea of escape is appealing. Everyone goes a little differently. Falling asleep means the night is over. Nothing more is said.

SEVENTEEN ONE-HUNDREDTHS
OF A SECOND

ABBY WANTED TO GO OUT TO DINNER. Two months were gone and winter was over and she was tired of sitting around waiting for dinner to show up. She was tired of the dinners that showed up, tired of lasagnas and potpies in crumpled aluminum trays, tired of casserole dishes popping with boiled chicken and burnt cheese, tired of crusted, store-bought cakes. She was tired of guests who couldn't cook, who couldn't stop asking her how she was holding up, who cried in her living room and made it all so much worse. She wanted to go someplace loud, she said, where the waiters didn't speak English, where she could have a drink without someone thinking it a sign of her depression. She was tired of her depression. "Pretend we're on a date," she told Jonah. "No one will know."

Jonah made reservations at Ginsu, one of those festive places where the chef cooked right at your table and then juggled the knives while you ate. The sun was dropping over the Great Salt Lake, a sparkling mirror against the Oquirrh Mountains and Antelope Island, still snow-covered from the late-spring storms. Abby drummed the table while the chef carved a radish into a tulip. Jonah watched the skin jiggle around her elbow and on the upper part of her arm, near her sleeve. A small sausage of skin, not there before tonight, rolled over the waistband of her pants. Her blouse was translucent blue and airy, her small breasts larger, more noticeable than ever.

He was not used to looking at her body, or rather he had tried for many years to avoid looking at it for too long. He had seen Abby naked once, in the dorms, when she stood up from Charlie's bed, and though she was the only woman he'd ever seen completely naked, and though the image returned to him whenever he grew lonely, he forced himself not to dwell upon it. Charlie was his oldest and closest friend and Abby was Charlie's wife, even still, even though Charlie was dead.

Abby dropped her chopsticks and moaned, "Ooh." She pressed her hand to her mouth.

"What's wrong?"

"Nothing," she said. "Just an episode." Charlie's heart had failed while he was swimming. It happened the first Monday in March. He'd just returned from a weekend in Moab, where he and Abby had gone to try, again, to get pregnant. In vitro had failed twice, and eighteen months of hormone injections hadn't made Abby's eggs any more receptive to Charlie's sperm. They'd made the Moab trip three other times. The doctor told them it was time to think about adoption, but that just made Charlie all the more determined to conceive. He viewed pregnancy as he'd viewed swimming: if he worked hard enough and put in the time, he could attain any goal. He had earned an unexpected spot on the Olympic Team his junior year in college, when almost no one, including Jonah, thought he had a chance. He had learned to ignore predictions, ignore odds, refuse to give up.

After Charlie died, the idea that Abby was pregnant seemed improbable, their three years of earnest trying a cruel joke. Abby never said another word about it and had held herself together when everyone around her had lost it, stiff-lipped through the ordeal at the hospital, and the crematorium, and even at the cemetery where, impervious to every wail and sob, she knelt on the Astroturf pad to fit the urn bearing Charlie's ashes into its tight copper hole. The closest she came to breaking down were these periodic waves of nausea. They drifted in and out like a fog, like a bad mood. Abby called them "episodes," as though they were just another part of her daily schedule. Her dam was leaking, Jonah thought. Any moment all that emotion would come gushing. He steadied himself to catch it, but Abby squeezed a sizzling shrimp with her chopsticks and raised it to her mouth.

Abby was still chewing when she gripped Jonah's wrist. He saw the color drain from her face. "It's back?" he asked. Abby stood up fast, knocking over her tall chair. Her hair swished across the back of her blouse and her hips swung around the chairs as she threaded through the room. A shaggy-haired boy in a white tux stood up from the next table to pick up Abby's chair. Returning to his table, he pressed his hand to his date's pale back and stroked the skin between her shoulders. The boy on his other side lifted his hand and the two gave each other high fives.

The other couples at their table looked at Jonah. He turned his watch on his wrist. Would a date go to her? He waited a minute and then walked to the women's room and pushed the door open with his foot. "You okay?" he called in. He could see the soles of her shoes and her calves and knees beneath the stall. He also saw two brown shoes and a pair of stretched black underpants beneath the stall beside hers. Abby gagged and Jonah saw her heels drop, her weight shift to her toes.

Even though the medical examiner had concluded that Charlie's heart was so wrecked nothing short of a transplant could have saved him, Jonah couldn't help but feel responsible for Charlie's death. He had known Charlie wasn't sleeping well, and when he got to sleep had a hard time waking up again. But rather than recognizing Charlie was sick, Jonah had seized on his lethargy as an opportunity to bury him in the pool. After twenty years of competition, he didn't give Charlie an inch. The slower Charlie swam, the harder Jonah pushed; he swelled, cocky and proud, when Charlie touched the wall gasping and clutching his chest. "Let's go fatso," Jonah had said, slapping the water. And replaying the scene of Charlie's last, gasping seconds, he saw a thousand instants in which he might have saved him. Had he only pulled Charlie's face out of the water faster; had he breathed into Charlie's mouth before sliding him from the water to the pool deck; had he not stopped CPR compressions to catch his breath. He stopped for no more than ten seconds after eleven minutes of compressions, but he was certain it had made a difference. When he resumed, Charlie's eyes had rolled back and looked like two halved almonds. Foamy yellow beads pooled in the creases of his mouth.

Jonah heard the water splash as he leaned against the doorway of the ladies' room. He felt his own dinner rise to the back of his throat and forced himself to concentrate on the light switch. "Take your time," he said. Sometimes he was afraid he was dying, too. The autopsy concluded that Charlie's congestive heart failure was the result of an infection, and whatever infectious air Charlie had breathed, Jonah must have breathed as well. He snapped awake at two o'clock in the morning, his breath catching. He recited every psalm he could remember, calling out to the ceiling of his bedroom, but none of it provided much comfort. His soul may have been bought, but what about his life? His time here on Earth?

How many times in the Bible had God swooped down and knocked a man dead? Now Abby was throwing up.

The brown shoes shifted and a moment later a plump woman with bright pink skin opened the door beside Abby's. She scowled at Jonah and hurried out, adjusting her skirt. "Give me a sec," Abby said. The toilet flushed. Her heels returned to the floor and the cuffs of her khakis shook loose. The door swung open and she pulled her hair behind her head. She turned on the faucet and leaned over the sink. She twisted her mouth to catch the water, swished, and spat. "I'm sorry you have to see me this way."

"I've seen worse," he said. Her eyes narrowed in the mirror. She filled her hands with water and rinsed her face, bowing into the sink. Each time she leaned up, her cheeks were more flushed and her mascara ran into stripes beneath her eyes, like long black tears. He watched Abby dry her face with a handful of paper towels, the bathroom's fluorescent lights buzzing and flickering above her, and he knew she was pregnant. Abby's eyes, when they met his in the mirror, knew it, too. He envisioned Abby in the delivery room screaming out from behind the drawn curtain, one hand gripping the railing of the bed, the other holding on to the nurse's gloved hand, while he, neither husband nor father, paced the hallway and waited for it to end. It had become his biggest fear: bearing witness to pain with no ability to act against it. He said, "Remember that girl who lived down the hall from us in the dorms? Amber Nixon. After her mother died she couldn't stop losing weight and was always throwing up in the bathroom by the lobby. Turned out she had hyperthyroidism. Her doctor had to kill the gland. By the fall she'd gained something like a hundred pounds."

"I remember her," Abby said. She smoothed the front of her blouse. "She sat alone in her room with the door open, and no one went in to talk to her. Dropped out at Christmas. That's a reassuring story."

"I just mean you shouldn't jump to conclusions."

"I'm not jumping anywhere."

"It could be a lot of things. A bug. Food poisoning."

"It could be," she said. "But it's not."

• • •

A warm wind was blowing in from the desert when they left the restaurant. Rather than shoot up the front side of Capitol Hill to Abby's house, Jonah drove through downtown and out along 300 West. Steve Miller's

"The Joker" was playing and he liked the warm air against his face. After Charlie died he'd taken a dozen long drives by himself—Highway 40 past Park City and Heber and behind the mountains to Provo; Highway 150 through the Uinta Mountains to Evanston, Wyoming—high alpine roads above the inversion where he could listen to music as he stared into the sun.

His car was a dark blue Chevrolet Caprice with a bench front seat and a bulky, outdated mobile phone fixed to the dash, the kind of thing driven by detectives in the movies. The car belonged to Song Pharmaceuticals. Jonah kept the trunk and backseat loaded with boxes of trial packets, ballpoint pens, polyurethane stress balls, all labeled with the slogan: "Sing a New Song." Key chains played the company jingle at the press of a button: *I will celebrate, sing a new song*. Song specialized in antidepressants and mood-stabilizers, a handful of anticonvulsants for epilepsy and Parkinson's. Jonah's two drugs were Mesodol, an antipsychotic that, due to its unique targeting of the midbrain dopamine receptors, more or less sold itself, and Prolift, an aggressive amphetamine for treating anxiety and attention-deficit/hyperactivity disorder. Prolift was the moneymaker. Each year more children and adults were diagnosed with ADHD, and the market was flooded with treatments. Jonah hustled to keep up. He gave packs of gum to the nurses and brought cookies and bagels and expensive lunches on gigantic black trays. The older physicians were cordial and accepted him as part of the landscape of medicine, but it was the overworked and underpaid residents who were most happy to see him. One resident told him, "Thank God for capitalism. We'd live off Doritos if it wasn't for guys like you." Once a week he held a dinner for the residents at a fancy restaurant. They all knew Song's song by heart.

Abby's bangs flapped over her eyes. She rode with her eyes closed, her elbow on the window. She looked as if she were asleep. She opened the door in front of her house and put her foot on the curb. The dome light filled the interior of the car, and the windows tightened in the dark. "It felt for a minute there like I was at sea," she said. "I'm still a bit dizzy."

"Maybe you should see a doctor," Jonah said. He turned down the headlights. "Just to make sure everything's okay."

"I don't want to be sure yet. I'm fine with the suspense."

A car turned up the street, and its headlights flashed across the bridge of her nose, her mouth and chin. "It's a lot to take in," he said.

"Look," she said, "don't tell me this is some kind of silver lining. Trying to get pregnant wasn't exactly the joyful experience I'd hoped it would be. The hormones made me sick, my periods were worse than ever, and I felt like shit all the time. I wanted to quit, but Charlie didn't. It got to be a thing between us."

"He didn't like to lose."

"No kidding. He had to prove his boys could swim. Our weekend in Moab was supposed to be a last gasp. After that we were going to take a break. I spent the whole time thinking *we* needed a break. One of the other conservationists at the Gardens offered me her guestroom, and I had planned to take her up on it."

"I had no idea," Jonah said.

"Neither did Charlie. I was arranging it while you were giving him mouth-to-mouth."

"I mean, he never indicated any kind of . . . strain. I thought everything was fine."

"In his mind, everything probably was." She fished through her purse for gum. She fed the neon-green stick between her teeth and rolled the foil into a tiny ball and dropped it into the ashtray. "The night he died, as awful as it sounds, I felt a little relieved that at least the baby-making fiasco was over. You might say that was my silver lining."

"You're feeling guilty," Jonah said. "That's all it is." He remembered his own guilty pleasures after Charlie died, the fleeting delight he took in buttered toast and television commercials and even—though he was embarrassed to recall it—the swollen sense of importance he took with him back to the pool, the way the other swimmers turned their eyes on him, touched his arm and shoulders.

"I feel guilty now, but I didn't then." Her cheeks were red, her freckles like constellations. "I just wanted a little time. Nothing forever. Now everything is forever."

He thought of Paul's claim in Romans that *all things work together for good*, but he didn't dare say it aloud. The hospital chaplain had given her a pamphlet titled "Letting go and letting God," which she'd promptly shredded in the ambulance bay, tearing each page into squares. Jonah breathed in and out through his teeth, two shorts and one long. "I can be your Lamaze coach."

Abby squeezed his hand and pressed her cheek to his. "Of course you can. This whole thing would be much worse without you." She kissed his cheek. Her breath was warm against his face, a comfort that spread down to his hands and knees. He had forgotten how it felt. He reached his arm out to hug her, but she leaned back. "Let's not find anything out for a little while, okay? Let me pretend a little longer. I'll go running tomorrow and see if it goes away. Maybe it's just a gut from all the slop we've been eating. Who knows, maybe I *am* Amber Nixon."

· · ·

The pool where Charlie died was perched high in the foothills of the Wasatch—in a vast, tiled room with big square windows overlooking the city and the lake beyond the airport and the mountain peaks rising suddenly into the sky. The adjacent outdoor pool sat drained and unused throughout the winter, the deep end a soup of snowmelt and rain. Drowned mice floated against the gutters, and on sunnier days geese landed to paddle about the oily puddles. In June the outdoor pool was scoured and filled, and when it opened for the summer Jonah volunteered to teach swimming lessons.

The lessons were offered through Jonah's church, Summit Bible Fellowship, as part of Pastor Jeff Miller's "stealth evangelism" initiative. Evangelicals needed to get creative, Jeff said, especially in Utah, where people had grown wary of missionaries knocking on their doors to talk about eternal damnation or promises of your own planet. The first scenario sounded like Halloween, the second like a pyramid scheme. Stealth evangelism meant gathering Christians and non-Christians together for secular activities, barbecues and movie nights, and allowing God to come up in the natural course of the conversation. "We're Christians and we're cool," Jeff said. "People need to see that we can relate." Jeff dyed his hair black and wore baggy pants; before becoming a pastor he'd been a marketing executive for one of the ski resorts. The skin around his eyes was bright white, the tip of his nose burnt red. "If the discussion goes well, invite your friends to come on Sunday. No pressure. We're selling God, not used cars." Jeff had rented the pool for the Vacation Bible Camp and offered free swimming lessons to any child who enrolled.

Jonah had taught swimming in college, and it felt good to teach again. It was a skill that had never left him. After the first day even the most fearful children descended the steps into the marble-blue water and made their way across the shallow end. Not a day went by without at least two or three mothers pulling him aside to tell him he was the best teacher their child had ever had. Jonah recognized, from a sales call to the mental-health outpatient clinic, a skinny boy with a pronounced overbite. His name was Titus, and as far as Jonah could tell, he was the only one who arrived for lessons unaccompanied by a parent. His silver BMX bike leaned against the chain-link fence. The handlebars were missing its rubber grips and the bare metal pipes glinted in the hot sun. The first day, Titus refused to take off his shirt or go anywhere near the water; he just sat at the end of a chaise and bounced his legs. Jonah coaxed him into the water the next morning, and by the end of the week Titus was swimming on his back and breathing to the side. Each day Titus swam a little farther and each day Jonah went home gratified. He was a good teacher and he knew it. Equally gratifying was showing up for work in a tank top and a pair of red shorts, his back and chest saturated with sun and radiating heat well into the night. He left the Chevrolet in the garage and rode his bike, a sack lunch and a big jug of water sloshing rhythmically in his backpack.

Parents dropped their children off at nine, picked them up at four. Some moms stayed for the lessons and sat with their ankles crossed on the plastic lounge chairs, legs oily in the sun. Games were designed to weave the Bible into the lessons. Jonah told the story of Paul's shipwreck on Crete and had the kids race across the pool as though making for the shore. The unruly were sent to "Patmos," a sun-baked square of concrete on the far side of the deck. In keeping with his name, Jonah let one class of seven-year-olds hang from his shoulders and neck and try to pry him from the wall. Now and again he caught one of the mothers staring at him from behind her sunglasses, eyeing his long arms and flat stomach. He wondered if Abby would one day sit this way, a Starbucks cup by her foot, the length of her thigh exposed to the swimming instructor as she crossed one leg over another, gabbing with other mothers while her child, Charlie's child, splashed and kicked. Jonah had never considered himself handsome, especially next to Charlie, whose broad shoulders and dark eyebrows made him look more like a quarterback than a swimmer. Jonah's nose was arched and rounded, his ears were too big, and he was too tall, almost six four. But he was thin at least, and strong, especially in the water.

The other counselors were teenagers, mostly girls but a handful of boys too, fourteen and fifteen, a year away from the summer jobs that would allow them to buy cars and go out on dates—a future that could not come fast enough. The girls wore bikini-tops beneath their T-shirts and used every spare minute to "lay out" on the lounge chairs around the pool, the tops of their shorts rolled down low. Courageous boys drifted toward the girls, their voices cracking, their chests slender and ribbed. The tentative sat in the shade and rifled through stacks of trading cards—not baseball cards, but some Japanese cartoon Jonah had never heard of. Only Jonah bothered to take in the scenery: the sky above the mountains a crystal blue so sharp it looked as though it might shatter, snowcaps liquefying on the upper mountain peaks and flowing through the cracks.

He missed Charlie more than ever the week of Vacation Bible Camp. All that time in the water washed up so many memories: of high school and the long bus rides to swim meets in Albuquerque and Santa Fe, the two of them slumped low in a seat near the back, whispering about girls and rival swimmers and college, about the glossy packets that arrived each day from some far-flung university in the East or North. Charlie could have gone anywhere, lots of schools wanted him, but Utah offered both him and Jonah scholarships, and Charlie thought they should stay together. "It wouldn't be the same without you, JoMo." Jonah also missed his own youth group where he went on Sunday mornings and Tuesday nights and Max Swenson, the group's leader, who told Jonah that God's plan was like a pair of headlights on a winding mountain road—enough light to see what's immediately before us, but not the whole path. Jonah lived at the top of a curvy road in the hills above Los Alamos where his mother sat with the Bible open on the coffee-table beside the classifieds—forced to find a job after his father had left Los Alamos for the Jet Propulsion Lab in Pasadena—rocking on her elbows as she prayed for a job that matched her skills, which, she admitted, were few. Some nights Jonah would drive home from Bible study with the headlights off, wanting to show God he could go without even a meager amount of light, that he could trust with the whole of his being.

For a time he had believed it all, the six-day creation of the Earth, Jesus healing the blind and leprous, Armageddon and the Antichrist, Leviathan rising from the volcanic trenches of the ocean. He knew some of it was far-fetched, even irrational, but everyone had irrational beliefs. Charlie was certain it was only a matter of time before a comet annihilated the Earth. An improbable belief was one of the marks of faith. But the End Times floated through his mind like science fiction—spectacular, but easy to dismiss. It was a belief that required imagination, but no real sacrifice.

Not the sacrifice of choosing the spirit over the flesh. His friends in the University Christian Fellowship described sex in financial terms, the body's sexual organs like savings accounts that accrued interest and on the wedding night doled out tremendous dividends in the form of boundless, unending sex. For the more serious, sex was a reenactment of Christ's devotion to the church; our true essences are entwined in our sperm and eggs, and when we join our bodies in sex we join both spirit and flesh, just as Christ joined His spirit with flesh when He descended to Earth to die for our sins. To have sex outside of marriage was to cheapen that sacrifice. Most tried, and most failed, to make it to the wedding night. Boys stroked their girlfriends' breasts, and couples showered together, or skinny-dipped in the pool, or slept over at each other's apartments, all the while fondling that gray area between purity and sin. Week after week, Bible studies were filled with twenty-year-old men crying into their hands for the sex they'd wanted and had and now regretted. But by the next week they'd weathered their guilt and had moved past it, and had taken their place among the squad lines of the fallen, the sullied, the normal.

Virginity was a choice made in the face of constant temptation. So many mornings he had woken up to find Abby's underwear on the floor beside Charlie's bed, tiny twists of violet or stripes or white lace, their bodies entwined beneath Charlie's blue twin-sized comforter, Abby's painted toenails, her milky, hairless calf peeking out the bottom. So many times Abby had told Jonah to close his eyes while she reached for Charlie's towel and scurried across the hall to the bathroom, and not once, *not once*, had he cheated and looked anyway. His two college girlfriends, both Christians and supposedly committed to their virginity, said they were ready if he was. It wasn't that he lacked the desire, it was just that the way it was offered—"We can if you want to"—sounded so plain, as though sex itself was fundamentally ordinary, and by participating in it he would become ordinary, too. At a bachelor party for a former teammate in Las Vegas, just after Jonah turned thirty, a woman in a nightclub had whispered rum-pungent promises to show him a good time if he took her upstairs. It seemed just the extravagant way to lose his virginity, and he made it as far as the elevator before he reconsidered. He stammered and apologized and then put her in the elevator alone. As the brass doors hissed shut, she called out: "You fag, you pathetic fag. Go upstairs and jack off." Her voice, her words, the hissing elevator door, the clanking slot machines in the casino all rang in his skull as he spilled onto the dazzling, parched Strip, his skin as tight as his grip on the steering wheel on the lightless mountain road, the pain in his thighs and belly and balls proof he'd made the right decision.

He knew he was different from other celibates, Catholic priests and nuns and even unmarried Protestant ministers, all of whom exchanged consummation for ordination and guarded their bodies as they guarded the altars and cloths of their faiths. A single layman in his thirties was another matter . . . virtue not translated into marriage can attract suspicious attention. Even among those in his own church, Jonah found himself transmogrified from the boy any father would trust with his daughter into the man who made parents nervous. Jeff Miller was surprised when he volunteered for the Vacation Bible Camp; some of the leaders during the week asked him if he had a job. "I had vacation time to use up," Jonah explained, "and I like to swim." It was a reasonable explanation, but not one that satisfied the questions about his motives. "Shouldn't you be camping or something?" one of the mothers asked. On Thursday afternoon he overheard two of the teenage counselors whisper a rumor they'd heard that he was secretly gay.

Camp let out early on Friday. The children went home with bags of candy and pocket-sized red Bibles. They dashed through the chain-link gate buzzing with excitement and sugar. Candy wrappers lined the deck and floated in the water, wrinkled translucent membranes that bent the sunlight. Jonah lingered to help pick up. Titus hung around, too, scurrying about the deck with his narrow back arched, his broomstick arms dangling toward the cement, carrying handfuls of wrappers to the trash can. After they finished Jonah asked, "Someone coming to pick you up?"

"I ride my bike," Titus said. "My mom doesn't drive."

Titus bounced on the balls of his feet, his arms twitching at his sides. His teeth chattered. He was on something—perhaps more than one thing, perhaps Prolift. Prolift was speed if given to normal children and adults, but it mellowed out wild kids just long enough for them to focus for a few hours at a time. It had its share of side effects, but all medications did: nausea and insomnia, aggressive behavior; in extreme cases, paranoia and anorexia. Side effects were managed with more drugs. "Where do you live?" Jonah asked.

"Down the hill, by the high school." Titus shoved his hands down his pockets and withdrew them quickly, like an outlaw drawing guns. "Where's your house?"

"East." Jonah pointed toward the mountains. "Close to Mount Olympus."

Titus stood as tall as Jonah's elbow. His large front teeth were yellow and overlapped his lip like a rabbit's. His body looked as if he were about nine or ten, though his face was older and his teeth too big. "How old are you?"

"Thirteen," Titus said. "I'll be fourteen in December."

Impossible, Jonah thought. He himself was almost six feet tall by the time he turned fourteen. He realized he'd seen Titus a few times at church, running up and down the staircase with children half his age, stealing sugar packets from the coffee hour. "Are you in the youth group?"

"Not yet. Pastor Jeff says I'm not ready. Maybe next year."

"Get your bike," Jonah said. "I'll ride with you to your house." Titus dashed to the fence and straddled his silver bike, his twiggy arms extended to the handlebars. He looked back and squinted, his teeth clamped down hard on his bottom lip, his eyes slits against the glaring light. He'd worn the same clothes all week, the same gray T-shirt and baggy jean shorts, hand-me-down swim trunks underneath. Jonah collected the candy and the Bible. "Don't forget this stuff."

Titus shook his head. "I can't carry it." Jonah stuffed both inside his backpack and unlocked his bike from the rack. "Okay," he said. "Let's roll."

A late wind had picked up off the west desert. Jonah's skin felt tight with heat and chlorine and sunscreen. A pleasant, physical smell seeped from his armpits and swirled around in the diesel fumes from the city buses. The skyline rose below, rings of copper dust around the mirrored windows. He followed Titus down a narrow street on the back side of the high school, the square blue dumpsters and graffiti-covered wall visible through the trees, and then up a cracked driveway beside a sagging brick bungalow, the front windows shaded by the wide porch. A necklace of oil spots stained the driveway from the street to the garage, a sagging, doorless shed where a faded green Ford Granada sat hunkered in the dust. "We live down there," Titus said. He pointed to the darkened basement windows, the window wells filled with leaves and sprouting weeds, the storm door cracked and propped open with a stone. The tiny backyard was littered with scraps of red paper, sheets of newspaper, splinters of wood. Gaping holes in the shrubs where the branches had been sawed apart. "Who lives upstairs?"

"Some old lady. I don't see her much. Come see my room."

"I should get going," Jonah said. He wanted to ride away, but it would've been a bad way to end the week. He remembered Titus's Bible in his backpack, and by the time he pulled it out, Titus was down the steps.

He ducked through the basement door and was immediately hit with a humid stench—maple syrup and urine. The green carpet was as littered as the lawn, the curtains drawn tight. A small television flickered a snowy reception, the warped voices of an afternoon talk show chattering against the wall. "Mom," Titus called out. "This is Jonah, my swim teacher." Jonah looked to the hallway, expecting Titus's mother to appear from a back bedroom. Instead a very large black-haired woman rose slowly from the torn recliner that faced the television. She wore only socks and a thin cotton nightgown, the stretched collar revealing the head and bust of Betty Boop tattooed on her enormous left breast. She was easily three hundred and fifty pounds. She wheezed and coughed and gripped the back of the chair. "Jonah," she said in a hoarse whisper. She made her way toward him. "Titus has talked about you all week." Jonah got a clearer look at her face as she neared him: swollen with fat, but still in possession of its angles and shape. Her eyes were a deep, glassy blue, and Jonah could tell she had at one time been beautiful. Her name was Rosalina. Jonah recognized her from church, though he'd never talked to her before. "Thanks for bringing him home," she said. "It's very Christian of you."

"It was no problem. On my way."

Titus disappeared down the dark hallway and Jonah could hear the echo of wood banging against metal. "I've been praying for someone like you," Rosalina said. "For Titus. He really needs a man in his life right now. I can't do it on my own. So many Christians talk about helping the needy, but very few ever do, don't you think?"

"I don't know," Jonah said. "I suppose that's true."

"Well it is. You think one person from our church helped us move last time? I had to call the Mormons just to get someone with a pickup truck to come over. What did everyone expect—I could do it myself?"

Jonah could only nod. He glanced at the door.

Her voice cracked and she wheezed, lifting her hand to her mouth. Her fingernails were all painted different colors. "Mormons aren't any better. I was Mormon when Titus got taken from me. No one came to help. He was gone for three weeks, but it was a bad three weeks. I didn't get back the same little boy. He was abused, Jonah, in all sorts of ways. Physically, emotionally, verbally, sexually. That sort of thing scars a kid."

It was a lot of information to volunteer to a stranger, and he wondered how much of it was true. He said, passively, "That's horrible."

"It's a really good thing you came along. Titus needs a man in his life." She rolled her beatific eyes toward the low ceiling. The drywall was cracked and splintered, and poked full of holes. Footsteps creaked along slowly above them. "I prayed for you and God answered." She smiled and reached out her swollen hand. "God is good."

"Yes," Jonah said, his hands in his pockets. "He is."

Titus reappeared in the living room and said, "Come see, come see." Jonah was thankful for the chance to escape Rosalina, even if it meant penetrating farther inside. He had to duck his head to fit through the hallway, the furnace duct low and swinging on its rusted ties. The kitchen was stacked with boxes, and plates of unfinished food were piled on the oven, the narrow countertop, and in a festering heap in the sink. Titus's bedroom was behind a tiny door just beyond the kitchen. Hardly six feet wide, the green carpet was faded yellow in spots, and from the room wafted the heavy stench of urine. The wooden frame of his tiny bed had been slashed to a pulp, the slivers of wood threaded into the stained carpet. Titus stood before the shelf fixed to the far wall and said, "This is what I wanted to show you. Ta-da."

The shelf was lined with homemade weapons, a sword whittled from a juniper branch, two halves of a mop-handle joined with a piece of chain to make nunchucks, a row of rusted metal throwing stars. Titus slid a star off the shelf and threw it at the wall. He gritted his teeth and screamed, "Hay ah!" The star thudded against the drywall and a thin stream of dust fell onto his unmade bed.

"Careful," Jonah said. He had seen many unfortunates at the hospitals: stray homeless men with more than one voice in their heads; women with borderline personality disorder who threatened to drink bleach if they were sent home; tortured children who, unable to measure what had been done to them, mutilated their own skin. A social worker told him of places like this, where the mentally disabled lived—old hotels converted into rudimentary apartments, the plumbing bad, the radiators rusted, the walls and carpets infested with mold. It had all seemed so far away, so strange, the patients like actors in a drive-in movie: a quick look to the right or the left and the world was normal again, doctors mumbling into the dictation phones, clerks ordering labs with the pens he gave to them. Now he felt sucked into the drama, trapped in this hidden cave beneath the earth. It was the kind of feeling just months ago he would have called Charlie to talk about. Charlie would have taken his voice up an octave, impersonated Hannibal from *Silence of the Lambs*. Laughed the whole thing away. Now all he could think about was telling Abby. He wanted to lie on his couch with a beer and talk to Abby. He touched the doorframe, tapped his sneaker on the buckled linoleum in the kitchen and looked down the dark hallway. "I need to get home," he said. "A friend is waiting for me. Thanks for showing me your room."

"Can I come?" Titus jumped up and touched the low ceiling.

"No," he said. He said it more quickly than he intended, and Titus flinched. Jonah's chest tightened, and he felt desperate for fresh air. "Sorry, buddy. Maybe another time, okay?"

"Is it your girlfriend that's coming?"

"My friend is a woman," he said. "Not my girlfriend."

"Ah, you have a girlfriend," Titus said, but Jonah was already backing out of the bedroom and ducking through the hallway. "Wait," Rosalina said as he crossed the living room, "I want to ask you something." Jonah did not stop. He tapped his watch and mumbled, "I'm sorry, I'm in a rush," and kept on until he had come back up to ground level, the fresh air, the sun.

• • •

From Jeff Miller, Jonah learned that Rosalina had spent much of her adulthood addicted to meth and heroin and that Titus was born addicted to both drugs as well. A few years later, she'd come to know the Lord, left the Mormons, and kicked the habit. Titus's father was gone, which was a good thing, since he'd been into some heavy stuff himself. Rosalina had turned so sharply from her old ways that she had disavowed both her maiden and married names; her name was Rosalina, period. The church computer had her as Rosalina Rosalina. Coming off the drugs had not been easy. She gained two hundred pounds and developed bipolar disorder. "More likely it was exposed," Jeff said. "Probably part of the reason she used in the first place." She took lithium, and painkillers for arthritis, something else for asthma. "Every time I talk to her she has something new," Jeff said.

Jonah talked from his car, on his way back from a call in Tooele. To his left the Great Salt Lake lapped against the gravel; to his right the Kennecott Copper smelter puffed smoke into the clouds. Titus had his own share of troubles, Jeff said. His early addiction had crossed some wires. He was an anxious kid. Night terrors kept him wetting the bed. "Do you know what he's on?" Jonah asked.

"No. I know the regular stuff didn't work so he's on something stronger now. I'm not sure what it is. He gets frustrated in groups and acts out. He's better one-on-one." Titus and his mother had bounced around from one basement apartment to another. State disability paid the bills. She'd been through a number of churches too, asking for handouts. "It's better than heroin." Static fuzzed in and out as he rounded the mountains. The city shone against the Wasatch. Jeff said, "Titus is in school and she knows God. Jesus came for the sick, not the healthy, right? Christ has won her heart, but not her son's. Not yet. He does need a father figure, Jonah." The way he said it, Jonah knew Rosalina had made the same appeal to Jeff and now the buck was getting passed. "I think it would help him get a better look at Jesus."

Jonah thought about that phrase "father figure." A figure, as in a specter, an almost, a not-quite. Like every other role he'd played: teammate, best man, representative, witness. He wondered what word he would possess when it came to Abby's baby. What would people call him? And all this talk of leading Titus to Jesus bothered him, too, for it hatched the irritating possibility that churches like his were the repositories for the weird and the desperate, and that among them he was just as weird and desperate. But he felt guilty for running out on Titus, and he was almost certain Titus was on Prolift. He felt like a dealer, the boy his needy little junkie. Titus was practically the same age as the teenage camp counselors, but invisible to them, shunted into a special school during the year and in the summer made to participate in the games and Bible lessons designed for children five and six years younger. He thought again of Charlie's child, already destined for a fatherless world. He'd read a study in which 69 percent of children without fathers suffer from a psychological problem, either anxiety or depression or full-blown psychosis.

So Jonah agreed to spend time with Titus. Tuesdays and Thursdays he finished work by three and picked up Titus on his way home. Titus waited for him crouched behind the glass storm door, his big teeth clamped down on his lip, a weapon—a sword, his homemade nunchucks—always in his hand. Whatever optimism Jonah had talked himself into faded quickly. Titus couldn't sit still for longer than two minutes, and he begged for money, and for candy, and for everything he touched in Jonah's house: an empty glass bottle, a frayed paintbrush, a coil of jute rope in the garage. Jonah tried to teach him to pitch a tent in the front yard, but Titus separated all the poles from the nylon and made spears, which he threw at the trunk of the elm. He asked Titus to help him scrub the window screens or sweep the driveway, but if the job didn't involve operating a piece of destructive machinery, the boy wanted no part of it. He'd grasp and clutch his chest and claim to have asthma, or a heart murmur, or a lung infection. After an hour or so Jonah would surrender, and Titus would pass the rest of the afternoon in front of the television. Jonah kept his wallet out of sight when he was there, and made sure anything of value was in the closet or locked up, but even after Titus was gone, he couldn't help walking through his house certain that something was missing. Everywhere he looked he found Titus's handprints: smeared on the windows, the television, the glasses in the cupboard—everywhere a translucent grime the air-conditioning hardened to a crust.

The second week of August Abby went with Jonah on the premise of taking Titus for a hike. She wanted to see the square-dotted blue butterflies, abundant in the high meadows. "With all the rain we had this spring, there should be some left," she said. It sounded like a ruse, though for what Jonah couldn't say. Abby and Charlie's wedding anniversary was the eighteenth, but when he asked her if that had anything to do with the hike, she said only, "I'm a biologist."

They pulled into Titus's driveway just in time to see him charge up the basement steps with a chrome cap gun, a roll of red cap-papers spooled into the open chamber. Titus extended his arm and closed his eyes and fired the gun as fast as he could, one loud pop after another, his teeth ground together and his head tucked. The cap-papers fluttered to the ground in smoking sulfurous flakes. "So that's him?" Abby said. "Violent little guy."

"You ought to see his bedroom." Jonah's hands tightened around the steering wheel, and the air-conditioner condensed a horizon of vapor against the windshield. "This might not be such a good idea."

"Oh come on," Abby said. "It's just a cap gun. The boys in my neighborhood when I was a kid torched an entire field because they were bored. They're doctors and lawyers now." She slid her arm beneath his elbow and pressed the horn. Titus jumped and dropped the gun, ran quickly to the car. The dashboard pinged as the door hung open and a gust of hot air pressed against the back of Jonah's neck. "Hey," Titus said, climbing into the backseat. "Who's this?"

"This is Abby," Jonah said. "My friend."

"Oh yeah," Titus said. "Your girlfriend."

"Not quite."

"He won't have me," Abby said, looking over the seat. "I'm damaged goods."

"What does that mean?" Titus said.

"Nothing, forget it," Jonah said.

"Where are we going?"

"Up the canyon," Jonah said. "For a hike."

"I know a good place to spot butterflies," Abby said. "Trust me, it's cool."

"For you," Titus folded his arms across his chest. Jonah shifted into reverse.

White clouds piled in the sky as Jonah wound up Big Cottonwood Canyon. Abby leaned her head against the rest and watched the rock-climbers spider up the granite walls, arms splayed, colored ropes hanging slack between their legs. Titus flicked the ashtray in the backseat, a sharp sound of metal grating against metal. He said, "How far up are we going?"

"Just to here," Abby said. She pointed to the side of the road. "This is the place."

A narrow trail threaded the trees, pines interrupted here and there by a clutch of yellowing aspens. The air was thicker than usual, and Jonah grew hot quickly. It felt good to sweat, to feel his heart in his chest. Titus lagged behind, moaning that he had asthma. Finally Jonah said, "You don't have to go any farther. Just stay here and wait for us." Titus flopped down on a log and let his hands dangle between his knees.

"You're gonna miss the butterflies," Abby said.

"Like I care," Titus said. "This sucks."

Jonah unzipped his backpack and handed Titus a bottle of water. "Promise me you'll stay right here. Just sit in the shade and relax."

"Okay."

"I mean it. It's easy to get lost if you get away from the trail. Don't mess around."

Titus nodded and dug in his pocket for his knife.

"Don't cut anything either," Abby said. "Please. This is national forest."

"You can whittle dead sticks," Jonah said. "Cutting into live trees can get you into big trouble."

"Who's going to know?"

"I will," Abby said. "I'm the law in these here parts."

"Okay," Titus said. He crossed his heart with his finger. "I swear."

Faster now they followed the runoff stream where the last of the melted snow flowed through the rocks as through a long drain. Jonah watched Abby ahead of him, the damp toungues of sweat emerging through her T-shirt, running down her sides, and disappearing behind her backpack. He watched the blue-veined skin in the backs of her knees twist as she scrambled over a rise of boulders, her calves and thighs now meaty and pressing against the cuffs of her shorts. He liked this part of her body, her broadened back, her ponytail swinging as she climbed. She was no longer the girl he met in college, but he could still see her if he looked closely.

He'd noticed her before Charlie had, in the dorm cafeteria, scooping rice into a bowl. She was on the cross-country team and had just come from the showers. Her red warm-up jacket was open at the collar and her wet hair was twisted up in a tight bun, exposing her long, flushed neck. Jonah invited her to sit with him and Charlie, and by the time dinner was finished, Charlie had won her. Jonah never had a chance. For a long time, he told himself it was better this way. Abby wasn't a Christian and she certainly wasn't a virgin. She and Charlie did it in a slew of semiexposed places: a dressing room at the mall, a bathroom on the top floor of the biology building, a study room in the back corner of the library. Charlie always told Jonah about it afterward, sometimes waking him up in the middle of the night. It was as though a story had to be told for it to have happened. They stayed awake for hours while Charlie rehashed the details, who saw them go in and who saw them come out, the way the room smelled, the threatening footsteps just as he was about to come. "She's a freaking nympho," Charlie had said. "It's awesome." Jonah thought he shouldn't hear this, but he couldn't help himself. His own desires caught fire and glowed while Charlie talked, and he drifted back to sleep imagining a woman—he tried not to imagine Abby, though it was difficult not to—sliding her underpants past her knees or pulling her shirt above her head.

Abby moved steadily, her center of gravity low and squared with the trail. They scrambled over a ridge of boulders and down into a grassy meadow. Clouds thickened to the west and heat lightning flashed over the desert, the thunder a faint rumble. Snowmelt collected into a pond against the rocks and was backed up by a dam of twigs and a pile of gray stones. Abby sat down on a rock and unlaced her boots. Her feet and ankles were startlingly white against her tan legs. She slid one foot into the shallow water and huffed against the cold. "I used to come up here all the time. I have a permit to collect seeds, but most days I just hiked. Can you believe I get paid to do this?"

"You ought to try my job. I drive around and bring people lunch."

"You're everybody's favorite guy. And hanging out with the kid earns you major points in the do-gooder race. Not that you need them."

"I doubt it. If he does something really bad, I'll be partly to blame."

"You worry too much about consequences," she said. She pulled her foot from the pond. Water dripped from her heel. "Take off your shoes. You'll feel better." She stood up from the rock and stepped into the meadow, the buckwheat as tall as her knees.

Jonah unlaced his boots and peeled off his socks. Abby sifted through the buckwheat with her hands, and squatted. It was an awkward position; she had to keep extending her foot to maintain her balance. But it was natural, in a way, like a peasant farming a small plot of land. She was at home here, close to the edge of the trees. She sifted through a pile of birch leaves and said, "Aha. Here." She turned over the buckwheat to reveal a curled purple leaf, the rings of a caterpillar's belly faintly visible through the white membrane at the narrow end, the fatter end crinkled around the wings. "It took me awhile to see them when I first started coming up here," she said. "I had to look and look. First there are none, then you learn where to focus, and they're everywhere." He studied the pupa in her hand, her belly a globe squeezed between her thighs and breasts. She ran her fingernail down the center of the cocoon and split it in half. "Watch this," she said. She peeled back the sides and a tiny blue butterfly, no bigger than her thumbnail, unfolded its wings. Abby blew on its wings, and for a moment the butterfly stood frozen, wet and stunned. Then, as though waking up, it lifted off from its cocoon, from Abby's hand, and was gone.

Jonah was amazed. "I didn't know you could do that."

"That's nothing," Abby said. She pressed her palms against her knees and straightened, holding her back. She unzipped her backpack and from it hefted a gallon-sized plastic bag full of gray silt. It looked as if she'd emptied her vacuum cleaner bag. Abby shook it. "It's Charlie. How do you like that?"

"You buried him," Jonah said, incredulous. "I held the urn."

"It was filled with ashes from my fireplace. I'm not one for graveyards."

"You buried wood?"

"It's all carbon in the end. This way everyone gets what she wanted. His mom can go see him whenever she likes, right in her own hometown. She'll never know the difference." She stepped into the pond.

Abby had always been hard to read. Some nights Jonah would show up for dinner and find broken glass in the trash can, Charlie sulking in the backyard, the air heavy with the fight Jonah had interrupted. And there Abby would be, chopping tomatoes as if nothing had happened. He didn't know how to read what they were doing now, whether she and Charlie had talked about scattering each other in the mountains, or if this was a mockery of the ceremonies of death. It seemed a private moment, but she'd been willing to bring Titus along. None of it made sense.

The water was frigid and mud oozed between his toes. A green cloud stirred up. Abby parted the seams of the bag, and ash collected around their ankles and calves; a ring of Charlie clung to their skin and to the stringy hair on Jonah's legs.

"You probably think I'm going to hell for this," she said. She shrugged, "Not that I haven't figured that already."

Jonah reached down and dipped his fingers in the ash, then lifted up his hand and studied it. Was this Charlie's leg? His pointed chin? His big wrecked heart? He imagined Charlie as he often saw him, his head slipping beneath the water at the start of a swim, the skin around his shoulder blades folded and rippling as he pulled his arms tight above his head, Jonah's own chest exploding a little as he pushed off behind him. Swimming was different without him. He didn't have the same fire, racing no longer had much point, and watching the ash settle and drift toward the little dam and down into the stream, it seemed sad that after all the times he had raced Charlie, this was what his friend had become. He hoped there was an afterlife for Charlie, some salvation for almost-Christians, or close friends of the saved, but somehow this felt like the end.

He looked at Abby, her eyes glassy and abstract. "What a bastard," she said. She pressed her finger to the creased skin around her left eye, then withdrew it quickly.

"He loved you very much," Jonah said. "You know that."

"Just stand here a minute." She reached for his hand. Her palm throbbed heat; it felt different from the other times they'd touched. "I want to watch the ashes disappear." Her thumb stroked the back of his hand.

Lightning flashed to the west. The clouds had drifted across the valley. A cluster of butterflies emerged from the buckwheat at the edge of the water, fluttering as they moved up and sideways, touching a bloom, lifting, circling back. Then, though blue skies were overhead, lightning flashed again, almost directly below them, a brighter flash and a louder crack than he could ever have imagined. They hurried out of the water.

"Spooky," Abby said. She wiggled her fingers on both hands. "God's coming for us. Think we can outrun Him?"

"No."

"Think the kid's okay?"

"I hope so." He stepped into his boots and pulled the laces tight. He heard a scream in the distance, a long, high-pitched screech. As it grew louder he realized what it was. "It's Titus," he said. "Must have struck close."

"Got him moving, didn't it?" Abby said. The sun was bright against the granite walls, concentrated there as the clouds rolled in. The wind fluttered her sleeve. "We're going to get wet."

There was no stopping it. Jonah could smell rain, and the cool air ran

79

a chill down his sides. He knew the dangers of getting caught in a light-ning storm, but he couldn't stop watching Abby. She held her hand like a visor over her eyes and looked down toward the valley. It was no longer sadness he felt, or anxiety—it was desire. Charlie's ashes were in the water, and Jonah wanted her. Abby shook the dried buckwheat from her boots, her neck bent, the bones arcing at the top of her spine. Jonah rubbed his own neck and imagined the skin and the bones he felt beneath it were hers. He imagined his lips there. She laid her cheek against her shoulder and narrowed her eyes at him. The hair stood up on Jonah's arms and around the knobs of both knees. "You feel that?" Abby said, though before he could say or do anything he heard Titus again, his voice loud and panicked, calling Jonah's name.

· · ·

That Sunday, Pastor Jeff talked about the lustful heart. Before Christ, he said, God's covenant with man was through the law, the Ten Com-mandments, and the instructions for how to dress and eat. Actions weighed more heavily than thoughts. Then Jesus came along and taught us the lustful heart is just as sinful as the body. Jonah wrote that down—*the lustful heart is just as sinful as the body*—in the margins of his Bible.

And yet, as he traversed the valley in the Chevrolet over the following weeks, he sinned with Abby a thousand times a day. He imagined her tak-ing him by the hand into the bedroom, undressing while he watched, pressing her breasts to his face. Other times he tore her shirt with his hands and unhooked her bra with his teeth. He remembered Charlie's sto-ries about where they had done it, though more than anything he returned to the night he saw Abby naked—Abby's pale, freckled breasts lit by the moonlight through the curtains, the dark strip of hair between her legs. He'd heard them doing it before, Abby's squeaky gasps and Char-lie's long sighs. His hearing, he knew, was part of Charlie's sport. But that night was no performance; Abby thought he was asleep. And as quickly as he could conjure her gasps and moans, he could imagine her dismiss-ing her mother's or her friends' inquires about him. *You mean Jonah?* He could practically hear her laugh. *Oh, he's harmless!*

But he wasn't, not like she thought. He'd never been able to turn the other cheek. His friendship with Charlie was always competitive, and competition forges a strange, often hateful bond, one that obligated Jonah to cheer Charlie home at the Olympic Trials even as he secretly hoped Charlie would lose, swallow water at the last second, slip on his last turn, or run out of gas in the final ten meters. Seventeen one-hundredths of a second separated Charlie from third place in the two-hundred butterfly, from staying home, from equivalence with Jonah's respectable eleventh-place finish in the mile. Seventeen one-hundredths of a second earned Charlie the right to have his picture taken with the President, to wave a toy American flag in the opening parade, to walk around campus in a Team USA jacket. Charlie never once bragged that he deserved it, and throughout their senior year he cheered harder than ever for Jonah's races. He did all that could be asked of a friend, but Jonah still felt a little burst of relief whenever Charlie had an off race. That relief was his only acknowledgment of his hatred, and he tried his best to force it away from his face, not to appear gratified by it.

The night he saw Abby naked, Jonah found his hatred so overwhelming that he did speak it. He whispered across the carpet that separated his bed from Charlie's, "I hate you." On the bookshelf attached to the wall above Charlie's bed sat three cans of Hormel Chili, a pile of papers and books, an unopened bottle of beer, and Charlie's MVP trophy. The brass swimmer atop the trophy glowed white in the moonlight. Jonah lifted it from the shelf and cradled the marble base in his hand, the sharp edge against his palm. Charlie's face was turned to the side on the pillow, his hair swirled above his ear. Jonah raised the trophy above his own head and, for just a moment, imagined bringing it down onto Charlie's face. Loyalty was a sham, sportsmanship a loser's word. He shelved the trophy and hurried across the hall to the bathroom, washed his hands and face, and for a good five minutes, studied himself in the mirror, his taut chest and stomach, his long arms. He balled his hands into fists and boxed the air, two rights and a left. He felt strong. He felt mean. He was not harmless, not at all.

In the eyes of Jeff Miller, though, Jonah was a hero. Word got around Jonah was "discipling" Titus, and congregation members began slipping him tickets for the last few Stingers home games or preseason lift tickets—things Jonah could get easily enough on his own and none of which Titus had any interest in. Rosalina drifted now and again through the Sunday service in a drugged haze, like a float separated from its parade, her oceanic eyes glazed, the skin beneath her neck folding as her head lolled from side to side. Some members slapped him on the back and shook his

hand. "You're a godsend," they told him. He'd gone after the sheep separated from the flock. No one needed to worry anymore about what to do
with Titus.

School started in September, and after a full day of classrooms and
books and forced times of prolonged concentration, Titus climbed into
Jonah's car twitching with rage. An explosive fury commanded his movements; riding in the car his hands twitched in his lap as if he was working
to defuse a bomb. The basement appeared more battered—a window broken, circular burns on the cracked cement, a trail of garbage leading from
the door to the trash can. One day Jonah lifted the trash can lid and found
it swarming with maggots. Rosalina never appeared when he picked Titus
up or dropped him off, even though he could hear the television blaring
when Titus shoved open the door. Jonah was full of nervous energy, too,
restless in the lingering heat and unsure of himself around Abby, certain
that every word he spoke in her presence betrayed his feelings. The next
time he saw her, things would be awkward. There were days his long-
battled desires felt so present and close to bursting that he punched his
mattress and pillows. In the waiting room of one of the clinics, a woman
spilled her purse, and when she leaned over to gather it back up, the collar of her blouse hung open and Jonah saw she was not wearing a bra. In
private humiliation he watched himself stand up from the chair and go
into the bathroom fully intent on doing what he did not want to do,
ashamed of his reflection as he passed by the mirror. Outside, the nurses
shuffled past the door. He knew the consequences of being caught, that it
would cost him his job, but he didn't care. He remembered some of the
things Charlie used to say when he came home from being with Abby:
"You've got to do battle with the world, J—each place you do it, you claim
as your own." Or, "It's why God gave men thumbs, lock and key." The
phrases always seemed beyond his understanding, and thinking of Charlie only caused him to picture Abby more, which just made it worse.

There was, then, a relief to his afternoons with Titus, the pure physi-
cality of it. Titus consumed the space of three people with all his dancing
around. It kept Jonah from thinking too much. Afternoons had a routine.
Jonah picked him up at three and took him to his house. He made Titus
a turkey sandwich. For the length of time it took him to eat, Titus could
sit at the kitchen table and talk. He asked Titus about his medications, but
Titus couldn't name any of them. He said he took seven pills in the morn-

ing, three more before bed. "Is one of them yellow?" Jonah asked. "Small and round?" Titus said he couldn't remember. Jonah asked about his friends at school. Titus said he had two, Nick and Brigham, both with green belts in karate. They backed him up during fights. "Do you fight a lot?" Jonah asked.

"Not a lot, but when I do, look out. I'm mean and real tough."

"Do you win?"

Titus nodded. "Yeah."

"Other boys pick on you?"

"Not so much. Most are afraid of me. They've seen me mess people up real bad."

Jonah inspected Titus's arms and face while he chewed his sandwich. Besides the usual scrapes and scabs, he saw nothing to suggest anything major. "You look tough," he said. Titus grinned and took a swig of Coke. He liked the idea of Titus telling stories to look stronger and tougher. It was proof Titus saw him as a man to measure himself against, and to measure up to, and Jonah felt in that one small way he had assumed the role of a father, not just the figure of one. He felt he should ask Titus if he knew Jesus, but he found it difficult to find an opening, and anyway, weren't these afternoons the model of Jeff's stealth evangelism? Wouldn't Titus come to know Jesus better through Jonah's actions than through a sales-pitch, a booklet, or the Bible spread between them on the kitchen table? After Titus finished his snack they'd watch television for a half hour while their food digested, and then he and Jonah would go into the front yard to practice Titus's "moves." Titus chopped and kicked and called out "Hay ah!" while Jonah bent his knees and stuck out his hands to block. Titus would occasionally narrow his eyes on Jonah's chest or neck and run hard, but Jonah always managed to get his hands up. It siphoned out most of his energy, and some of Jonah's, too, and on the way home, Titus curled into a ball on the front seat and fell asleep, helpless as a wingless bird. Jonah's arms and hands were always sticky after his afternoons with Titus, as was his car, his kitchen table, his doorknobs. He wiped it all away with a soapy rag, though what had once seemed like grime and filth now seemed less toxic, the oil of human touch.

· · ·

The Botanical Gardens held a party at the end of every season. This year the staff decided to make the party a baby shower for Abby. "I told them I didn't want one," Abby said. She stood before her bathroom mirror working a clip in her hair. Her belly drooped beneath the hem of her maternity blouse, a small moon emerging from behind a cloud. "They insisted. Now everyone in the whole goddamn place will be there."

"Think of all the presents," Jonah said. "You haven't bought anything for the baby yet."

"Last minute is better. Just in case." Her blouse tied in the front. Abby lifted her breasts with her arm while she unlaced and retied the ribbon. "I actually do like this party. It means we've made it to the end of the summer and that the Gardens are still in okay shape. I spend months picking trash out of the beds. You have no idea how many candy wrappers and wads of gum we find. Ant mounds spring up overnight. And the concerts! We practically have to send one of the maintenance workers swimming in the koi pond just to fish out the beer bottles. Not to mention the condoms and cigarette butts we dig out of the trees. You'd think people would have a bit more *respect*."

Jonah laughed. "You sound so protective."

"Don't let the big shirt fool you," she said. "It may be a shower, but there'll be plenty of booze and dancing, and someone usually faints or pukes. The single folks pair up and wander out to screw under the open sky. Enough gossip to last until spring." She lifted an eyebrow. "Who knows, J, you drink enough to let your guard down and someone just might take advantage of you."

"I'm skilled in the fine art of evasion."

"Yes," she said. "I know."

From the Gardens' hilltop perch, they could see the valley spread out below, city lights twinkling all the way to the Oquirrhs. Headlights crawled like ants up the graded slope of the Kennecott Copper Mine. A strip of pink stretched across the far shore of the lake, the water shimmering like foil. It was just after dusk. They climbed the winding path through the gates to the Orangerie, its tall windows suffused with a creamy glow. Fruit trees planted in stone pots climbed toward the ceiling, limbs entwined with twinkling white lights. Partygoers milled along the buffet line. "The director is Mormon, so he won't spring for liquor," Abby said as they walked in. In the center of the room, a couple danced clumsily, stepping on each other's toes. "It's BYOB, but almost everyone *B*s and some starting drinking before they come." She rolled her eyes. "Be alert."

Gifts were stacked on a table against the wall, at the end of which sat a gigantic cake, as big as a wedding cake, ornately decorated with icing flowers and poached apples curled into roses. Beyond it sat the liquor table, magnums of wine and slender bottles filled with vodka and gin and tequila, a mound of limes in a ceramic bowl. Abby introduced Jonah around. The other conservationists were mostly women with sunburned cheeks and noses, their hands rough inside his palm. Jonah forgot their names as soon as they were spoken, except for one woman he recognized from Charlie's funeral—Gretchen. "Oh yes, *Jonah*," she said. Her brown hair was French-braided down the center of her back. "I remember you now. Abby talks about you all the time. The saint."

"Not quite," he said.

"Abby says you're a real sweetheart. You knew Charlie well?"

"Since high school."

Abby stood before the drink table filling a glass with Coke. She was too far away to hear. Gretchen scanned the room. "I'm sorry," she said. "It was just horrible." Jonah nodded. "And just that morning—" she stopped talking when Abby returned with two glasses. "Mine's unleaded," Abby said, extending one of the glasses to Jonah. "But I put a little gas in yours." She was followed by a man with silver hair carefully styled into a frozen wave that glinted beneath the lights. The tip of his nose was round, like a marble. "This is Mr. Johnson, the director."

Mr. Johnson extended his hand. "Don."

"Jonah Moore."

"Glad you came," Don said. "Food's good. I can't vouch for the spirits."

"Thank you for having me."

"I'm going to steal Abby for a dance."

Jonah shrugged, and Don led Abby away. Gretchen stepped close and said, almost into his ear, "Watch out for that one. He's a real flirt."

"Yeah?"

"He's a bishop in his ward or stake or whatever it's called. I know he's got seven kids. See that woman over there, the frump?" Gretchen pointed ed to a homely woman seated alone near the drinks, her plain, elongated face angled toward a half-emptied glass of water. "That's his wife. If she could hear half the things her husband says. He believes that because he's some high-and-mighty in his church, he can say whatever he likes. Maybe it's his name. Every Halloween he comes to work in his white suit and pink T-shirt shirt and says, 'it's not a costume.'" She rolled her eyes. "That's right, *you're* Don Johnson."

Jonah laughed. "Never get tired of making jokes about that, do you?"

"It's all bullshit," she said. "Any one of us could run this place better than he does, but the legislature insists on a man. We're a garden, for God's sake."

"Well, Eve fouled that one up for you," he said.

Now it was Gretchen's turn to laugh. Jonah watched Don Johnson press his hand against the center of Abby's lower back. He was less than six feet tall and had a paunch. His belt pushed against Abby's belly, and they moved together slowly, like a game in which two people carry a ball across a room without using their hands. Gretchen's arm brushed against Jonah's. He hardly noticed. She said, "So, you two?"

"We're just friends," he said. His voice sounded plaintive. "I'm a stand-in."

"Abby doesn't need a stand-in," she said. She allowed her arm to rub against his again. Her silver bracelet dragged across the cuff of his shirt.

Jonah stepped to the side, "Sorry."

"Abby's tough as nails. I've tried to get her to talk, but she doesn't say much. Maybe she's better with you."

"Hardly."

"I know she's alone in all this, but she won't crack." Gretchen leaned toward his ear and lowered her voice. Jonah dipped his head to listen just as Don Johnson unfurled Abby to the ends of his arms, then reeled her back. "Her heart is a little black box. No crash can break it. Not me, no sir. I still cry sometimes thinking about it."

"I miss him," Jonah said.

"With Abby to console you, I don't know how you don't." She squeezed his wrist and swept his empty glass off the table. A couple in the shadows on the other side of the floor stole a quick, furtive kiss. "Let me refill this for you."

The biologists all chipped in for a crib and changing table, and besides the big stuff, Abby wound up with things Jonah had never known were necessary for a baby. A bathtub small enough to fit in a kitchen sink, a floating thermometer, tiny fingernail clippers, a folding vibrating chair. He stacked the boxes into Abby's arms and carried the crib down to the car. The wind pushed against the crib box, like a sail on the steep wooded path. Gretchen had brought him a stiff second drink, and then a stiff third; they had danced to a few songs, and in the breeze he could still smell her perfume. He felt a little drunk. He said to Abby, "Your boss is a horn-dog."

"Don? Oh, he's a little touchy-feely. Charlie never liked him either. He has a good heart, I think. Lots of kids. His oldest daughter is twenty-seven so he thinks he can comment on women's clothes or figures and still sound like a father. It's not like he'd ever try anything." She inserted the key into the trunk, popped it open. The dim bulb lit her hands and stomach. "Plus, he's a bishop. Teenagers have to confess to him when they've done the deed. Can you imagine? I'd have been kicked out of that church when I was thirteen."

"Thirteen?" As young as Titus, he thought. Still he imagined it, her young body.

"My older sister was a bad influence."

"Gretchen doesn't think Don is so innocent."

"Gretchen isn't so fond of men at the moment. Her last relationship came to a messy end. You seemed to be changing her mind, though."

"We just danced," he said. "For lack of other partners."

Abby stabbed his chest with her fingernail. "Wake up, Jonah. People get attracted to one another. It happens. You don't need a star to fall from the sky to know it." Jonah's star had already fallen, so he leaned in and kissed her, just once, softly behind her ear. He could still claim it was friendly. The open trunk bounced in the wind, and he steadied it with his hand.

"See?" She leaned against him. "Not so hard."

They drove home in silence, Jonah in the passenger seat. The traffic thickened as they crossed through town, the other cars filled with other couples out on a Saturday night. Abby's hand rested on the gearshift and then on the inside of his thigh. He could feel her pulse through his skin and through his pants. Her long, earth-damaged fingers moved back and forth ever so slightly, and he worried that she might bump up against his erection. A thousand tiny abandonments fluttered in his soul, like the butterflies over the buckwheat, declaring not a presence, but the absence formed by desire. He knew what was happening, what would happen when they got to her house; he had time to stop himself, but he did not want to. He said, "Gretchen was who you were going to stay with. Her guestroom?"

Abby kept her eyes forward. Wide maple branches arched over the street, showering leaves. "That's right, she was the one."

She pulled into her driveway and killed the headlights. The house sat hunkered in the dark. Formally and in silence, Abby led him through the front door and up the staircase to her bedroom. She flicked on the lamp beside the bed, the lavender comforter pulled tight beneath the pillows. He had the brief sensation that this was how the married made love, ascending the stairs in unspoken agreement about what would take place at the top, approaching each other beside the bed they shared on angry or ill or tired nights. Abby turned and kissed him. He felt her tongue, still cold and sweet from the Coke, slide into his mouth and explore his teeth. The last tongue to come inside his mouth was Charlie's when the CPR compressions had pushed his bloated tongue out of his mouth. "We probably shouldn't," Jonah said.

"We're doing it, Jonah." It was his name she was saying and it rang in his ear. "I can't wait forever. And now I've got competition." She dropped her arm from his neck and took his hand, then turned him to sit on the bed. The comforter exhaled beneath his weight, and his erection pressed uncomfortably against his zipper. "Try not to talk too much."

"You know I—"

She lifted an eyebrow to scold him. "I know. Don't worry." She unlaced the black bow on the front of her blouse, then crossed her arms at her waist and slid the whole thing up over her head. It fell to a heap at Jonah's feet. How many times had he imagined such a motion? Touched himself in the dark for want of that single unfurling? Abby's nipples were thick and dark beneath the cups of her white bra, and her belly was much larger unclothed than he expected, divided down the center by a crimson line. A web of purple veins crawled toward her navel. She pushed her skirt down her thighs. She turned to the mirror on the dresser, cupped her belly with both hands. "Aren't I a pretty picture?" Her white underpants strained at the seams. "I feel like I've been eaten from the inside out," she said. "*Consumed.*"

"It's good," he said, awkward, his mouth dry. "Beautiful, I mean."

She reached around him to untuck his shirt. Jonah worked the top buttons until together they yanked it over his head, oxford and undershirt together. She unfastened his pants and used her thumbs to slide both his pants and underwear past his knees. The belt clicked against the floor. Embarrassed, he watched his bent erection point toward the door, but Abby looked at it plainly, no more special than a hand or a toe. *Thirteen,* he thought. *Jesus.* She unfastened her bra and stepped out of her underpants, her pubic hair abundant between her legs and up the slope of her stomach. Abby cupped her hand between Jonah's legs. He felt his pulse against the pressure of her fingers. "There now," she said. "You're doing fine."

He moved backward on his elbows. Abby lifted her knee to the bed and lumbered forward. Jonah kissed her sternum and then the top of her belly as she moved above him. He took the knob of her navel in his mouth. "I can't quite see down there anymore," Abby said. "I don't have a mirror in the shower."

"It's beautiful," he said. "All of you."

"I feel like a whale."

"Does that mean you're going to swallow me inside you?"

"You need to work on your pillow talk, mister."

"I mean the story about Jonah and the whale. From the Bible."

"I know. You might want to leave the Bible out of this for a few minutes."

She sat back on her knees. Her breasts hung like two sacks against the top of her stomach. She guided Jonah's hands there. "Your hands are too soft. Be more insistent. I wouldn't mind it if you hit me."

"I could never do that. Charlie—"

"No more of Charlie. For Christ's sake."

"No more."

She leaned forward and he took her nipple in his mouth, making her wince. He pulled back. "I'm just tender," she said. "Don't stop." Then, "I don't know if I even remember what this is like."

"Like I do."

"We're both new at it then. Virgins."

Jonah looked down to her stomach, his erection rising to meet it. "I don't think you qualify," he said. "Technically."

"Do you feel okay?"

"Yes," he said. "I'm fine."

And he was fine. As Abby dragged her hand down Jonah's stomach and guided him inside, slowly working him in, lifting and settling until she sat squarely upon him, he felt better than ever. She was heavier than he expected and that felt good too, her weight spread over his entire middle, enveloping him in warmth. Abby locked her elbows on either side of his head. Jonah closed his eyes and, to his surprise, his mind drifted to the night in high school when the swim team climbed to the roof of the natatorium, unscrewed the skylights, and dove through the dark to the pool below. Charlie dove first, and when Jonah stood on the edge and looked down into the nothing, he heard Charlie call up, "Come on, jump!" Jonah was afraid, but dove anyway. He felt himself falling now through the same black and humid void of his own fear. Then he felt the bottom coming, and gripping the bottom of Abby's stomach, he emptied quickly, fluttering up inside her.

Afterward, they lay stretched on either side of the dark stain of what they had done, and listened to the house creak in the breeze. Now and then a car downshifted and worked to climb the hill. Abby rolled to her elbow, her enlarged breasts drooping toward the mattress. She asked, "You've never done it before? Really?"

"No."

"Never once, just to see?"

"Never."

"But you've come close, right? You could have had you wanted to?"

"I came close," he said. "I fled the evil desires of youth."

"How close was close? The one that could have happened. How close was that?" She was tickled by the idea, and proud of herself. Her mouth curled at the edges.

"I got drunk enough at Nick Houseman's bachelor party to follow a woman out of a club," he said. "She had even bought condoms in the bathroom. I made it as far as the elevator, but I didn't go up."

"What stopped you?"

"Charlie."

She laughed, plumbed his navel with her finger nail. Jonah felt a current travel from his abdomen to his balls, as though a wire connected the two. "You give Charlie too much credit. He definitely would have gone up," Abby said.

"He did."

"What?"

"Got into an elevator with a woman," he said. "Someone he met in the club."

It was a secret he'd kept for years, even when he thought Abby deserved to know it, even when he was sure she did know, somehow, that Charlie had told her. He'd kept it because he knew Charlie couldn't be alone. Charlie would have suffered much more to have Abby leave him than he would living with the burden of his conscience. What made Charlie fun also made him weak: his need to be loved, to impress, to dazzle and delight. He bought drinks for the bachelor party and for the group of women that crowded into their booth at the back of the club. Charlie drank until his eyes were red and his mouth hung open, until the young woman, maybe a year or two out of college, wearing a strapless red dress with glitter sprinkled across her chest and neck, led him onto the dance floor and slid her hands inside his back pockets while they swayed and bumped. When the song ended, she took Charlie's hand and moved in the direction of the door and Charlie followed her out of the club and into the bright lights of the casino. The ringing bells and falling coins should have brought Charlie back, but they didn't. He didn't want to be brought back. He got into the elevator and turned to face the closing doors. That was when Jonah saw him, just before the doors drew shut. The look on Charlie's eyes said, *Don't judge me for doing this.* The alcohol wasn't to blame; Charlie knew what he was doing. Jonah was awake when Charlie returned to the hotel room the next morning. Charlie was weeping. He told Jonah he thought he had a disease.

"Like AIDS?" Abby touched her stomach.

"No . . . sex," Jonah said. "He couldn't get enough."

By telling it, he meant to tell Abby he and Charlie were, finally, very different. He was stronger than Charlie, and by giving her what he had given to no one else, he was telling her he loved her. He wanted to say those words, *I love you,* for he had never considered the possibility that he felt anything but love. But he felt himself rising again, wanting her more than ever, more than he had the first time. Abby lay still on her side, her breasts gleaming atop her belly, the orange streetlight dividing her thigh in half. He put his hand in the moonlight, then on her leg, and slid it upward. Abby winced, and he felt her thighs constrict around his hand. "Stop," she said. "What are you doing?"

"I thought you knew what he was like," he said. "I thought you liked it."

"You thought I liked it? You thought I liked my husband fucking strange women when he went out of town? That's how you think I am?"

"Yes." Of all the ways he had envisioned himself with her, this was the version he had most wanted, and he knew it. "Aren't you?"

"Maybe so," she said. She rolled onto her back and opened her legs. "Go for it." What he did next surprised even him. He rolled on top of her, fumbled forward, and slid inside, never once saying a word. Abby held her eyes locked on his, sunken and hateful. Her top lip curled slightly, unmoved. He had to lean up on his hands to make room for her belly, though his arms soon grew tired and he gradually descended until his weight settled down on top of her. What had tingled every nerve just hours ago now felt deadened and mechanical. Abby lay with her hands flat against her sides. Their pelvic bones ground together and pinched his balls. Just as he was about to finish, he felt a kick at the base of his stomach, hard enough that he looked down. It took him a second to understand that it came from inside Abby, from the baby. Did it know what he was doing to her? Jonah tried not to think. Instead, he sped up and hurried to finish.

He pulled away and Abby stood up in front of the open window. She flicked on the light, a too-bright flash that snapped Jonah's eyes shut. He covered himself with his hands. She said, "Congratulations, Jonah. You went from virgin to asshole in just two screws. That's got to be a record."

"Abby," he said. "Wait."

She stood in the doorway of the bathroom, lingering there as though considering whether to turn back. Jonah waited, not speaking, studying the place where her arched spine met her ass. He wanted her still. She stepped inside and flicked the door shut behind her, rattling the knob in the latch. Jonah waited for a minute in the hallway for the sound of Abby crying in the bathroom. He considered knocking and whispering through the oak. But the door was silent; whatever noises she made beyond were absorbed. The entire house felt trapped in that oaken silence. Would a real lover wait to apologize? He could not handle her opening the door only to tell him to leave. He fumbled back into his pants.

It was past three when Jonah slipped down the stairs with his shoes in his hands. He looked up the staircase once to make sure Abby wasn't there. He opened the door and closed it hard, so she would know he was gone. A delivery truck was parked facing uphill in the middle of the street, blocking Jonah's car. A man in white pants and a yellow jacket jumped when the door slammed, jostling his dolly of milk. He watched Jonah walk all the way to his car. "Need me to move it, man?"

"I can wait," Jonah said.

"I can move it quick and quiet. She won't even know you're gone."

"She already knows."

"That's right," he said. "Let her know how it is. She'll beg you for it that way." He rocked the dolly back to vertical and set the brake with his foot, then hopped over and climbed inside the cab. He slid the truck into neutral and drifted backward toward the curb.

· · ·

Jonah steered the Chevrolet down the back side of Capitol Hill and then out along the quarry and the refinery to the shore of the lake, the black water rippling over the marshes, its lowest point of the year. He could see the airport across the water, the planes tucked into the gates, the runway lit up. He drove the freeway a few miles, then exited and drove back the other direction. He wasn't going anywhere, just waiting for the sun to rise. He could manage returning to his empty house if there was light in the living room and he could brew coffee and scramble eggs and watch the television programs intended for the waking, rather than the infomercials and phone-sex ads aired when only the lonely and desperate were watching. He did not yet feel shame, or even regret, though he felt the tide of both ebbing back, preparing to sweep forward. He passed a police cruiser staked out on a feeder road, and he straightened his back and eased off the accelerator, careful not to apply the brake. He felt like a drunk driver.

Before long he saw the paperboys riding their bicycles up and down the streets, slinging papers, and a handful of runners puffing moist clouds of breath as they passed beneath the streetlamps. The mountains appeared as though out of nowhere, a line of orange rimming the peaks.

Jonah felt the need to sleep coming on hard when he turned onto his street. He blinked and forced his eyes to stay open. Titus sat on the front steps when he pulled to the curb in front of his house. He felt the spark and crackle of anger as he withdrew the key from the ignition. Titus's showing up seemed just the punishment he deserved. "For Christ's sake," he said to the windshield.

Titus's bike lay on its side in the grass. Jonah started up the walk, and Titus stood up and folded his pocketknife closed, shoved it down his front pocket. His small eyes were scanning and he bit down on the corners of his mouth. His teeth were speckled yellow, and purple creases streaked the outside of his cheeks. Jonah could tell Titus had been scratching at his face. Jonah saw a "T" etched in the concrete by the step. "I've got new moves," Titus said. "Wanna see?"

"Not right now," Jonah said. "Maybe another time."

"Can I come in for a while?"

"This isn't a good time, buddy." Titus winced. The wind stirred the trees and spread the leaves across the grass. "I'm sorry you rode all the way here, but I've had a long night."

"Let me have a Coke then. Something." Titus bounced on his toes and shook his hands. "Come on. I'll just sit on the steps and drink it."

Titus stopped bouncing, but his eyes and lips could not hold still. Jonah asked, "Did you take your medications?"

"No," he said. "I'm not taking them no more. My mom locked me out of the house and called the cops. Screw her."

"You need them. They help you. Ride back home and take them. Come back tomorrow."

"No!" Titus shouted. He ran up and gripped Jonah's arm. His hands were grimy; his mouth and skin smelled of syrup, and of something feral and rotting: of sickness, not childhood. "They're coming to take me away. I'm not going."

"Calm down," Jonah said. "No one's coming." He pried Titus's grip from his arm. Jonah's skin was white and then it flushed red. He backed Titus up a few steps and then stepped backward himself. "Your mom's not going to send you anywhere." It was possible the police or social services or whomever you called to take a kid away were already pulling up to the basement door. The truth was a larger burden than the lie right then. "Ride home and see. You'll be all right."

The curtains parted in the window across the street. The woman who lived there, an immaculately neat widow whom he had never formally met, stared out from behind the glass. Titus jumped and backed up a few steps, then withdrew the knife from his pocket and unfolded the blade. It was rusted, but the edge was scuffed clean, sharpened on the cement. "You have to let me in," he said. "They're after me."

"No one's after you," Jonah said. "Go home." He walked over to Titus's bike and lifted it from the grass. He tapped the sod back into place with his foot. "Go on."

"No!" Titus screamed again. He threw his knife at his bike. It landed close to Jonah's foot, the chipped handle rising from the grass. Jonah pulled it out, folded it up, and put it in his pocket. "Go home before I call the police," he said. "Right now."

Titus dug down inside his pocket and produced one of the throwing stars, a little rusted saw blade he pinched between his thumb and the side of his index finger. He raised his hand, narrowed his eyes on Jonah's chest, and screamed "Hay ah!," and Jonah knew Titus wasn't playing. This was for real.

He moved his arm to cover his face. The star hit him in the soft flesh near his elbow, and then fell back to the grass. Jonah rolled his arm and examined the blood trickling toward his elbow. He caught the blood in his hand and looked at it on his fingers and in the lines of his palm. Abby would be awake soon and would rise thinking of him with malice. He felt Charlie watching him, stirring the trees and guiding Titus's bicycle to his house, the messenger of his revenge, the boy's pockets filled with metal. An old hate rose sharp and fast from Jonah's stomach to his throat, and he ran hard to Titus, four fast steps Titus did not try to dodge. He gripped Titus by the neck, said, "You little shit." Titus wriggled in his hand, and turned and looked up, his face turning red. Jonah felt Titus tightening, bracing himself. A half-smirk smeared across the boy's crooked, over-bitten mouth. He was here for this: he had come to Jonah's house not to show his moves or to eat or even for asylum from the police, but to be beaten, just as he had been beaten by everyone else he had grown to trust or love. Titus's eyes stopped moving and his pupils grew wide. He was afraid, but relieved in his fear. Fear he knew and understood; love he did not. It was a test. Abby had been a test, too, and Jonah had failed both. He threw Titus to the pavement as hard as he could. Titus's head bounced on the cement and then curled toward his knees. Titus lay still and Jonah backed away from him and backed up his front stairs and went inside the house and called the police.

Jonah walked outside with his wallet in his pocket, his hands at his sides. A crimson streak of blood had dried between the wound in his arm and the tip of his elbow. Two officers climbed out of the cruiser, a compact man with a long chin and a young woman who wore her blonde hair pulled into a tight bun, exposing dark roots. The widow across the street stood in her doorway in a green housedress, her arms folded across her chest. The male officer called to Titus by name. "Can you stand up, Titus? You okay?" Amazingly, Titus rolled to his back and sat up. The side of his head and a fanned spot in his hair were smeared with blood. The officer helped him to stand and he rose cautiously, dazed. The officer held his shoulder and walked him in a circle.

The female officer approached Jonah with a hand on her belt. Her bulletproof vest bulked beneath her uniform. "You want to tell me what happened?"

"I pushed him," Jonah said. "I threw him down."

She noticed Jonah's arm, then looked up at his face. Her eyes were brown, her mouth small and pink; she wore no makeup. She turned her head a little when her eyes met Jonah's, and he could tell she was probing him. He was certain that the night and the morning, the things he had done and said, were painted all over his face, that he reeked of it. She said, "How'd that happen?"

"He threw a star at me." It still lay in the grass, and he pointed to it. "Right there." He dug inside his pocket for the knife and gave it to her. "I took this from him, too."

"You know Titus?"

"We go to the same church. We've been spending time together. I came home this morning and he was here, off his medications. I couldn't calm him down."

"Where were you?"

"With a friend."

"Got a name?"

"Abby O'Gorman." The officer nodded, wrote. She tore a page from her notepad, then folded shut the pad and tucked it in her belt. She handed him the slip of paper. "We'll take him with us. Looks like he'll need a few stitches, but the fact that he's up and walking is a good sign. Here's a number to call if you want to press charges."

"Me?"

"It's your property, isn't it? He attacked you. Is that not the story?"

"No," he said. "It is."

"We know Titus." Her belt screeched and she turned the dial on her radio. "I can't tell you how many times we've been to his house. We're not stupid. I'm pretty sick of it, to tell you the truth." Her partner collected Titus's bike from the lawn and loaded it into the trunk of the car. He led Titus by the shoulder, opened the back door, and helped him to sit. Titus leaned his head against the window and closed his eyes, then opened them and concentrated on the butt of the shotgun holstered beside the radio up front. He turned and looked out the window at Jonah's house, his head small behind the glass, his teeth clamped down on his lip, already an image of the criminal he would become.

· · ·

In December Jonah learned Abby had given birth to a boy, William Charles O'Gorman. He thumbed through the phonebook until he found the address of The Baby Boutique, where he bought three pairs of fleece sleepers with matching blankets. The more extravagant items sat against the front window of the store, singing swings and human-sized stuffed animals, and for a second he considered buying one of those as well. He had wanted to apologize, to beg Abby to forgive him, but it was too late for that. He was no longer the old, dependable Jonah, the good guy she had once known. He felt ashamed when he thought about that night, but more than shame, he felt aroused all over again, as though an addiction had been awakened in him. Wanting Abby more than ever, he watched the women moving through the store, bellies pressed against their sweaters, breasts swollen two sizes too large. Sin had him; he was in its jaws. He asked for the package to be gift-wrapped and mailed. The clerk handed him a card to fill out, and inside he wrote only, "Congratulations," and his name.

Abby wrote back two weeks later, a thank-you card that arrived on Christmas Eve. It was filled with sentences Jonah could tell she had written many times: *Thank you for your lovely gift. William looks adorable in it. I don't know when I'll sleep again, but he's a blessing. All our love, Abby.* Included was a photograph of William in his hospital bassinet, wrapped in a blue-and-pink striped blanket, his hands clenched into tight fists near his eyes. Jonah studied the picture at his kitchen table, William's misshapen head and flattened nose, and tried to decide whether he most resembled Charlie or Abby. For a time he'd allowed himself to believe he had, in some small way, helped to make William—not in the sex he'd had with Abby, but by his proximity during those seven months when the distance between him and William was an ever-thinning veil of skin. Jonah saw his own face nowhere in William's, and though William's father was dead and Jonah was alive, Charlie would live on in photographs and Abby's stories and her patient explanations about how babies are made. If William were ever to see Jonah in a photograph, it would be to the side of Charlie, off-center, slightly out of focus. Snow fell thick and silent, illuminated as it passed through the amber halos of the streetlamps. No cars drove down his street, and the snow accumulated undisturbed until the lawns and the sidewalks and even the asphalt disappeared. Everything felt shut down, as though a switch had been thrown, and Jonah felt that stillness invade his heart. He belonged to his solitude as a prisoner comes to belong to the blocks and bars of his cell. Solitude was his natural place in the universe.

As a swimmer he had always been a team of one. His race, the mile, was always slotted at the end of every swim meet when no one was around to watch; it was always just him and the other milers going at it, lap after lap. He qualified for the Olympic Trials alone, at a Sunday time trial, the lights off in the natatorium, swimming through patches of shadow and sunlight, looking upon an empty deck and an empty stack of bleachers whenever he turned to breathe. Though he knew of men who married for the first time in their forties or even their fifties, both marriage and fatherhood were dangerous in his hands, and he did not trust himself with either. He ran into Gretchen from time to time, in the supermarket and the lift lines at the ski resorts, and though she was cordial, he never asked for her phone number. He came to see his life without sex not as a punishment, but as a preparation for a life that would always belong to no one but himself, and to God. He wished he'd had the strength to save his virginity forever, for now he knew he wasn't afraid of being alone. His night with Abby exorcised that fear, though it also wrecked the faith he once knew. He no longer felt God in his body, in his skin and blood, and would never again trust enough to drive in the dark without the headlights. It was as though the Holy Spirit had leaked out of him. Although he could not abandon his beliefs—even without faith he still believed—God, for him, had been reduced to ideas. Perhaps a depraved faith was real faith, he thought one night as he stood in his darkened hallway, *the conviction of things not seen.* Or felt.

Some nights he fell asleep wondering what it would feel like when his heart stopped. His car was parked in the garage, his lights timed to turn on and off automatically. How long would it take anyone to miss him? What would his body look like when the fire department broke through his front door and entered his bedroom? He took his cross-country skis up the canyon and disappeared among the pines, aware of the dangers of avalanches and getting lost, but not afraid of either, skirting the ridgelines with his left knee bent, descending through a narrow stand of trees. His two closest friends were gone, and he had never gone back to church. Neither Jeff Miller nor anyone else had ever called to ask why. Surely word had gotten around about what had happened with Titus, and somehow he felt everyone knew about what he had done to Abby, too. He could hear the congregation whispering during the coffee hour: *I knew there was something strange with him. We never should have let him around our children.*

When Abby moved to Denver the next spring, Jonah figured he would never see her again. He felt a muted delight that what had happened between them had been damaging enough to drive Abby away, and the knowledge that she was gone filled him with a gust of relief, like the first breath of air after a long time underwater. He lifted his bike down from the hooks in the garage and pedaled up the roads that skirted the foothills. Unlike the spring of Charlie's death, that season was bright, blue, and filled with constant sunlight. He zipped along behind the hospital where three young doctors were tossing a Frisbee in a triangle while a fourth smoked against an ambulance. He dropped into City Creek Canyon where the last of the snow clung in the gullies between the river birch, and then, descending past the capitol, he emerged into the grid of downtown. Temple Square bloomed; the streets were awash with people crossing between the Temple and the Convention Center, squinting, dazed by the mountain sun. He dashed a yellow light, turned east, and stood up on the pedals, hungry for pain.

He didn't lose touch with Abby, though. Charlie's life insurance had allowed her to pay off her mortgage, and since she owned her house outright, she decided to keep it and rent it out. Now and again Jonah drove by the house—most often in times of need and lust to stare up into the second-story window where he had loved that one night—and found a couple or a young family unloading furniture from the back of a U-Haul, angling mattresses and tables to fit through the front door. Abby returned to Salt Lake once a year to look in on the house, and when she did, they got together, sometimes for dinner or lunch, other times for only a few minutes in the park, Jonah and Abby standing with their arms crossed while William played on the swings. Over time, William grew into a miniature version of his father, slender in the hips and broad in the shoulders, his nose off center as though it had come out already broken. The visits felt obligatory and chaperoned, but still he went.

Abby bobbed her hair to her chin and colored it brown. She had never fully shed the weight of pregnancy, and wore it now as though she'd never looked any different. In the way she curled her lip or slipped two fingers beneath her collar to adjust the strap of her bra, Jonah knew she'd had other lovers since she moved, some for a single night or a single weekend, others for months at a stretch. Her encounter with Jonah had been subsumed beneath the weight of the other bodies, the stain of Jonah's most sinful day washed away in a sea of strange aftershaves. Abby seemed to hold nothing against him, though the lack of malice was almost worse than the burden of it. He thought what had happened between them now ranked among a list of her other unsatisfying sexual encounters, a joke to tell at a party, an odd little secret to tell to another man—in the end, nothing. And having watched Abby undress, having felt her skin and breath, he could too easily imagine the scene re-created in another place with another man. His pain wasn't the thought of Abby with someone else, but rather of himself forgotten in that moment. If Abby thought about anyone else while making love, it was surely Charlie, not him. Jonah's entire life felt pushed farther and farther inside Abby's body where it became as useless as an appendix, not worth the effort of cutting out.

He craved sex still, but it was only his body desiring it, not his spirit, and his body could be pacified in the solitude of his bathroom. Instead, his soul's desire for love was replaced with the need to swim. Daily he returned to the pool like an animal born of water, waking hungrily in the dark an hour before dawn and driving to the pool with the radio off, preserving the silence through the locker room and onto the deck where the blue water lapped into the gutter and gurgled down through the pipes. He swam hard, driving his legs off the wall and stroking faster and faster until at last he would stop and retch into the gutter. Chlorine was his drug and he used it like an addict. Early morning appointments that kept him from swimming left him feeling anxious and greasy. Some mornings he swam long enough to feel the chemicals drive the moisture from every pore in his skin. Later, as he was merging onto the freeway or unfolding the paper wrapping of a sandwich, the sun would light across his hand and remind him of the big satellite map of the Salt Lake Valley that used to hang above Charlie's desk. The dehydrated pores wrinkled around his knuckles and wrist looked like the earth folding into the mountains, the back of his hand a smooth plain between the bones. Abby had given Jonah the map; he'd framed it and hung it in his spare bedroom. When he studied it he thought of Charlie's ashes traveling through the narrow runoff canals that cut between the houses and the park and dumped into the Jordan River, which flowed by the airport and out to the Great Salt Lake, the dust of his friend spilling out into the shallow water, floating on the surface as though waiting to be taken up into the atmosphere and carried off to another sky.

• • •

One August Jonah saw a flyer seeking a swimming coach for the high school team. He applied, and during the interview the principal looked across his metal desk with nervous black eyes and a thin upper lip and spoke of the responsibilities of coaching teenagers, the roles and boundaries of a mentor. "They'll tell you things," the principal said. "You won't believe it. Some will try to cross the line. You have to be the one to hold it." He asked if Jonah had a criminal record. Jonah shook his head. The principal extended his hand, "Good luck."

The job was part-time and paid a measly thousand dollars for the season, which Jonah rolled over each year into the team's equally measly budget to buy new warm-ups and suits. The season lasted from September to January, workouts from three until four-thirty, four afternoons a week. Most swimmers were there by default, castoffs from other sports that required more skill or coordination or fitness to participate. A few had been cut from the marching band; others were there to lose weight. Each September a nervous mother placed a clandestine call to ask Jonah to be patient, but also firm—her son or daughter was lazy and needed prodding, a teenager with a fragile ego. One of his swimmers, Owen, had Down syndrome, worked part-time bagging groceries at the supermarket, and on a good day could beat most of the team. And one or two found a fluid stroke and put on muscle in the weight room—emerging as real swimmers—cocky and fast, eager to race. Jonah did what he could to help. He prepared lists of season-best times and mailed them to colleges; he helped the swimmers fill out their applications; he called college coaches and spoke on their behalf. A few earned scholarships to schools they would otherwise never have been able to afford. Shaking their hands at graduation and wishing them good luck, Jonah felt, for that one instant, he had done something good again.

He was liked. Some swimmers arrived before workout to talk and sat next to him on the bench beside the pool. At first he thought they wanted his advice, as they wanted the advice of their teachers and parents, but soon he realized they saw him differently and were there to confess what they couldn't tell a teacher or a parent. Most were Mormon and had been born into their beliefs; some kept their faith without questioning, while others dispensed with it but knew they'd break their mothers' hearts if they said so. Abandoning their beliefs, or perhaps in impatience for its promises, some had had sex in a friend's basement or in the back of the family van and now walked through school feeling suddenly too adult, hollow and bruised inside, worried that they were pregnant. Girls cried and tried to lean into him, but Jonah kept them at bay by standing up and propping one foot between them on the bench. At the end of each season, before the state championships, he had the team to his house for a spaghetti dinner. He encouraged the boys to shave their heads and the girls to shave their arms, and after dinner he showed the tape of Charlie's two-hundred butterfly at the Olympic Trials. Jonah tapped against the television screen as Charlie closed in on the field and moved from sixth to second in the last four meters. "That's how it's done, folks," he'd say. The swimmers stared at the screen, their faces washed in blue wonder.

He attended a coaches' meeting once a month at the high school. He walked through the crowded hallways packed with bodies, caterpillars of backpacks weaving between lockers, the corridor ripe with perfume and paper and body odor. Boys and girls touched each other constantly; they pinched and tickled and kissed behind the columns. Many hugged their goodbyes when leaving for class as though they were aware of the speed at which they were changing, certain the next time they saw one another everything would be different. Jonah looked for Titus, scanning the smallest, darkest heads. From a distance he'd often see him, only to draw closer and find the boy's nose too long or his teeth too small. Titus was never there. He could have forgiven himself had he seen him, or known through some other channel what had become of him. He had driven by Titus's house on several occasions, and once, after almost a year had passed since that awful morning, he worked up the courage to knock on the door. No one answered, and the next time he drove by, the house was for sale, the mutilated bushes cleared out, the Ford Granada gone from the garage. Had he and his mother moved again to another basement across the valley, within the boundaries of another school? Or, had Titus been sent to the juvenile facility where instead of chemistry and algebra and American history he learned to operate the metal shop machines or to tinker with engines, to play basketball in a windowless gym and fight with the other boys who, like him, were troubled enough to have to live behind bars and wire? He watched the news and on slow mornings scanned the newspaper for stories involving acts of vandalism or violence or gangs. He was glad when he didn't see Titus's picture or name.

He was thankful for those isolated afternoons, for the stretched mountain sky, the elm that blanketed his lawn with its freckled leaves, for his swimmers and their little tragedies—how their braces shifted their teeth while their bodies thrust and lurched and trembled into adulthood. The fire truck that raced up his street while he was eating dinner felt like a warning, and he was careful not to miss it. He downed the last of his beer, washed his plate and fork, and flopped down on the couch.

• • •

In December, Abby called. "We're back for a few weeks," she said. "Merry Christmas."

"Merry Christmas," he said. "How's Denver?"

"We're through with Denver. On to L.A. now, after New Year's. Our house sold faster than I expected, and Salt Lake is between renters, so here we are."

"Still with what's his name?"

"Benjamin. He's fine. Coming next week."

"Engaged yet?"

"As a matter of fact. No date yet, but it's his job we're moving for."

"Congratulations."

"Thank you. I hear you're a swim coach now."

"This time of year I am. Part-time."

"What would you say to giving William a few lessons? He's been itch-ing to learn butterfly, and now that we're moving someplace warm, he's really eager. He took lessons in Denver, but his teacher couldn't swim but-terfly, let alone teach it. I thought maybe, if you had the time."

"Sure," he said. "How's Wednesday?"

"My schedule's clear. It'll be good to see you."

He waited for them on the bench beside the pool. The last storm had left the roofs and lawns frosted, the asphalt shining. The American flag whipped in the wind. The sun warmed the glass behind him, and he watched the swim team gather in the corner by the diving boards. Tim Cannon, his assistant coach, led the team through the stretches. Workout didn't start for another half hour, and the swimmers trickled onto the deck one at a time, dragging their equipment bags and playing catch with a tennis ball. Owen swung his arms in a circle, his tongue lolling outside his mouth. Jonah dismissed all the thoughts he'd entertained since he talked to Abby: that she was bringing William here because he was the closest thing to Charlie; or better, though Jonah rejected the thought as soon as it came to him, that the lessons were just an excuse to see *him*. No, none of that. William was seven and he liked sports. He'd heard enough stories about his father the swimmer, and measuring himself against a leg-end, he wanted to be a swimmer too.

Nevertheless, when Jonah saw the hallway door swing open and William cross beneath Abby's outstretched arm with a towel draped around his neck, then stop and stare down into the water where the sun-light shimmered over the black-tiled lines, he wondered what William knew of his father's death. Did he know that it happened in this water? Had Abby explained in the vague terms used to talk to a child, *His heart quit working and without a heart you can't live?* Neither William nor Abby could know how it had looked, Charlie's final involuntary spasms, his skin turning green and then blue and then purple. Charlie's death, for Abby, was the hospital emergency room, the ventilation tube, the blanket folded and tucked beneath his shoulders. The pool was Jonah's alone. Jonah stood up from the bench, smiled. "Hey, William. You remember me?"

"Oh, sure," William answered. His face was rounder, his hair shaped like a bowl.

Abby wore a red sweater with a green Christmas tree sewn on the front. "Thanks for doing this," she said.

"It's no problem."

She scanned the pool. "That your team over there?"

Jonah nodded, rubbed his bare stomach. "We're big enough that I got an assistant this year. He gets my little paycheck. He'll get the team started and I'll join them when I'm finished here." He turned to William. "Ready to swim?"

"Butterfly," William said. "That's what we're doing, right?"

"Those are my orders."

"My dad did butterfly. He went to the Olympics."

"I know," Jonah said. "I watched him make the team."

"Jonah almost made it himself," Abby said.

"You did?"

"I tried out, but I didn't make it."

"Grandma O'Gorman says I can go to the Olympics, too. It's in my genes."

"You listen now," Abby said. She lifted the towel from William's neck and set it on the bench. "You're here to learn. We can play another time."

"Okay," William said. He bounced on his toes. He wore a pair of green goggles. He jumped into the water.

"We'll be fine," Jonah said. He entered the water feet first, sank to the bottom and looked up at William's legs churning, Abby's bent and elongated frame leaning over the water. He surfaced and directed William to hold on to the wall while he gripped William's ankles and pushed his legs through the dolphin kick. "First rule of butterfly," he said, "where your head goes, your body will follow. Say it back to me."

"Where your head goes your body will follow."

"Good." Next he held William flat on the water's surface, a hand around his head, the other gripping the waist of his trunks. He pushed William's head down and lifted his shorts up, then sank his hips and lifted his head and shouted, "Breathe!" William gasped and allowed his head to follow Jonah's hand beneath the water. When they stopped, Jonah pressed his hand against William's chest and could feel the rapid flutter of his heart. When William's heart slowed and his breathing calmed, he said, "Okay, try that dolphin motion. Arms at your side. Use your hips. Where your head goes your body will follow." William pushed off Jonah's knees and botched the motion by lifting his feet and head together. Jonah righted him and said, "Try again."

THE END OF THE STRAIGHT AND NARROW

Thirty minutes passed this way, William flopping in the water, Jonah catching and correcting him. Charlie, he remembered, had never needed much instruction. Butterfly came to him like music. When the time was up, Jonah waved to Tim Cannon, circling his index finger to say "round 'em up." Tim clapped his hands and shouted for the team to get in the water. "That's enough for today," Jonah said. "We'll do more next time."

Swimmers poured into the pool. Three boys in a row did can openers from the blocks, and within seconds the surface was churning. Little waves broke over the lip of the gutter and the drains gurgled loudly. "Wait," William said. "I haven't done the arms yet."

"That's next time."

"Can I try now? Please."

"Okay," Jonah said. "Stay in this lane. Where the head goes—"

"The body will follow."

"Show me."

William pushed off the wall and rocked forward, his chin lurching and his arms swinging so forcefully he pushed himself backward with each stroke. Jonah climbed out and dried off, slid his jeans over his Speedo, a T-shirt over his head. The team churned back and forth in the lanes beside William. Abby said, "I can't tell you how much I appreciate this. He really wanted to learn."

Jonah dried his hair. "I'm glad you asked me. That you'd want me to teach him."

"Well," she said. "The stars aligned."

William had reached the middle of the pool and hung his arms over the lane rope, his mouth open and panting. The lane beside his was packed with swimmers in both directions. The lead swimmer, Anthony Mickelson, that year's captain, turned at the wall, streamlined under the water and came up swimming butterfly, flicking his wrists as he worked toward a sprint, showing off. William leaned over the lane rope as Anthony tucked his head and chopped the water with his hands. William leaned far enough to look Anthony in the eye, to see his mouth fall open, the backs of his wrists rise from the water and swing forward. Jonah held his breath. He saw it coming—the knob of Anthony's wrist shattering the plastic of William's goggles, William's head snapping back, his body falling toward a rhombus of sun on the bottom of the pool—the collision he'd watched for and braced himself against since the day he'd lifted

Charlie's face from the water and rolled his friend to his back and found his lips bloodless and blue. Jonah leaned forward, ready to dive.

But William, by instinct—or was it genetic?—pushed back from the rope and let his belly float to the surface. Anthony sailed by, unimpeded. William paddled back to the wall where Abby waited with a towel. "Lift me, Uncle Jonah," he called out. *Uncle* was good, more than he expected. Jonah took hold of William's wrists and hoisted him up, water gushing from the pockets of William's trunks. Abby wrapped him up tight, tucked the flap of the towel around his neck. She moved William toward the bench where his clothes waited in a pile atop his shoes and jacket. She gathered up the pile and pressed it against her chest while William wriggled out of the towel and slung it around his neck. Together they headed for the locker room. When she passed by Jonah, she reached out and touched his arm. Her palm was wet from William's head and lingered on his bicep just long enough for Jonah to notice the skin on her wrist bunched around the band of her watch and the delta of veins fanning toward her fingers. "Thanks, Jonah," she said. "This was perfect." It wasn't grace he felt, or forgiveness either, but it was something close to both, an echo from long ago. He waited to see how long it would last. Across the pool two boys had stopped to fix their goggles. They both propped an elbow up on the deck while they fiddled with the straps, neither one in a hurry. Tim Cannon came up behind them and clapped his hands and shouted, "Let's get back to it." The boys resumed swimming and the vast sunlit room was filled with the sounds of soles smacking against the wall, of drainpipes gurgling and water sloshing over the gutters, washing Jonah back upon a familiar shore.

PART II

THE EYES TO SEE

THE GUESTS TWIRLED beneath a cosmos of artificial stars: the oak trees in my grandparents' backyard wrapped in miniature white lights. Larger bulbs, like those from a carnival ride, the filament a white-hot squiggle in the center of the core, had been strung overhead, between the bedrooms to the east and the great room to the west. The glowing skeletons of the trees reached and grabbed at the dark, and leaves fell between the lights, as though from nowhere, landing on the tables and lawn and the checkerboard dance floor. Beyond the party, the garden was all deep shadows and amber haze, a maze of brick pathways and twisted, naked statues, eccentric things my grandmother had shipped back from Europe to ornament her azaleas. Couples slipped away to wander the winding paths, which had an irresistible pull, and when they emerged from the shadows and stepped onto the dance floor, their fingers were interlaced and their collars were wrinkled. Star drunk, whispering in each other's ears, they pressed their bodies together, shoulders to shoulders, hips to hips, as though the dance floor was an alien surface that could be crossed no other way. They unfurled to the ends of their arms, and coiled back, and then, because this was Texas, two-stepped toward the bar. On the way, they passed my mother, dancing alone, the universe shining in her prosthetic eye.

This was new behavior, and strange. Most years my mother weathered the party against the terrace railing where she could remain visible, but out of the way. If she mingled, she kept her elbow linked with my father's, or with Kay's. She wore a matte-black dress that hung nearly to her ankles. It fit her like a shadow. She was a head taller than everyone else, including the men. She spun, two-stepped backward, and raised her palms as though to press them against the night. It seemed my grandmother had been right and the rest of us dead wrong: the party was just the lift in spirits my mother needed.

"What on earth is she doing?" my grandmother asked. She gripped the terrace railing beside me. Her gown fit snugly against her chest and stomach; only up close could one discern her age, by the creases in the skin around her mouth and clavicle and where her arms overflowed her dress. She was fifty-seven, tonight.

"Dancing," I said.

"I don't like the looks of this."

"She's having fun. Celebrating life. Isn't that what you wanted?"

"Not quite what I had in mind." My grandmother looked toward the garden and frowned. Through the trees a woman's earrings glittered, along with the Oyster watch face of the man reaching up to touch her chin. "You'd think people would get the hint. The band is the edge of the party. *Noli intrare.* I only turned the lights on for ambience."

"Pretty hard to hurt brick just by walking on it," I said.

"Don't sass me, Rowdy," she said. "It's my birthday."

But this was no birthday party. Candles and cake and presents my grandmother considered narcissistic. "Can you honestly imagine me unwrapping gifts in front of people?" she asked me once, and honestly, I could not. Andrew Carnegie said fortunes that flow in large part from society should in large part be returned to society, and my mother's ruined eyes had given my grandmother the perfect opportunity to return her fortune to society. This was the fifteenth year of the Cordelia Sterling Jarrett Vision Foundation. And when it came to this party, she spared no expense. In the center of the hors d'oeuvres table was an ice sculpture of the Port Isabel Lighthouse, chiseled into shape that morning inside the freezer in the cook's kitchen, rendered down to the tiniest detail: the three square windows interrupting the smooth cylinder of the tower, the double-bar railing around the observation deck just below the lantern, even the giant star announcing the lighthouse as the entrance to Texas. The sculpture was, like the party itself, a reminder that it was our responsibility to bring light to dark horizons, and that our time was short.

"I wish she'd sit down," my grandmother said. "Save her strength. I had half a mind to tell her not to even come." Of course, not coming was never a possibility. My grandmother had called Doctor Berkeley herself to make sure my mother was well enough to attend. If guests were going to give to the Cordelia Sterling Jarrett Vision Foundation, they needed to see Cordelia Sterling Jarrett. The foundation's inability to restore my mother's sight had made it strong, its cause noble and tragic, just as images of charred and decimated rain forests brought in far more money than pictures of healthy trees. The foundation funded the fight against retinal detachment, and against retinopathy of prematurity, a condition that occurred, ironically, in premature infants. My mother's name was attached to an ophthalmology fellowship and an endowed professorship at the Texas Medical Center, more than a half dozen research grants. Several grant recipients milled among the guests, discernible by the shapes of their eyeglasses (round), their slightly wilted collars, and the strain in their faces as they attempted to explain their science to partygoers who feigned interest, and feigned it impatiently.

I feigned disagreement with my grandmother. "It's good to see her having fun," I said. "God knows she's needed to get out." By the time I finished saying it, I believed it myself.

"Regardless," she said. "Kay should stay with her. What is she paid for?"

Kay had lived with us since the September after my mother lost her vision, since I was three months old. She had been with us for so long Jill and I often thought of her as our mother, too. Jill, in fact, was known to tell people she had two mothers, which led some to worry that she was the daughter of lesbians. Her friends' parents were often relieved to learn our mother was blind. Kay sat with my father at a table on the far side of the yard. My father leaned toward her bare shoulder, her gown backless and purple, his mustache crinkling around his mouth. Kay nodded, then cupped her hand around her mouth and spoke into his ear. For months they had been talking like this, off by themselves. I assumed it was the way you talked about cancer, like it was a secret, and in their hushed whispers they were planning for the worst, for all the forms the worst could take. My mother breathed into a champagne flute, fogging the glass. A waiter brought her a gin and tonic and she drank it down like water.

"I saw that," my grandmother said. "Heavens."

The way I saw it, so long as my mother remained in sight, there was nothing to fear. Almost everyone at the party was an old-line Houstonian, rich on oil or inheritance fattened by oil, and had no trouble tolerating eccentric behavior so long as it was not disruptive. My grandmother scanned the floor. "Where's Jill?"

"I don't know. She was behind us when we came in, but I never saw her come out. She must be inside watching TV."

She clicked her tongue. "That girl floats on the weather." She had me right where she wanted me. "I need a favor from you, Rowdy. I need you to keep an eye on your mother. It seems no one else is up to the job. You think you can do it?"

"Okay," I said, though I had been watching her all along. Ever since she had come home with the prosthetic eye, I had been unable to take my eyes off it. I had seen it on the bathroom vanity, oblong and silicone, not at all the glass marble I had expected. An implant had been imbedded in her socket where it was attached to the muscle; the prosthetic fit over the top. She had to take out the eye and rinse it with saline to keep it moist until her tear ducts adjusted. I watched her hold the eye in her palm, and fit it in the hole in her face. She turned to me and asked, "Is it straight, Rowdy?" I hadn't told her I was standing there. Spooked, I answered, "Yes, ma'am."

"No problem," I told my grandmother.

She tucked a fifty into my breast pocket. Folded into a narrow rectangle, it slid down my pocket like a tongue. "I'm counting on you," she said. "Eyes like a hawk."

"None other," I said. She tightened her eyes and I corrected myself. "Yes, ma'am."

• • •

If the party commemorated anybody's birthday, it was mine. On the day I was born, I blinded my mother in the backyard of our house. I was two weeks past due. All summer long she had suffered through corneal edema, pulsing headaches that spiraled around her occipital bones, swollen ankles and feet, and an aching back. Her doctor told her to avoid aspirin, and my father said he'd heard Tylenol could cause birth defects, so she took neither. After my due date passed, she attempted to coax me out with chili peppers soaked in balsamic vinegar, with blue and black cohosh, with sit-ups in her underwear. At night my father drove her down the unpaved, potholed roads into the country toward Tomball and

Magnolia, even as far as Brenham, bouncing over every bump, desperate to jar me loose. But I remained reluctant, stubborn.

Our house sat at the end of a gravel road, abutting fifty acres of uncut pines and backing up to a bayou, a smaller and wilder tributary of Buffalo Bayou, which flowed past my grandparents' property. Trees surrounded our house on all sides except where the bayou slid away from the lawn. Beyond the bayou were more trees. At forty-two weeks, her doctor scheduled an induction. My mother consented grudgingly and awoke that day nervous about her pale skin and the thought of her legs spread before a man she had known only as long as her pregnancy. Hoping for a little color, she carried a collapsible chair to the backyard, naked, her bathing suit too small and not worth the effort of putting on. It was July, mosquitoes blood-plump and hovering, heat rippling from the dogwood and grass. She rubbed sunscreen across her belly and breasts, her face, and lay back in the sun. She felt the heat on her chin, felt me turn and kick, and felt a pain shoot up her spine to her face. Her belly leaped and twitched. She touched the towel between her legs and found it wet. Her eyes burned from the sweat and sunscreen that had seeped beneath her eyelids. When she opened her eyes and saw the world through a soupy green jelly, as though looking up from the bottom of a pond, her first thought was to blame the sunscreen. Only hours later—after she had arrived at the hospital, her hands and knees still bleeding from her crawl to the backdoor, after the ophthalmologist had dialed his pinpoint of light into her pupils and gasped—would it become clear that the sunscreen was innocent.

What wasn't known until the night of my birth was that during the course of her pregnancy she had developed subretinal neovascularization—tiny blood vessels beneath her retinal tissue. The formation of those vessels was not my doing, though pregnancy and its pressures most likely brought them on. And it was my movement that ruptured them, and hemorrhaged her retinas away from their moorings. I wasn't awake yet; I wasn't conscious, but labor is a decision made by the baby, not the mother—anencephalics, for example, must be induced, for they lack the brains to tell them to birth. I decided to come when I did, and because of that, my mother was blind.

This fact is never spoken of, and the story is almost never told. My mother told it to me only once, after a period of insistent begging, and the look in her eyes had frightened me. She looked at me as though I had cheated her in a way that motherhood kept her from admitting. She stared while she spoke, perfectly focused, which forced me to look back. She never said she forgave me, or that she didn't blame me, for to say either thing would have been to acknowledge I had done something wrong in the first place. Instead, what passed between us was a silence. I was to keep silent about her blindness and she was to keep silent about my role in it. I was six years old, and Kay had lived with us for longer than I could recall, and Jill was three and not ready to know such things. The fact that we lived in a house with a blind mother and an extra woman in the bedroom above the garage was not to be seen as odd in any way, but as ordinary as the grass and leaves.

. . .

For years we lived in that ordinariness, even if it was an ordinariness that recognizes its special place in the world—getting along under a weight others would deem unbearable. We did not shush Kay when she spoke during movies, narrating the scenery and costumes, nor did we question the dabs of hot glue on the thermostat and stove. Before Jill or I learned to talk, we learned to guide my mother's hand to what we wanted, to press it to our lips if we were hungry. We learned to read by listening to books on tape, just as my mother listened to her own books and even her magazines on tape. She could be moody, but so could my father, and so could Kay, and so could Jill and I, and our moodiness had nothing to do with blindness.

That summer, when I was fifteen, she began to disappear. She walked down the hallway between the kitchen and the bedrooms with a shoulder pressed into the wall. She stepped into closets and stood there for hours. She wandered into the woods behind our house and vanished among the pines, reappearing on the other side, on the shoulder of the highway, her clothes dirty, her hands bloody and full of slivers. Mrs. Stevenson, our neighbor across the street, brought her home. She told us she saw my mother step onto the highway. A car swerved to miss her. "She appeared out of nowhere," Mrs. Stevenson said. "Boom, there she was."

My father had the hardest time with this behavior. There was no science to it, as far as he could tell. He was a neurobiologist at the Texas Medical Center, and what others explained with psychology, or decaying morals, or bad upbringing, he explained with chemistry. When Jill wet the bed, he consoled her by explaining that she lacked the proper amount of antidiuretic hormone. Her kidneys didn't know to stop producing urine during the night; she couldn't help it, even if she wanted to. This made Jill feel better, even when she peed her pants at school. His own work constellated around the transmission of a single substance, GABA, which floated between the synaptic neurons—a space so small it had to be measured with dye and deduction, with cause and effect. GABA was linked to convulsions. I had gone with him to the Epilepsy Study Center at the Medical Center, small rooms monitored by video cameras and clicking machines, patients wired to EEG and CPAP. On the monitor in the control room, I watched them seize, their veins bulge in their necks, their muscles spasm and twitch until their tongues bled. My father studied the images of their brains, isolated in black-and-white on a separate monitor. He pointed to something I couldn't see and told me this was the problem. "So much suffering," he said. "Such a small thing." He saw no patients, considered no extenuating circumstances, weighed no environmental factors. There was no environment. There was only GABA, floating, deficient. His universe was a series of one-by-three-inch glass slides, and beyond that lay distraction, and fear.

When I was eight, he caught me lighting fireworks at the edge of the bayou. My fingers were black with powder and smelled of sulfur. I held the firework until the fuse burned all the way down, then threw it up to watch it burst, a white-hot flash against the white-hot sky. It was an irresponsible thing to be doing: we hadn't had rain in weeks; the bayou stream was down to a damp strip of mud, the grass and dogwood were as dry as kindling. My father took me to the stove, sprayed a sheet of paper with my mother's hairspray and then dropped it to the burner. It ignited with a whoosh. A corner lifted to escape the gas, but the gas pulled it back. Flakes of ash floated up and then drifted to the floor. He said, "Imagine this is your mother's hair. It can set fire just as easily. You have to watch, watch, watch. All the time. Do you understand?"

I pointed to the faded scar on his forearm, three concentric half circles. He said, "I got this in college, in my first lab. Set my arm on a hot plate. I was careless, but lucky." He rubbed the scar. "Now I think twice before I do anything. Before I cross the street." His work was defined by others questioning his every decision. His research was seen as too narrowly focused, and because of that he lived off of grants rather than regular funding from the medical school. During the years his grants were up for renewal, he stomped about the house turning off lights and dialing down the air, fearful that this time his money would not come through. He was too proud to take money from my grandparents. Even my mother's disability check, which paid Kay's salary, was shameful. His father was an airplane mechanic, his mother a violin teacher; they lived for forty years in the same house in Philadelphia, rarely traveled, and refused to move when their neighborhood went from blue-collar to inner-city slum. My father claimed it made him tenacious with his work. Also for that reason, he hated this party.

. . .

In July my mother disappeared in the Galleria. She and Kay were shopping in The Limited when my mother wandered off. We learned later she drifted all the way to the Westin Hotel, took the elevator to the lobby, and wandered out the front door. The bellman put her in a taxi, and the taxi drove her down Highway 59 to an open-air furniture tent. My father, once he arrived at the mall, said what we all feared: that she had been led away by a strange and menacing hand. We would find her body raped and mutilated, if we ever found it at all. When the furniture-store owner brought her back to the mall, my father was hardly relieved. He took her face in his hands and squeezed her skull between his palms. "Cory," he said, "what were you thinking?" We were in the security office, the captain standing with his arms crossed by the door, Jill and I slumped, exhausted, in the chairs against the wall, Kay sobbing by the water fountain. We had gone store to store for hours. My father pressed his forehead to my mother's forehead and his nose to her nose and looked into her eyes, close enough for her to make out his shape. (Her right eye, in good light, could see the outlines of objects, bright lines on a dark road.) "We're going in for a CAT scan," he said. "And blood work. Something is definitely wrong." My mother didn't say a word. My father's eyes filled, and he shook her shoulders, lightly at first, but harder when she did not respond. "God damn it," he said. He shook her again and my mother's hair—that flammable hair—came out of its clip and spilled across her face. "God damn it."

The CAT scan showed nothing, but two weeks later, at our annual eye exams, a mass was found on her choroid, the back of her left eye. Doctor

Berkeley said the melanoma explained the disappearing. The pressure on her optic nerve had likely affected her orientation, though she had never once complained of disorientation. Since the eye couldn't see, he told her the best thing would be to take it out—a procedure called enucleation. The cancer could get to her brain otherwise, and why go through chemotherapy and radiation? For a time, my mother resisted. A blind eye is better than a hole, she said; just like a crippled leg is better than a stump. Not always, my father argued. We all worked to convince her. Kay pleaded on her knees; Jill clung to her neck and begged her not to die. I offered her my left eye. I'd take the prosthetic. That way, we'd each have one.

"No thanks," she said, "I don't need it back," and I quit that line of argument.

Though it wasn't a joke. My entire life I was concerned about my role in the suffering of others. I bussed dirty tables at McDonald's to keep the employees from getting stuck with the job; I voted for every student-council office candidate so as not to pick one over another; and that very fall I had been asked to the Sadie Hawkins Dance by Chevonne Duncan, my lab partner in biology. Chevonne played center on the girls' basketball team and was the only girl I have ever met who was taller than my mother. She was a good two-and-a-half inches taller than me, and until the night of the dance I had never seen her hair in anything but a knot. I didn't want to go, but I couldn't say no. My phone rang eight different times with no one on the other end before I finally heard Chevonne's voice. Kay said, "It's just one night; you'll have fun," and when I said I didn't think it would be fun, she said, "Be a gentleman, Rowdy. Make it special." Chevonne bought us matching Tommy Hilfiger shirts, stiff button-downs that looked as though they'd been assembled from a dozen scraps of leftover material. Mine was extra large; I think Chevonne's was extra large tall. The night of the dance she got her hair permed and picked me up in her brother's truck. She paid for our dinner at Pappadeaux's and for our pictures at the dance, my hands folded around hers, our heads leaned together. I could tell the night meant a lot to her, like it was her first date ever. It was my first date ever, but not at all how I had imagined it. In the cab of the truck in the parking lot, she leaned in to kiss me. Startled, I leaned back. She said, "Sorry," and looked down toward the gas and brake, and I saw just how easily I could ruin her night. I said, "No, I just thought we'd wait until we got home," and then leaned in. Her tongue was rough and tasted like Dr Pepper and Doritos, and I wondered why everyone was so eager to tongue-kiss when it was really rather gross, especially when I thought about the Doritos—the GABA of high school—drifting between her mouth and mine. But I didn't stop, not even when I could feel people moving past the windows, looking in at us. Not even when I could hear them shouting. When Chevonne looked at the clock and said, "I'd better get us home," I kissed her once more and said, "Thanks for a great night." Was this the right thing to say? I didn't know, but I understood that guilt is a force equal to love.

• • •

Combined, there is no stronger power. I had been given a job to do and I stuck to it. I watched the hem of my mother's dress swish around her ankles, her flat-soled sandals, her brightly painted toenails. Kay had done them that afternoon. Painting her nails was one thing my mother couldn't do herself. Years ago Kay had strung beads on safety pins, which she attached to the hangers in my mother's closet; the more beads, the darker the garment. Sometimes she'd put on too much eye shadow, or it would glob in the corners, and Kay would smooth it out with her thumbs. Kay always looked her over, just to make sure.

My grandfather stood with three other men, all singing, *What's it all about, Alfie?* The source of my mother's height, his silver hair gleaming, he drifted through the party like a giraffe, his big lips nibbling from a small plate in his hand. Out on the floor, my mother let her head roll around on her neck, and when I drew near her, she smelled like champagne and gin and perfume. After two hours of steady playing, the band members' faces were shining and moist. "Mom," I said.

"Who is it?" she said. As though she didn't recognize me.

"Me. Are you okay?"

"Do I seem like I'm not?"

"Are you having fun?"

"Who do you think has the best time at a football game?"

I thought about saying, "The couple beneath the bleachers," but I didn't want to get slapped. She had a kind of radar when it came to me being crass. I said, "The winners."

"Those big dumb animals that do all the flips," she said. "Though I bet those costumes get hot. Thank God for fall." She pinched the front of her dress and fluffed it with air. Then she stopped moving and her prosthetic eye glinted. I stepped back. Since the eye had come out, she'd quit wandering, but now she was disappearing in a different way. Entering the house, I would call her name and get no answer but the click and whirr of the air-conditioner, though moving through the house I'd find her at the kitchen table, staring at the wall. Like the wandering, this too had an explanation: the Vicodin given to her to soothe her pain after surgery.

It was an explanation still current as I watched her finger her pocket, drag her hand from her hip to her mouth, lift her chin, and gulp. "Does your eye hurt?" I asked, relieved.

"Nothing hurts, Rowdy. I'm pain free."

"Do you want to go sit down? Have something to eat?"

"If I wanted to sit down, I'd be sitting. Elizabeth prefers I be front and center." She threw up her arms. "We've got spirit, yes we do! Go Cyclops!"

I laughed, though I shouldn't have. "Have you talked to many people?"

"Not one." She huffed. "Easier than—"

Just like that, she was no longer there. She shuffled left, then right. The dance floor felt like the bottom of a bowl, the terrace above us on three sides, the band on the fourth, tables spread out on the lawn, voices everywhere. I heard low male voices grumbling, controlled, another man who kept pleading, *oh baby, oh darling*, a group of women laughing spasmodically. The French-horn player turned away and sneezed: I heard the horn quit, and I heard him sneeze. When I looked, he was playing again, and everyone else at the party looked delighted. Every dress glittered. It wasn't Halloween yet, but it felt like a costume party, everyone dressed up as they wanted to be, the awful world festering underneath.

· · ·

Eventually my mother did tire enough to sit, and I went inside to use the bathroom. Standing before the toilet, I heard a shuffling inside the walls, and I knew Jill was close. My grandparents' house had been built with spaces between the walls for accessing the bathroom pipes and for circulating fresh air, a technology considered cutting-edge before air-conditioning. My mother told stories of large fans set before the openings, metallic air and dust and bees drifting through the vents. Now the vents were sealed into the air-conditioning, leaving behind the narrow passageways, which only Jill could get through. She was skinny as a stick, her arms so bony that once I pretended to snap her wrist in my hands. Jill screamed and I let go. I hadn't meant to hurt her.

I knocked on the wall—one, two, pause, three, pause, four. Through the wall I heard her say, "I'll come out."

I went to the bathroom at the back of the house. The panel at the back of the linen closet had been removed, the space between the walls a black void of warm air. I heard Jill coming, and a moment later she appeared, her hair and the front of her dress spangled with dust. "What were you doing?"

"Hiding notes," she said. "For the children." If I was the cause of my mother's blindness, Jill was its consequence. She feared invisibility. She auditioned for every school play, ran for office every year, volunteered to care for the class rabbit during Thanksgiving and Christmas breaks. Whenever we went to Galveston, she wrote her name in the sand with a stick, in letters large enough passing planes could see. Lately she had taken to creating time capsules for her descendants. She buried her dolls in the backyard, along with a photograph of herself, and a baggie filled with hair pulled from the bathtub drain. She pilfered every trash can on our street for weeks, gathering wine and soda bottles, then stuffed the bottles with notes and set them to float in the bayou.

She held a folded square in her hand. I asked to see it. *Dear Children,* it said, *I hope you're having a good life. May you be in heaven a half hour before the devil knows you're dead.*

"What's that last bit?" I asked.

"I saw it on a plaque in the other room. You should write a message, too." She stepped into the bedroom and returned with a paper and pen. I took it from her and scribbled, *Go back from whence you came.*

"I like that," she said. "A warning. Here, I'll hide it for you." I gave her the note and she ducked beneath the opening. I don't know how many notes she managed to hide back there, but I know it was a lot. Whenever I drive down my grandparents' street and find the house changed in some way, I think of the people who own it now opening a wall and Jill's notes fluttering out like paper butterflies—her name everywhere among the house's history. I had long hoped for exactly the opposite. I would rather have been forgotten. In the mornings, I watched my mother pour her coffee with the tip of her index finger curled over the lip of the mug so she could tell when to stop, and when we went out I watched other people watch her, at first unaware of her blindness and then suddenly surprised by it, averting their eyes from hers or slowing their speech, the entire time a voice in my head repeating, *You did this to her*. She was a blind woman; it was impossible to see her otherwise. I understood her disappearing, at least in this one way. Unable to see, she hoped to slip by unseen.

Jill stepped out of the hole, unbent herself, and brushed the dust from the front of her dress. "It'll take a real sleuth to find those," she said.

"What's the point of writing them if no one will ever find them?"

"The future Jill in the family will know where to look. You should see all I've found back there."

"We'd better head back outside," I said. "It's almost time."

. . .

My grandmother stood on the bandstand in an even slimmer-fitting red dress. She made a point to change at least twice a party. Glitter sparkled in the creases around her eyes. Guests stood together on the floor, several more seated regally in the chairs turned to face the stage. A waiter passed around champagne. An effervescing flute was offered to me and I took it. My grandmother prided herself on never telling the same story from one year to the next. Each year's speech, though a cousin of the speeches it followed and preceded, was uniquely scripted: this year, it was the horror of cancer. In past years she had used the phrase "the horror of blindness" to describe sights my mother had missed—my sister's newborn face, for example, and the salesgirl who tried to swindle her by telling her the twenties she produced from her wallet were really fives. For the present, however, blindness was a lesser enemy. She wasted little time:

> Friends, this has been a year like none other. Cordelia was discovered to have cancer in her eye, and while she won her war with the disease, she lost her eye in the battle. The prosthetic artist did a miraculous job matching her new eye with her old, and I'll wager that none of you can tell which is which. And I'm not telling! Seeing her here tonight, I am reminded that we are blessed to be where we are in this life, and that we cannot allow our talents and gifts to go to waste. We must fight harder than we've fought in the past. We can no longer content ourselves with making small differences; we must make larger differences. Blindness

is not the world's foremost affliction, nor are cancers of the eye, but both are fights we can win, and having won them, we can look clearly toward the next. For that reason, we've decided to expand our efforts. We will soon break ground on the Cordelia Sterling Jarrett Eye Center, to be located in the Texas Medical Center. With your help it will become the epicenter of ophthalmologic research. With your help, it will bring light to darkness. We hope you will join us.

It was a shorter speech than other years, and the guests made it through without becoming distracted. When my grandmother stopped speaking, they applauded loudly, roused and inspired, for philanthropies attached to buildings occupy the world fixedly and make for lasting legacies. Buildings meant walls with plaques and photographs. Jill understood this and said, "Cool. Maybe people will kiss Mom's picture like they do Elvis's statue at Graceland."

"They do that at Graceland?"

"From what I've heard." She took the champagne flute out of my hand and downed the last of it.

"I think we'd all like to hear from Cordelia," my grandmother said. Each year, in a routine unfailing, my grandmother would call my mother's name, and Kay, or my father, or my grandfather, would lead her to the microphone, and my mother would thank the guests and say she was praying for scientific advancements and look uncomfortably nervous, for which she was promptly forgiven. Tonight she did not heed the cue. The guests waited, but my mother did not come forward. My grandmother said, "Cordelia, are you out there, honey?" She scanned the floor and terrace with her hand shading her eyes. I looked, too, but could not see her.

• • •

Besides my family, no one understood the gravity of her absence. My grandmother said, "Well, she must have stepped away. We'll hear from her later," and then descended the bandstand's steps. The music, and the party, resumed, hardly a step missed. After a half hour had passed and all the doors in the house had been opened and lighted and my mother had not materialized, something approaching a panic swept through us. The fact she was not inside the house meant she was outside the house. She was in the world. Only a mile from my grandparents' house was

Westheimer, a six-lane jugular crossing Houston, filled with bars and men's clubs and transvestites. I thought about the pills in my mother's pocket, and how her black dress drew her into the shadows. My father said he and Kay were going out to look for her and told me to stay put in case she came back, a job I immediately passed on to Jill. "She might be down in the azalea garden," I said. "I'll make a loop and come back."

Jill shook her head, but that was all.

The trees and shrubs were bent and twisted. I had heard stories of thieves entering the neighborhood by way of the bayou, waiting in unlit hallways until the owners went to bed. Every half step I saw a body rise, strange eyes blinking from behind a tree. In every case it was a statue, a fountain, a whorled topiary. My grandmother had enlisted the valets and caterers to search the grounds, and across the garden I saw other flashlights floating in the dark. I heard my mother's name, *Cordelia, Cordelia.* It made the search seem absurd, as though she would roll out from the bushes and say, "Here I am; you found me! I was here all along!" She would only be found when and if she chose to be found. She had a way of fading into the background and reemerging suddenly, of popping into and out of conversations. I'd be at the sink or on the phone, someplace where I thought I could see all around me; I'd blink, and there she'd be. I never knew where she'd come from, and I never knew what she knew.

I lowered my voice. "Mom," I said. "It's Rowdy. Tell me where you are. I won't give you up." I turned one corner and then another, scanning the oaks, half-expecting to find her reclining on a branch, grinning like the Cheshire Cat. In the distance I heard, "What a pile of horseshit. Keep her on a goddamn leash." Then I shut my eyes.

This was a game I played in the woods behind our house. I never once thought the game had anything to do with my mother's blindness, but of course it had everything to do with it. Any behavior that could be remotely construed as mocking, including walking around with my eyes closed, earned a quick slap from Kay. In the woods I could try my hand at blindness, and measure my ability to adapt to it when it came for me, as I was sure it one day would. I would walk blindfolded from one end of the woods to another. At first I walked with my hands out, touching a tree, stepping around it, touching another, but in time I grew courageous and kept my hands at my sides. Woods are noisy places if you listen, and in time I came to hear the trees: small silences in the air, masses the wind had to move around. I, too, learned to move around them. If I heard cars, I knew I was near the highway; if water, I knew I had traveled along the bayou. Other times I let my mind wander and imagined coming upon a secret cottage nestled back there, inhabited by a strange old woman, or a deep ravine with a waterfall like the one on *Fantasy Island,* or my favorite, an uncharted inlet of the Gulf of Mexico, complete with sand and sun-baked kelp and oyster shells. Since I was fifteen, I also imagined coming upon scenes more sinister and voyeuristic: young, naked bodies bathing or playing in the water. I could conjure it so vividly I'd open my eyes and want to weep at the sight of only trees. The rare times I got hold of magazines with naked women inside, usually from the older brother of a friend, I took them with me into the woods.

I listened for my mother's measured breathing, her stillness. I heard the leaves rustle, a squirrel climb a tree. I stopped when I heard water. Buffalo Bayou was iridescent as oil, and as wide across as the freeway. Autumn floods had brought the water up around the bases of the pines and willows, and beneath the surface flowed a second stream of garbage, of cans and cigarettes and twigs. I watched the fog thicken on the grass and over the current, and I imagined my mother making it here, a breeze over her feet, the Vicodin rattling in her pocket. I watched until I was certain I saw something move beneath the surface—a body long and sleek, propelled by a tail. I said, once, "Mom," and then, because I, too, was part of the search, "Cordelia," and then I said both names again. The bayou made no response. A minute later a cigarette floated by on top of a can, smoke rising from its still-orange tip. I gasped, and then I turned and ran.

· · ·

When I returned, the band wasn't playing, and only a few people sat around the tables, talking into their sleeves. The tower of the lighthouse had thinned and collapsed; the fallen lantern lay melting into the violet linen. Through the glass doors to the study, I saw my father and Kay standing with their backs turned. Extending from Kay's right elbow was the telephone cord. My father stood to her left, his elbow locked tight to support his weight against the desk, his nose and mouth not far from Kay's ear. Kay was shaking her head, but my father was nodding his, and the sight of both gestures at once made me think the worst. My mother had wandered into traffic and had been struck by a car, or had been pulled from a back lot by the police. The call Kay was making was the first act of the aftermath. I stood still, not wanting to enter, not wanting to know. My father put his hand on Kay's lower back, on the flat, indented area where the muscles pull together, the skin exposed by her leaning forward. It's an area I've come to know as supremely erotic for its proximity to other parts of the body and because a hand there controls both movement and posture. Kay looked at him and then looked back at the phone. I assumed any touch between them, or between anyone else, would be the touch of comfort, of grief. I opened the door and braced for the news. My father looked up. In an instant his hand was in his pocket. "Find her?" he asked. Kay turned, too. When I said I hadn't, I couldn't tell whether or not they were relieved.

· · ·

Jill was the one who found her, in the bathroom of the cook's kitchen, a room that had been searched twice before my mother appeared in it. She was curled up on the floor with her knees pulled into her chest, her sickness lining the toilet. The caterers stood together near the range, pots and pans hanging overhead. Kay helped my mother to her knees. "We'll get you home," she said. She smoothed the hair from my mother's forehead and wiped her mouth and chin with a folded square of toilet paper. "It'll be all right."

"How many Vicodin did she take?" my father asked. He stood on the opposite side of the toilet.

"I see three in there," Kay said.

"Three more than that," my mother groaned.

"Jesus, Cory," my father said. "What were you thinking?"

My mother shook her head.

"Should I call an ambulance?" Kay asked. "Who knows how much she drank."

"Not yet," my father said. "If she threw most of them back up she should be okay."

My mother sat back on her knees and turned her face to Kay. Kay let out a short, pitched gasp. I didn't know why until my father moved to flush the toilet and Kay grabbed his wrist. "Don't," she said. "Wait." My mother touched her face, her left cheek and eyelid. The eye had come out.

"It's in there," Kay said. Her eyes rolled to the toilet. Before my father or Jill or I or anyone could react, Kay reached her hand into the toilet and fished out the eye. She did this without emotion, without disgust or pain, and watching her flush the toilet and stand to wash her hands and the eye in the sink, I realized how little I knew her. Where had this stoic strength come from? Fifteen years she had lived with us, and I had never met her mother, or understood where her father had gone, or seen where she had grown up, or considered what she would be doing if she were not with us. I couldn't imagine her not with us. She set the eye on the vanity while she dried her hands. I stared at it, fixed in its gaze, and was relieved when she wrapped it in tissue and slipped it inside her purse. "We'll just take this home."

My grandmother appeared in the doorway with her hands laced together. "Oh, Cordelia. I knew it was too soon for you to be out. This is my fault." She turned and shouted into the kitchen. "Someone please call an ambulance."

"She doesn't need one," my father said. "She just needs to go home."

"She needs her stomach pumped, Lee," my grandmother said.

"They won't pump her stomach. The hospital will give her charcoal to drink and send her home. She'll do better sleeping this off."

"You're the doctor." My grandmother's voice was sarcastic; my father was not the kind of doctor she trusted. She stepped forward, pressed her knees together, and bent toward my mother. She rubbed my mother's back. "Think you can stand up, honey? Think you can walk?"

"Happy birthday," my mother grumbled.

"Oh now, don't say that, honey. You're not well. It's my fault. I wanted you to come, but I shouldn't have pressed so hard. It was too much. Lee and Kay will take you home." She turned to my father. "Should she stay? It'd be no problem."

My father shook his head. "She's drunk, Elizabeth. She needs two aspirin and a good night of sleep."

My grandmother lifted my mother's arm from the toilet and looped it around her neck, helped my mother to stand. "Here we go, honey. Just take your time."

Kay wrapped her arm around my mother's waist, and together she and my grandmother walked my mother out of the bathroom. My mother's head drooped between her shoulders. She tried to lift it, but couldn't. Her remaining eye was bloodshot. As they passed me, my grandmother looked at me and pursed her lips and then looked away. I was supposed to have been watching my mother.

. . .

An ambulance waited in the driveway with its engine chugging, called despite my father's insistence. The paramedics both held orange tackle boxes. When they saw my mother, they came toward her. "Never mind," my grandmother said, waving them off. "We don't need you after all."

"You should have called to tell us," one said. He wore a blue cap low on his forehead.

"Well, I didn't," she said. "Send me the bill."

The valet brought the van around and my father slid open the back door. My mother tried to step up, but fumbled and tripped forward. My grandmother squeaked and said, "Help her, Rod," and my grandfather, stalwart and silent, appeared—I can't really say from where. He lifted my mother into the van. Backing away from the door, he straightened up and placed a hand on my father's shoulder. "Drive safely, Lee," he said. "Take care of my little girl." My father nodded, then looked at me and said, "You drive, Rowdy. I've had one more than I should have." I had my permit and could have qualified for a hardship license because of my mother's blindness, but I had yet to prove myself a responsible driver. I flinched easily and drove too close to the line. Twice I'd taken a corner too fast and put the van in the ditch. It didn't occur to me that my father was willing to risk our safety for the sake of a satiric gesture. He said, "We're in Rowdy's hands. God be with us," and then climbed in the back beside Kay.

Jill climbed in up front and said, "If you get lost, I'll guide you. I have the map in my mind." She tapped her temple with her finger. She had a map of the world taped to her closet door and a map of Texas on her wall. She often lost entire afternoons thumbing through the Houston street guide.

But the night had taken a lot out of her, and before we made it to the freeway, she was asleep, curled up with her head on the armrest. Soon, so was everyone else. My father's head was craned back, his mouth gaping. Kay sat straight up, her purse in her lap, her eyes shut as though waiting for a gruesome scene to pass. My mother's skull rolled against the glass. The radio was off, the windows were rolled up tight, and the soggy plain of Houston merged with the darkness, distant rows of lights hovering at the crease of earth and sky. The world had never felt so big, nor I so alone in it. Oh, we were a moody bunch! I thought about my mother's prosthetic eye inside Kay's purse, the toilet paper clinging to the silicone, the eye unblinking, unemotional, ever focused. An eye without a body is certain of everything. It hides from nothing. Had it sat beside me on the dashboard, it would have seen everything I could not, the unformed suspicions that lay at the bottom of my stomach where the seatbelt crossed my lap: what would happen next, and next, and next, and finally. I angled the rearview mirror to see my mother. Her eyes were open, staring at me, her left a cavern of muscle and blood. I jerked the wheel, and Kay's eyes shot open. "What the hell are you doing, Rowdy? Trying to kill us?"

"Sorry," I said and set my hands at ten and two and focused forward, avoiding the mirror. Before me lay the chain of streetlamps, the lines in their unending Morse code of dots and dashes, billboards rising over the road. *Don't Be Sad!*, one said. *Experience the Flame Broiled Difference. Who Cares If They're Real? . . . They're Real Close.* Fog was condensing on the hood and the windshield and the asphalt. I felt the road turning slick. I tried to keep my hands steady on the wheel.

SWEET TEXAS ANGEL

AS SHE CROSSES THE HIGH POINT of the suspension bridge, the water below brown-green and streaked with sand, Kay feels the wind whistle through the floorboard of her Toyota and drum against the soles of her sandals. It is not yet seven o'clock, and the eastern horizon ahead of her is orange and red. Alone in her car, her car alone on the bridge, everything she sees appears poised to fly: the gulls standing with their necks craned on the bridge railing; the flaming refinery towers licking holes in the low, stretched clouds; a piece of paper trash drifting over the water. Even her steering wheel feels loose, as though the tires have lost contact with the road, and if she were to pull back on the wheel in just the right way she could steer the car upward above the bridge and the refinery and the whole sprawling Houston skyline, dewy and gray and infinite. She yawns, checks her rearview mirror, and watches the amber streetlamps feed like a necklace into the darkness she has left behind. Through the dashboard vents she can smell the Gulf, the salty air.

She's made good time. She'll arrive at her mother's by seven-thirty. She left earlier than usual, having never really gone to sleep, slipping through the back door and through the tunnel of pines to the highway in the predawn black, the dew just descending to the lawns. She has left everything in place. Her bed is made, the spread folded beneath the pillows, the corners tucked in tight. She's set out bowls and plates for breakfast, folded the napkins into triangles and weighted them with spoons, filled the coffee maker, and scrambled eggs in a bowl. All Cory will have to do is pour the mix into the skillet and move the spatula back and forth. Jill will pour the orange juice. Lee will fix the coffee. Rowdy will do the dishes without being asked. Everything will function without her.

The Toyota glides easily, picking up speed as the road curves back to earth. The highway before her is wide and straight and goes all the way to Florida. She could be gone before anyone thinks to miss her.

Crossing this bridge on other Saturday mornings she has dreamed of herself doing exactly that, missing her turnoff, slipping the Texas border, disappearing to some distant city, a different life. It is the consequence, she supposes, of how she spends her Friday nights, her car parked beneath the sea of neon billboards lining Westheimer and Richmond, in the tight jeans and bright makeup she only wears when going out, her back against the bar as she leans close to the ear of a stranger so he can hear her over the music. No man has ever asked her last name and when he asks her first, she calls herself whatever she likes. The result is the same, his desire no less present in his fingers. Speaking a different name into the ear of a man she doesn't know, she feels pulled out of her body, allowed to hover above herself—through the bar and across the parking lot and into her car, the headlights glowing in her rearview mirror illuminating her forehead and nose, following her away from the city to the winding farm-to-market road to the gravel pathway through the trees. The house sits at the end, hunkered in the pines. "This your place?" the man asks, standing shielded by the door of his car, surprised she has led him to a house so far out of the city, so big and so dark. Unsure of whether or not to trust her.

"It's where I live," she says. "I don't own it." She and Cory have an understanding. Weekends she can do what she likes, including bringing a man to her bedroom, so long as he is gone before the children wake up. Cory would rather Kay bring a man home than stay out all night. "So we know you're safe," Cory said. "And so you don't show up with your underwear in your back pocket while we're eating breakfast." Kay lifts a finger to her lips, points to the windows where Jill and Rowdy sleep, and leads him around the house to the back door, the stairwell in the garage fumy with gasoline and wet grass, the slow antifreeze drip from the van. Her bedroom is at the top. "There's a room here?" the man asks. She nods and opens the door. The ceiling slants sharply across her bed; on the other side three tall windows look over the acres of pine that surround the property, the low water in the bayou a silver thread in the moonlight. The clothes are hers, as are the frames on the dresser, the stack of cassettes, the tape player, and the stained glass sun-catcher in the shape of Texas suctioned to the window. The rest—the bed and dresser and nightstand—belongs to the house and will remain after she is gone.

Though in a way, the entire house is hers. She decides when to set out the china and the silver, what to grind in the food processor, when to use the oven. She moves freely through the bedrooms and closets and even into the big bathroom in the master bedroom, soaking in the sunken tub when no one else is home. On sleepless nights she walks the long tiled hallways, touches the doorknobs of the children's rooms, drinks orange juice from the pitcher with the refrigerator hanging open. No one minds. Lee has told her he sleeps better knowing she is there to watch over them. She's something like an aunt, but not. A stranger they have long grown used to. They tell her she's like family, which means she's not family at all.

• • •

She had a year to go toward her nursing degree when she answered an ad to look after a blind woman and an infant. The pay was low, but it included room and board, a bedroom above the garage that smelled of paint and window tinting, brand-new furniture, her own bathroom. She figured she'd stay a year, stockpile her tiny paycheck, and go back to school. Lee was a researcher at the Medical Center, and he said he could get her a break on tuition. But a year passed and then another, and in the third year, Cory was pregnant again, and Kay boxed up her books and her stethoscope. Fifteen years later she is a kind of nurse, though one who moves between the infirmary of the mad and the penitentiary of the blind. Most of her life feels like that, filled with the things she wanted, but not quite what she wants.

Even when Rowdy and Jill started school and it seemed the right time to go, something always happened that prevented it. There was the time, for example, she steered *around* a car accident. They were on I-10 headed to the Galleria when a pickup bounced off the guardrail, spun across the lane, and broadsided a Buick. Kay pumped the brakes, swerved, and cleared it. The car behind her ran smack into the pileup. Jill said it was a miracle. Even the neighbors walked by the house to marvel at the van. People didn't worry about hepatitis in the suburbs, or tuberculosis, or silicosis; they worried about the dangers of cars and freeways, about cancer, about bankruptcy. When Steven Stevenson, the dentist who lived across the street, got wind of how Kay had avoided the accident, he spent a good hour circling the van, kicking the tires, propping the hood to stare down at the engine, tapping his gold A&M ring against the radiator and the engine block. He declared the van "a fine machine" and told Lee the

Chrysler Corporation would be very interested in hearing about how its vehicle performed. "And give your help a raise. Watch out or I'll come steal her away from you." Kay was standing outside and Steven Stevenson had winked at her.

. . .

For months Cory claimed to have seen slivers of warped light in her left eye. She followed the light into the woods, into the stockroom of the supermarket, into a taxi outside the Galleria. Rowdy said his mother was disappearing, as though unable to see, she could not herself be seen. Turn around and she's gone. Kay thought she was just being selfish. When the tumor showed up, choroidal melanoma reproducing itself like mosquitoes in a wet ditch, Kay wanted to slap herself for missing it. She wasn't a doctor, but she should have known something was wrong. It was what she was paid to do and had done for a decade and a half, watching the stove and the scissors, sweeping her bare foot along the tile floor to make sure it was dry so Cory wouldn't slip, standing either in the yard or at the kitchen window while Rowdy and Jill climbed the sycamore to the roof or played too close to the bayou where cottonmouths lay curled in the tall grass. Rowdy and Jill had entered their teens without so much as a stitch, and Cory, too, had avoided every danger of blindness. Now blindness threatened in the one way Kay had been unable to anticipate, and she felt certain, watching the ophthalmologist dial his scope into a pinpoint of light and lean into Cory's pupil, the melanoma was just the beginning— all the dangers she had fended off were closing in. The car, strange men lurking in the park outside of Jill's school, the cancer that, once Cory was opened up, would be found everywhere, everywhere.

She wanted to hold Cory's hand in the hospital, to write her name on Cory's palm, to tell her *I'm right here.* Cory sat expressionless in her hospital bed with her hands in her lap. Kay sat for hours in the chair beside her bed, never sleeping, waiting for Cory to turn to her, to reach for her hand. But she didn't. The nurses came in and dropped the rails on Cory's bed and wheeled her down the hall. She came back with a square of gauze taped over the hole where her left eye had been, her lips rigid, her face an empty page. Lee touched Kay's shoulder and said, softly, "I don't know where she is." She turned and saw that his eyes were full.

Medication kept Cory calm, but not better. She went home with a prosthetic eye and parked herself at the kitchen table, where she buried herself in her headphones, listening to books-on-tape that arrived by the bundle from the Lighthouse Ministries. Each book was read by an inmate at the penitentiary in Huntsville. Lee used to joke that the prisoners had sexy, bad-boy voices and his wife probably had a crush on a few. Now he stood at the doorway and twisted his wedding ring around on his finger.

Last night, after they got Cory home from her mother's party, Lee laid his hand on Kay's shoulder, and she didn't shrug it off. Not even when he let it slide to her back, around her waist. He was starting to cry again, gusts of hot air against her neck. She said goodnight in the kitchen, but left open the door between the house and the garage. She hung her dress on the hook on the back of the bathroom door and was waiting when she heard his footsteps on the stairs.

. . .

Heading south along the shoreline of the Ship Channel, she smells diesel and molasses, rotting fish. A rusted pipe with a mouth as wide around as a car tire spews a creamy foam over a pile of concrete slabs. It is October and so the shrimp trucks are out, white, their compressors chugging. A man hauls two bags of ice back from the Circle K. She looks for the wooden pylons, once the legs of fishing piers and boat docks, where her father used to keep his shrimp pots. On Sundays her father and mother and Kay would drive the peninsula to take in the catch of gigantic gray prawns fattened in the warm water. Her father rolled his overalls above his knees and waded out to the anchor lines, which he pulled in fist over fist, careful not to snap the line. Kay followed him out in her bathing suit until the water got too deep for her to touch the bottom, then turned and waved at her mother who stood stroking her belly on the shore, the green water lapping against her ankles, her neck and arms peachy and freckled and not yet scarred by disease. Her father was already showing signs of hepatitis, but he wore long pants and sleeves most of the time, so the jaundice was hard to see.

Two miscarriages and a brother that came stillborn at twenty-three weeks and after that her father was too sick to try again. He did not trust hospitals or doctors and avoided both. Every oil worker got something, he said, and so accepted his disease as part of his predetermined fate and surrendered to it without a fight. For years Kay watched him wander their neighborhood naked, some nights attempting to swim across the Channel, other nights loading and unloading his pistol in the back bedroom of their cinderblock house in a movement so practiced and rhythmic it looked unconscious. When he knew his time was up he drove to a motel. The night the police arrived at her house, Kay checked the metal case on his closet shelf. It was heavy. She would not have agreed to ride in the police car to identify him had the gun been missing.

Her father's mouth was open, exposing his tobacco-yellowed teeth, but his eyes were closed, and in the hazy fog that drifted across the windows from Galveston Bay he looked almost peaceful. She imagined some essence of him escaping through the O of his mouth, his spirit swimming upstream against the air-conditioning and through the grates and into the air. She touched his cold beard, his wooden lips. "That's not him," she said.

"You're sure? We have a driver's license."

"No, I mean, it's his body. Just not *him*. He's gone."

"Right," the officer said. He rubbed the corners of his mouth with his thumb and index finger. "No soul in the shell."

"However you say it."

But it was a good way to say it, one she thinks of still as she crosses through town, the storefronts dilapidated and tired, the same old Chevys and Fords parked diagonally against the curb, a Starbucks grossly out of place on the corner where the hardware store used to be. It is the same town she knew as a girl, only now emptied of the people who populated her girlhood, full of people she almost recognizes but does not quite. A city of shells, she thinks.

• • •

Her mother sits in the living room in the rocking chair, her legs covered with a frayed afghan. She watches *Good Morning Houston* with the sound off. The plastic blinds are sun-bleached and cracked and the room smells of mold. The flowers Kay brought last time sit wilted almost black in a vase of syrup-green water. Her mother's hair is thin as thread and knotted around the crown of her head. "Hey, Momma," Kay says.

"Sheila. You're back." It's been a year since her mother remembered her name.

"It's Saturday."

"Is it?"

"Got any of that coffee left?"

"Heck, no."

"They threw it out? Well maybe you have some tea in the cupboard. I need *something*." The apartment has no teakettle, so Kay sets water to boil in a small pot. The bottom is rusted, but it will do. She dials open the blinds and throws the flowers in the trash, fills the sink with hot water and Joy and throws in the bowls and silverware on the counter. Every flat surface—the kitchen table, the end tables by the couch, the top of the fridge and microwave, even on either side of the door—is covered with *Watchtower* and *Awake!* magazines, the new issues stacked right on top of the old. There is a Bible on the table—not the New International Version Kay keeps in her own nightstand drawer, but the New World Translation, the Jehovah's Witness version. But the magazines are what engulf the room. They look as though they've been arranged as a barricade against some unknown evil, possibly Kay herself. The two women who share her mother's house, Ava and Charlene, converted her mother when Kay was sixteen, just after her father died. When Kay left for nursing school, they moved in and emptied her mother's cupboards of alcohol, her refrigerator of meat, and got her walking a little each day, all of which has slowed the progression of the disease. For that much Kay is thankful. But the women also keep her mother fearful of hospitals and have convinced her it was sex that made her sick and it is sex that keeps the disease alive inside her. "If you want to get better," Ava told her, "your daughter shouldn't come around. The Bible says to remove the wicked from among you." To avoid any conflict, Kay now comes in secret, on Saturdays, when she knows Ava and Charlene will be out all day knocking on doors and handing out tracts to the boys skateboarding in the park. What do they think when they come home to find the house clean and the cupboards full of food? A miracle? Manna from heaven? They never say.

Kay scoops the pamphlets into a trash bag, ties it shut, and sets it by the door. "You think those two could pick up after themselves every once in a while."

"They're busy."

"I thought cleanliness was next to godliness."

"Let me help you." Her mother pulls the afghan from her lap and stands. She looks tired, but lucid, better than last week. Her green eyes hold their focus. Kay watches her mother's swollen ankles and the bottoms of her blistered edematous legs as she shuffles across the dark carpet to the kitchen, her faded nightgown in a bunch around her middle, the hem against the floor. Her feet slide; even this short distance is too far to walk. She holds her hand against her side. "You feeling okay, Momma?" Kay points to her abdomen. "Does it hurt here?"

Her mother's eyes widen. "I know what you are trying to do and it won't work. Your father says I am doing the right thing. God told him so. He talks to God all the time."

"They have new procedures now, Momma. They can do it without blood transfusions. If you got a new liver you'd feel better."

"Ha! Kenny says that's all hogwash."

"I'm not sure Dad's talking to the right people."

"Shows what you know."

"Momma," Kay says. She lifts her mother's hand from the counter, rubs the bones between her fingers. She can almost touch her index finger to her thumb with her mother's hand in between. She cannot not try. "Don't you want to get better?"

"God's plan is God's plan."

"But you could get better."

"Oh, Sheila. Let's find you something to drink."

Her mother rights herself and her nightgown shakes loose. The cloth beneath the armpits is yellow and the folds of her lap are sour. Kay wonders when her mother wet herself, how many days she's worn the dirty gown. "Look at you!" Kay says. "Didn't they see your nightgown?"

"They don't see my body, just my soul."

"Well, I'm sure they smell more than your soul. How about we take a bath today?"

"We did that last time."

"It's a whole new week, Momma."

She guides her mother into the bathroom, sits her down on the toilet lid. A layer of hard-water grime rings the sides of the tub and clumps of gray hair are tangled in the crosshairs of the drain. Kay picks them out and scrubs the tub with Ajax and bleach, rinses, turns the water to warm, and plugs the drain. While the tub fills, Kay brushes out the knots from her mother's hair. "Maybe after your bath we can go get something to eat. My treat." Her mother gets monthly disability checks, same as Cory, but Kay doesn't know what happens to the money.

Kay takes her mother's hands and lifts them above her head. "Hold here a sec," she says and lifts the nightgown over her head. Her mother's body no longer alarms her—the dark bruises on her thighs and sides and the mass in her stomach where her liver swells—Kay's used to these things by now. Even to the hair between her mother's legs, still dark and abundant, the last place on her body she looks alive. Kay lifts her mother from the toilet and helps her to drop slowly into the water. The water folds around the wrinkles in her neck as she slides her hair below the bubbles. She lifts her belly and lets her feet rise to the surface. She almost smiles. "Feels good, doesn't it?" Kay says. "Nothing like a hot bath."

With a washcloth and a bar of soap, Kay lifts one leg, washes it, lowers it back. Then the next leg, then an arm, then the other arm. She presses her hand to her mother's back and helps her to slide up to sitting. She washes the arch of her hunched spine from the back of her hairline to the base of her coccyx. The water turns gray and filmy. Her mother has hardly left the apartment, if at all, and Kay wonders how she collected so much grime by just sitting around.

Kay looks away while she washes between her mother's legs, ashamed to touch her mother there, but knowing if she does not, she won't be clean. She cleans close to her mother's ear. She looks at the back of her mother's head and whispers in her ear, so softly she can hardly hear the words leave her own mouth. "Momma, can I tell you something?" She lingers there, pulls her head back a little and waits. Her mother makes no movement, no noise. She's listening. Kay leans in again. "I slept with Lee." But it is not enough to simply say his name; he was not just a man. "Cory's husband," she whispers, even softer than the first time. "The children's father. I let him touch me. In my bed."

She sighs against her mother's cheek. In that moment she feels better, as though she has released the bad Kay from the good. The good Kay kneels on the bathroom floor soaping her mother's deflated breast while the bad rises with the steam and evaporates against the lightbulb. She leans her mother back in the water. Her mother's eyes are open and wild; they scan the ceiling and the top of Kay's head. Made greener by her pale skin and ashen hair, her mother's eyes look deep as globes. But they do not recognize her. Her mother pulls her arms tight against her chest, flattening her breasts. "Who are you?" she says. Water splashes down the front of Kay's blouse and jeans.

"It's just me, Momma. Calm down."

"Get away. Get away." Her mother tries to stand up from the tub too quickly. She teeters and Kay reaches for her. Her mother shakes her elbow. "Don't touch me. Oh God, *please*."

"Momma, it's okay. It's me. It's Kay Lynn."

"Help me, Kenny!"

"Okay, okay." Kay drags the towel from the rack and opens it to catch her mother. "Let's dry you off." Her mother snatches the towel from her, suddenly strong, presses it against her chest, and then lets it fall into the water. She teeters forward and then backward and flails with both hands out, grasping at the air. Kay wraps her arms around her and lifts her from the bathtub. Her mother screams, "Oh God! Oh Kenny!"

"It's okay, Momma." Kay steadies her with one hand and reaches for another towel beneath the sink, spreads the towel and wraps it around her mother's shoulders. She holds it tightly so her mother cannot flail and drops an arm to her knees, lifts her mother up. She is light, more wind than body, less body than ever.

The bedroom is stuffy and hot and smells of cigarettes, an odor that lingers in the carpets and the walls like the ghost of her father. She sets her mother down on the edge of the unmade bed. Her mother lays her head against the pillow, pulls her legs into her stomach, and shivers. She kicks her feet beneath the blankets and Kay helps her pull them up to her neck. The sheets smell of rotting fruit, the nightly shroud of a decaying body. She had plans to take her mother to the Laundromat, but that can wait. She leaves the lights off and backs out of the room.

· · ·

She'd promised herself she wouldn't to talk to Lee today, but in the kitchen she dials the number to his laboratory. Even on a Saturday he's there. She can hear voices in the background, the whirr and beep of the sequencer, the techs chatting while they pour the slides. It takes him a second to recognize her voice. "I was just thinking about you," he says.

"I hope I didn't interrupt."

"It's not very busy. Are you okay?"

"My mother doesn't know who I am. She forgot my name months ago, but now it's more. My face. She talks to my father all the time."

"I thought he was dead."

"He is."

"Oh. . . . Where is she now?"

"Asleep."

"Meet me."

"I need to go to the store and she needs her clothes washed. This place is a sty."

"Give yourself a break. You'll be back before she wakes up. It's early still."

"Where?"

"Warwick Hotel. In the restaurant."

"You can get away?"

"I'll make something up. I'm the boss. Leave a note for your mother. She'll never know where you've been."

"Even if I leave a note she'll never know."

It scares her to think that soon her mother will be dead. Maybe she'll make it to the summer, maybe only Christmas, but either way, it won't be long. It's not the same as when her father died. Even if her mother does not recognize her, Kay recognizes herself by going to see her; her mother and her old house remind her of a past that does not belong to Cory, or the children, or Lee.

She knows she's on a fool's errand. Lee really isn't her type. She's never gone for the businessmen in expensive suits who hide their wedding rings in their breast pockets and set the keys to their BMWs on the bar. Her heart has always been for the wrecked and the injured. Beat-up roughnecks with chemical burns and discolored tattoos, longshoremen with slipped discs and broken thumbs—these were the men she took home or followed back to small trailers with wood-paneled bedrooms, tiny houses beneath the freeways. She knows injury, where to lay her hands and mouth, where to look and where not to look. The father of her child lost his left hand and wrist in the rigging chain of a shipyard crane. In the bar where they met, he tried to hide the absent hand in his pocket. Only when Kay pressed her hand against his thigh did he let it appear. She closed her palm around it like a doorknob, twisted, leaned close to his ear and told him she had a car. She spent three days in his motel room in Galena Park. His stomach was compact and tight, strong from the job he could no longer do. A scar from an earlier accident ran from his chin to the base of his throat. She wondered how he was alive. She let her head rest against his forearm, his truncated arm hidden beneath the pillow. She could feel his absent fingers on her cheek, still warm as the real hand cupped over her hip. He told her the crane lifted him over a hundred feet in the air and left him dangling over the Channel for nearly thirty minutes before he could be brought down. "It only hurt at first," he said. "Then I couldn't feel my arm no more and it felt like I was flying. I thought I was dead. Took nearly a month before I was convinced I wasn't. My hospital room was all white. I thought it was Heaven." She watched his chest swell as he talked, how he breathed all the way out.

She realized she was pregnant in the Jarretts' bathroom. She had been there a month. Cory's stomach and breasts had shrunk back down to size, but her eye sockets were ringed with purple from the surgery to reattach her retinas. Bedsores the shape of footballs covered her stomach and thighs from the weeks she spent immobilized, sandbags packed around her head. Each day Cory could do more, but it was becoming clear she'd never see again, at least not very much. A kaleidoscopic fragment of color, a soda can label, the shadow in the sun, but no more than that.

For weeks Kay slept with a pillow beneath her shirt, envisioning a crib in the corner, the smell of pines wafting through the open windows, her child learning to crawl up the staircase. She almost told Cory about it, but then she didn't. She called the motel, but no one there had ever heard of him. "Uneven beard," she said, "missing a hand. Ring a bell?" But no.

One afternoon when the pines were dropping needles onto the porch, Kay watched Cory undress Rowdy and carry him to the kitchen sink. Rowdy was big enough for the bathtub, but the sink was deep and Cory could manage it better. She filled the sink with water and a tablespoon of baby shampoo. Cory slid Rowdy from her shoulder, loosened the towel, dipped him in the water. Rowdy splashed, soaked the front of her shirt, then settled his head into his mother's palm. Cory squeezed the excess water from the washcloth with one hand and rubbed it over his chest and stomach. She dipped it again, wrung it out, and lifted his bottom to wash between his legs and the backs of his thighs and knees. She set him down in the basin and water splashed across the top of his face and he began to cry. Kay moved to help, but stopped herself. These little tasks were the vehicle of Cory's recovery, her adaptation to blindness. Cory picked Rowdy up, cradled him against her shirt, then lifted him close to her face. Her eyes scanned as if trying to see. Then with a strange, almost ceremonial movement, she lowered him back into the water, submerging his chest and shoulders and finally his head. The room went silent.

"Cory!" Kay lunged from the doorway. Rowdy was above the water before she even reached the sink, coughing, his eyes wide, his mouth open in silent gasps. It took him nearly a minute to scream. Cory breathed in shallow huffs.

"I almost had him," Cory said. "I almost saw him. He was almost there."

Kay spread the towel and wrapped it around them both. "It's all right. He's all right."

Cory cradled Rowdy in both hands and handed him to Kay. "You should take him."

"No," Kay said. "You're his mother. You're going to put him down."

"I don't think I can. I'm sorry."

"You don't have to apologize," Kay said. "Just do it." Cory lifted him back against her chest. She looped an arm through Kay's elbow and allowed herself to be guided to the nursery.

"I don't know what would have happened if you hadn't been there."

"You would have pulled him up. You lapsed. You didn't mean it."

"Your voice pulled me back. You saved him."

"I didn't," Kay said.

"You did. You're my guardian."

"No, I'm not," Kay said. "I'm your friend."

Still she could imagine it: the strange pietà of a woman drowning her own son in the kitchen sink, Lee arriving home to find Cory curled in a ball on the floor, Rowdy's body floating. She had seen babies in the hospital who had been hurt by mothers whose horrors were less real than Cory's. She knew what could happen. And the house, when she looked around it, was suddenly dangerous, the light sockets and the drawer of knives, the hot water in the faucet and the gas hissing up from the stove. She was afraid for Rowdy, but she was even more afraid for Cory. For weeks she dreamed of Cory opening her wrists in the bathtub while Lee slept unaware in the next room, or tumbling down into the bayou behind the house, or swallowing her entire bottle of pills at once. She knew if she looked away for even a second, Cory would do it. She knew it with the same sinking certainty with which she had first touched her stomach and cupped her breasts and known she was pregnant. How could she choose one over the other? Nonetheless, there was a choice to make, for it was selfish to have thought of bringing another child into the house, to impede herself with pregnancy and then distract herself with a baby. She went to Rowdy's room and watched him sleep, his lips puckered, thought-less as a fish. What would happen to him? It is almost impossible to meas-ure what would be against what already is.

The next week when Cory's mother came to take her shopping, Kay said she had errands to run and drove north through the pines, staying off the highway, passing through Tomball and Navasota and Bryan and Hammond, all the way to Waco. She stole a phone book from a booth, spread it open on her lap and circled the block until she found the clinic, not far from the Baylor campus. She parked across the street at the dough-nut shop. People stood beneath a cluster of scrub trees that shaded the parking lot. They held posters and walked back and forth in a line. Oth-ers held candles close to their faces and were quiet, heads bowed in prayer. She went unnoticed until she stepped into the near-empty parking lot and headed toward the front door. "Hey, mom!" someone shouted. "Let us talk to you for a minute! We're praying for you!" She looked back and saw a young woman in a Baylor sweatshirt, blonde hair, an almost beatific face. The girl's bottom lip quivered, on the verge of tears. Behind her a man waved a Bible and shouted, "Don't kill your baby!" She turned and went inside.

The doctor wore green scrubs and smelled like soap. He sat down on a stool at her feet, examined the sonogram, nodded, said she was eight weeks along. Through the back of the picture Kay saw a white oval, small-er than the tiniest shrimp her father trapped in Galveston Bay. It sat at the bottom of a dark sea that undulated beneath the fluorescent lights. "Where are you from?" he asked her.

"I live in Houston."

"Long way from home."

"That's the idea."

"You made it through that mess outside?"

"Yes."

"They don't know anything," the nurse said. "They don't know what you've been through to get here. We'll walk you to your car later on."

"In Houston what do you do?" the doctor asked. "You in school?"

"I was. Now I take care of a family. The woman is blind and she has a new baby."

"That's a good thing," he said. "What did you study?"

"Nursing." The nurse smiled and touched her shoulder. "I'm sorry," Kay said.

"There's no need to apologize," the nurse said. "No one here is accusing you of anything."

The doctor gave her a shot of lidocaine, and when her cervix was numb, he slid a succession of small, tapered dilators into her cervix, each one larger than the one before it. Kay flinched only once, but hard, rustling the paper sheet. The nurse squeezed her hand and the doctor threaded a small plastic tube into her uterus, the tube connected to a pump in the palm of his hand. "It won't be long now," he said, and squeezed.

· · ·

The hotel is red and U-shaped, a circular garden with a gazebo out front, the upper floors shaded by the eaves. The entrance is obscured by a row of azalea hedges and a line of live oaks along the curb. It has an air of mystery and secrecy, a place where oil executives meet with politicians. Lee waits for her in the lobby. He's wearing khaki pants and a yellow Izod, a kind of camouflage among the other aimless hotel guests. His arms are brown, his mustache neatly trimmed. He pretends to read the *Houston Chronicle* while holding the plastic rectangle of the room key like a tongue between his thumb and the knuckle of his index finger. He's new at this. She does not stand too close. "I have until noon," he says as he looks around the lobby. She follows him into the elevator, where she studies the comb rows in his hair, the flecks of gray in his temples and above his lip. He presses the button and they rise, slowly first and then more quickly, accelerating as they climb.

The curtains in the room are open to the skyline, the roofs of Rice University rising above the oaks. It is a nicer room than she is used to, twice the size of her bedroom, the chair beside the window upholstered with leather and accompanied by an ottoman large enough to be a bed itself. Unlike the motel rooms around the Channel, built for uncomfortable sleeps and hurried fucks, this room feels almost like the bedroom of a home, extra pillows and blankets stacked on the shelf, the windows turned southward to face the main thoroughfare of downtown and the museums and the park. "Can you afford this?" she asks.

"There's a university rate," he says. "And I have a travel budget; I can slide it in and no one will know." He untucks his shirt from his slacks, unlaces his shoes, a repetition of the motions he went through less than twelve hours ago. He hangs everything in the closet. Even his undershirt he folds up and sets on the shelf. Kay can feel a ritual forming—what their meetings will be like, how this slow act of undressing will count as foreplay. She hopes he will bring her back to this hotel, though to a different room. There are more angles to see, more streets to look down upon.

Last night they touched each other slowly, carefully, crawling over each other as if they were made of glass. Now she watches his thin chest and stomach, and she longs for the heavy longshoremen with blackened fingernails and sunburned tattoos. Men with weight to push against her, to pin her to the earth. She'd do it on the floor if he'd go for that. She sees him testing the mattress with his knee, and when he crawls onto the bed, Kay pulls him over and forces him to crawl over her. She presses her palms against the square of his back, pulls him down. "Whoa," he says. "Slow down. We have longer than ten minutes here."

"I wish you were heavier."

"I'm sorry to disappoint you."

"It's fine. Just don't stop."

He looks down at her eyes, his face yellowed by the morning light through the curtains. "What are you thinking?"

"I'm not."

"Your mother?"

"Do you want this or not?" She has spoken too harshly, and when she looks up, she sees his remorse. She feels selfish with guilt; she wants it all to herself. "It's been a hard morning," she says. "I want to feel something different. That's all."

"Okay."

But she *is* thinking about her mother, calling out to her father to swoop down and rescue her from the living. She is that far gone. Anyplace seems better than that damp bedroom, that phantom smell. All those hours alone there in conversation with her father have perhaps allowed her mother to believe it is not death that's coming for her—at least not the deaths of refinery explosions and hepatitis—but something less horrible, less bleak, more like leaving. Crossing a channel, like her father stepping out of his overalls and wading into the water with his maddened eye fixed on the other side. It's not so crazy that her mother talks to him. Perhaps his spirit is still trapped on the peninsula between the Channel and the Bay, between this world and the next, urging her mother to come toward him. She never heard her own child's heart beat and still she talks to it sometimes, not in the way her mother talks to her father, but comforted by the idea that it can see her and all the people she touches.

Lee locks his eyes on hers and she can see him hating this moment as much as he feeds on it. He is the kind of man who would never figure himself an adulterer. His wedding ring is still on his finger. All the same, here he is, afraid of himself. Kay lifts her head and kisses his bottom lip, says "Oh" for him. He smiles, closes his eyes. She lets her head sink back into the pillow. It is possible to become someone else, she thinks, or something, if it is required of us. It is possible to move across.

· · ·

It is the thought she carries with her through the remainder of that stretched, gauzy day. Filling a shopping cart with cans and bags of vegetables, transferring her mother's wet clothes to the dryer, the long drive across the city. Later, cooking dinner she watches Jill sit cross-legged before the television. Rowdy emerges from the bathroom with a towel around his waist. They ignore their mother, perched on her elbows at the table. Kay thinks, these are the things my child would be doing now. Her mother would live with them, too, bathed daily and medicated, eccentric rather than demented—all the things she gave up to keep safe these children who are too big to protect, to guide a woman who stares blankly at the wall.

After dinner Kay takes a beer from the refrigerator and ascends her staircase. Her open bedroom windows pull the heat up from the garage. She feels her resignation in her stomach and legs, her body too heavy to hold up. She sits on the top step, her car keys looped through her pinky finger. She rubs her foot on the carpet, looks into her slanted bedroom, the dresser and bed, the bathrobe over the door. It looks like a hotel she never checked out of. The wall glows silver in the moonlight, and through the windows she hears the distant zap and sizzle of mosquitoes frying on the bug lights. She speaks into the humid dark, the void. "I never should have given you up. If you were here I could go."

It does not always answer her, but tonight it does, its voice soft and faint and reassuring. Her sweet angel. "You did what you had to do. Stop second-guessing yourself. For all you know, we might have ended up living in your car."

"I'm going to end up there anyway. Only this time I'll be alone."

"Not yet. Not tonight. Put your keys away."

"They'll get along fine without me."

"They only think so. They don't know what would happen."

"I've thought about having another child," she says. "I could handle it now. I'm older."

"There'll be time for that later. You're getting ahead of yourself. You're young still. Trust me."

"Should I have left when I had the chance?"

"You already know that answer."

"What I'm doing now is worse. I should go."

"And leave them? You've got more here than you think. The children are your children, this life is your life. You can't pack as fast as you think you can. They need you too much. It was Cory at first and then it was the children. Now it's Lee." Below her the garage door opens and the headlights flash against the wall. The engine of Lee's car revs and she feels it fill the air below. "He doesn't know what he's doing. You cannot just run out on him, on any of them. Not now."

She hears the car shut off, the door open, Lee's heels against the garage floor. She waits for him to pass by the stairs and look up. She wants him to find her there. "No," she says. "I cannot run out."

CONSEQUENCES OF KNOWLEDGE

THE BAYOU BEHIND OUR HOUSE was cut twice a year. The city of Houston would drive out a big tractor with rotary blades that stuck out five feet on both sides and could mow the entire slope in three passes. We were due for the tractor to come again. The grasses on the banks were wild from the rain, and on warm days the cottonmouths climbed the banks to curl in the sun. The bayou was the one place my mother feared above all others—more than the woods that cut a wedge all the way to the highway, more than the supermarket with its high echoes and slick, narrow aisles, more than the tunnels beneath downtown. Those places she had memorized well enough when she could still see. The bayou was the last thing she saw before she went blind, and that single fact was enough to make the entire place deadly. She warned us that cottonmouths could bite through the toe of a shoe and that after a hard rain the water ran fast enough to pull a man under. But what most scared her was the way the bayou echoed the sound of absence, of nothing, the fact that she had never been to, or seen, its other side. Because I knew I'd caused this fear by blinding my mother, I tended to stay away from the bayou. Because she knew it was hard for my mother to hear down the slope of the bank, my sister liked to take her friends there to tell secrets.

My mother used to scream if she smelled the bayou on us. She knew the mud there, the smell of rotting crawdads and turtle shells, the texture of dogwood on our hands. Since the eye had come out, she hadn't yelled about anything. She sat at the kitchen table with her lost eye focused on the wall she could not see. Jill colored a picture and hung it there to brighten the room, and my mother seemed to watch it for hours. She could sit so quiet and still I was tempted to hold my finger beneath her nose. Kay once snapped her fingers in front of my mother's face and my mother did not even flinch. When my father came home, Kay told him my mother had "checked out." She looped her finger in a circle next to her ear. She thought Jill and I didn't see her do this, but we did.

Jill played in the bayou a lot more after that. She came home with grassy knees and muddy socks, mosquito bites on her wrists and elbows, fists full of wildflowers she pressed flat between two boards. I found her there on a Saturday in February, straddling her bike on the top edge of the bank, her back to the house. It was the first warm day we'd had since Halloween and the bayou hill looked like a sheet of burlap poked through with violet and yellow. The water was frothy and thick along the edges, though it ran clear in the center. The silt that lined the bottom glittered like flecks of gold. "What are you up to?" I asked. Jill knew she was caught and ignored me.

"I see you," I said. "Give me a break."

"I'm riding my bike," she said. Both her bike and the cuffs of her jeans were covered in mud and grass, dogwood tangled in the spokes of both tires. She let the front tire rock over the lip of the bank. "Idiot."

"Mom will scream if she catches you here."

"No, she won't."

"Cottonmouths come up on days like this," I said. One time a cottonmouth slithered all the way to our front door and curled up on the mat, rested its chin on the threshold like a pet waiting to be let in. Jill had found it when she opened the door. It had scared her enough to keep her out of the bayou until the tractor came. "Aren't you afraid?" I said.

"No." The side of her jaw tightened at the snap of her words.

"You're still young enough to die if you got bit."

"And you're not?"

"I'm too big," I said. "I'd get sick, but I wouldn't die."

"You mean you're too fat." She turned her eyes to me, slowly dragging them up from the bayou, a mimic of the look Kay used to flush out a lie. People said Jill's face was a clone of my father's, a resemblance usually lost on me. Now in Jill's strange look, I did see it, his smooth forehead and pointed chin, his flushed cheeks. Time had changed her in other ways: her T-shirt folded into the center of her chest and she had lost some of the skinniness that, just a summer ago, made her look so breakable. She looked more teenager than girl. The freckles on her arms and face gave her skin a tougher look than I remembered. I'd missed the emergence of all these things though we shared a bathroom and our bedrooms shared a wall.

I had avoided Jill since October when I walked into the backyard and saw my father standing naked in Kay's bedroom window. Kay was naked, too, though she stood behind him and I could see less of her. My father watched the moon over the pines and the shaved slope of the bayou and the water, and when he looked down he saw me standing there. He woke me up the next morning before anyone else was awake and drove me all the way down to the mouth of the Ship Channel for breakfast. We sat at a table against the window that overlooked the turning basin where the shoe-shaped ships unloaded their freight, reloaded new freight, and headed back down the Channel to Galveston Bay. He ordered two cups of coffee and said he owed me an explanation. I said he didn't. He said my mother lived inside a shell no one could get through. Not Kay and not him. "We're doing this to not leave," he said. "To stay. We both love your mother and this is what we need to do to get through. You understand, Rowdy?" I didn't, but I said I did. I wanted to watch the tankers change directions, but he kept his eyes low and said it was important I keep this between us. He was nervous. He promised that so long as I didn't blow it, he'd make things right again in good time. He reached his hand across the table for me to shake on it. "There are just some things men have to keep to themselves," he said. "You'll find this out yourself one day." I took his hand. I shook it.

When we returned home, I went into Jill's room and tried to pretend everything was normal. I asked her about the science fair and whether the Russian was treating her any better at ballet and about Todd McGann. Todd McGann was the only boy in her school as tall as she and my sister's perennial square-dance partner. Every teacher since the first grade told my parents Jill and Todd were a good match, as though their equal height and the ability to do-si-do without tripping made them soul mates. The joke had grown boring and we'd quit teasing Jill about it. When I said his name, Jill looked at me and said, "Who cares about him? What's with you?"

"Nothing," I said. "I was just wondering."

The children of blindness, Jill and I could communicate with just our eyes. There was the time, for example, when I was caught breaking windows inside one of the unfinished homes on the far side of the neighborhood. I arrived home in the back of the sheriff's patrol car, in handcuffs. When my father walked me into the kitchen, Kay touched the base of her throat and my mother gasped. I couldn't think of a good reason. There were other windows broken in the house, so I figured I would break one myself. The sound the glass made when it shattered was sharp, electric, and so thrilling that I found a two-by-four and broke as many as I could before the sheriff dragged me out by my belt loop. I couldn't say that, so I sat at the kitchen counter and tried to sound sorry. Jill came in, looked at my eyes, and said she'd seen a group of older boys giving me a hard time at the Stop N Go. My father asked her who they were and Jill said she did-n't know, but they had purple hair and wore nasty T-shirts with pictures of bleeding skulls and snakes and flames. My father looked at me and said, "That true?" And all I had to do was nod.

In her bedroom, Jill had looked at me with the same eyes, saucer-shaped and green, eyes that understood my truths before truth had words. She said nothing but her face said, "What's wrong?" What I knew I could-n't let her understand. My mother was in the laundry room across the hall, and Kay was in the kitchen. I said, "Never mind," and I left. I kept my distance from her after that.

On the bayou's edge, Jill said, "I'll ride where I want to. I don't need your permission."

"What's with you?"

"I'm tired of you acting funny," she said. "Just come out with whatev-er you're hiding."

"I'm not hiding anything," I said.

"You are. I know it." Her voice seemed on the verge of translating intu-ition into knowledge, as though all she needed was one suggestive hint and the puzzle would be solved. "You're hiding something about Mom and Dad, maybe about Kay, too. I know it."

I wondered how good I'd really been at hiding anything. Maybe my secret-keeping was a charade, a game played against me. I thought about spilling it to her. Jill seemed like the right person to tell. But I'd promised my father, and I was certain my silence kept the last threads of my fami-ly from unraveling. "I can't," I said. "I'm sorry."

"Come on. *It's me.* I won't tell a soul." Her arms were flexed and taut as they extended to the handlebars of her bike, her knuckles white around the grips. She twisted her neck and said, "If you don't tell me, I'll ask Mom."

"Just keep your mouth shut, okay?"

"Tell me and I will."

"I can't tell you and you can't say anything. This is important. You need to forget it."

"How can I forget what I don't know? You tell me first and then I'll forget. Or else I'll find out another way." The ring in her voice startled me. It was sharp-edged and cutting, the sound of glass. When she looked at me again and squinted into the sun, she looked stranger than ever. I feared her ability to wreck everything before it had a chance to get right again. I feared that the chance for things to get right was becoming less possible. My mother continued to sit day after day at the kitchen table; my father and Kay had a million reasons for leaving the house within a half hour of each other. Sometimes they even held hands when they watched TV. I felt cold suddenly, the sun behind a cloud and a wind through the pines. I lifted my foot to the back of her bicycle seat. The bike rocked beneath my weight. "Stop, Rowdy," Jill said and rolled herself forward. When I felt the front tire dip over the lip of the bayou I pushed as hard as I could. Gravity did the rest. Jill yelped as the bike carried her down, her voice helpless. It lacked all its toughness and was filled with the fear of a little girl. She tried to run with the bike, but the pedals knocked against the back of her legs and she fell forward, her chest against the handlebars. The handlebars twisted hard left and the bike flipped. Jill's long legs spun into the sky and the bike followed her body around. For half a second she was upended and vertical, her arms extended to catch herself, her body tangled in the bike. I heard the pop when she came down—a sound much different than glass: neither high nor sharp, but low and dull and in the bottom of my stomach.

Jill lay motionless in the grass with her eyes open wide. Her feet and ankles were in the water and the left handlebar of her bike had been driven deep into the mud. The rear of her bike rose from the water, the tire spinning around and around. Her chest and stomach rose and fell, but her eyes made no response. Blindness was always a potential danger for both of us. "Are you okay?" I said. "Jill?" I waved my hands in front of her face.

Her eyes blinked and she saw me. Her pupils widened and her irises darted from side to side. "I'm sorry!" I said. I reached for her shoulder, but she winced and I backed off. She withdrew her arm from beneath her back and lifted it to her chest. Her wrist was caked in mud and the bone had moved to the center of her arm. It made a knot beneath her skin like a joint in a tree limb. Jill brushed her fingers over it, pressed slightly against it, and screamed.

"I'm sorry," I said again. "I didn't mean it!"

Her only answer was to scream louder. We both knew I *had* meant it. Her lips curled back over her teeth. White strings of saliva fluttered across the open chasm of her mouth as she gasped for air. I brushed the hair away from her forehead. "Take a breath," I said. "Try to breathe." Her chest heaved. "Can you sit up?" She folded herself at the center and lifted her chin. I slid my hand beneath her back.

"Don't, Rowdy," she said.

"Let me help you."

"No."

"You need help," I said. "We need to get you home."

"Not from you," she said. "Don't touch me. I'll get myself home."

Jill supported her weight with her good arm while she pulled her feet from the water and worked to stand. I pulled on the handlebar of her bike until I got it free of the mud and then dragged the whole thing up from the water. Mud and rushes filled the hole at the end of the bar. The handlebars were bent all the way to the side. "Leave it," she said. "I don't want it anymore."

"You don't want to know about anything," I said. "If I had told you, you would have wished you hadn't heard it." Jill clutched her wrist, squatted down against her knees and wept. She looked at me once more and then turned up the hill.

. . .

I kept my voice steady when my mother clicked off her cassette. I didn't breathe too hard. I said, "Jill fell."

Behind me Jill only cried.

My mother said, "What does 'fell' mean?"

My mother's blindness taught me that truth was a function of story. The blind world is a narrated world, a listened-to world. Sounds and words can mean more than one thing. Weak lies left gaps. I didn't leave any gaps. I told her, "Jill and I were riding our bikes in the bayou. She hit a rock. It was totally covered up. The grass is really wet and all clumped together. There was no way she could see it. I wouldn't have seen it either. Evil Knievel wouldn't have seen it. It popped her tire and flipped her right over. I heard her wrist pop." I snapped my fingers to mimic the sound. "I was right there."

"Pop?" My mother rose, panicked, scraping the chair against the tile. She circled the table and stopped in front of Jill. "Show me," she said. I lifted her hand and guided it to Jill's wrist and the small knob the bone made where it had separated. I held Jill's arm from underneath, loose in my palm. She couldn't pull away. I was gentle. I controlled the weight of my mother's fingers against my sister's skin. I said, "Here."

I looked at Jill, as if to say *Please.* She looked away.

My mother wrapped ice in a dishtowel and told Jill to hold it on her wrist. Jill held it to her wrist and wept into a pillow on the sofa while my mother called the clinic. When she hung up, she said to me, "You'll have to drive. Can you make it that far without killing us?"

"I will," I said.

"I'm dirty," Jill said. "I landed in the mud. I can't go like this."

"Help your sister change into clean clothes," my mother said. "Hurry quick."

"No," Jill said. "You help me. Not Rowdy."

My mother came back to where I stood by the counter. She walked right up to me and stood with her nose less than an inch from mine. The sutures had faded and were only visible up close. The prosthetic eye was brown and its pupil perfect. I wondered if it could be bionic. It surprised me a fake eye could look suspicious and angry. She said, "What *really* happened?"

"I told you," I said.

"Jill?"

Jill nodded. My mother kept her eyes fixed on mine. "Speak up," she said.

"Yes," she said. It was the smallest, weakest lie I had ever heard.

I was taller that year, but still not taller than my mother. We were both six feet, our shoulders the same height. When she stood before me, her knees touched my knees. She pressed her thumb and index finger into the soft skin beneath my jaw. I could feel the pulse in her thumb. "Did you do this, Rowdy? Tell me the truth."

"An accident," I said. It was the most truth I could muster right then. "We should not have even been in the bayou."

She released her hand from my throat. I had been too afraid to notice how much air she had cut off until the rush of it filled my lungs. "If you're lying, I'll find out." I thought of what Jill had said: *I'll find out another way.*

My mother put her hand on Jill's shoulder and guided her down the hallway to her bedroom. Her movements were so fluid I was sure she'd been acting in the weeks after her surgery when she walked with her shoulder or arm against the wall. When they came out Jill had her hair pulled back and wore clean jeans and a navy-blue button-down shirt, the sleeves wide and airy, room enough for sliding over a cast. Something I never would have thought of. My mother collected her sunglasses and her keys in one motion with her left hand as she guided Jill with her right. "Come on, Rowdy," she said and I followed them out the door to the garage. The blind, the injured, the guilty.

• • •

The emergency room was packed, and broken bones go last. Jill sat in a vinyl chair and closed her eyes against my mother's shoulder. I helped my mother fill out the paperwork and described the people who sat around us in the waiting room. When I was first learning to talk, it was a way of learning colors and letters. Now it was a responsibility. I told her about the old man asleep with his mouth open, his top row of teeth missing, the snap of his shirt undone, showing a yellowed undershirt beneath. His wife's hand trembled as she rested it against his thigh. A girl in a cheerleader uniform sat alone with her legs crossed. Her blonde bangs were glitter-frosted and she wore big hoop earrings to go with her big boobs. "She could be pregnant," I said. "Who knows?" I imagined the circumstances under which that might be true, a Chevy Suburban parked out in a field, her jeans and underwear balled up on the front seat.

"Shut your mouth," my mother said.

I whispered my description of the boy who sat opposite us. I said, "Bowl haircut; Astros T-shirt; eight or nine years old." I said, "Missing his front teeth." I did not tell her how many teeth the boy was missing, or that the teeth were bloody and clinging to their thread-thin roots and sat in a line on the towel spread across his lap. I did not describe his swollen purple eyes, and the man and woman who sat beside him and dabbed with their fingertips at the corners of their eyes.

A nurse led us down a linoleum corridor to a room. The nurse looked about my mother's age, maybe forty, her hair dyed bright orange. Jill lifted the dishtowel, and the nurse cradled my sister's arm in her hand. The nurse turned Jill's arm slowly, as though it were made of ashes. Jill winced and the nurse said, "I'll get the doctor. Don't worry, honey. He'll fix you up right and tight."

I expected to wait awhile but the doctor came in just a minute later. He was black and a good inch shorter than Jill. He wore a yellow necktie with a rubber Snoopy doll wrapped around the tube of his stethoscope. "So," he said. "Bike accident?"

My sister nodded.

"Happens every year. First warm day and we play too hard. You ever seen *E. T.*? Be nice if bikes could fly." He slid his fingers beneath Jill's arm and lifted it from her lap. He whistled "When You Wish Upon a Star," softly, while he turned her arm in his hand and felt the break with the tip of his thumb. His whistle sounded odd to me, as if he wasn't paying attention, but it seemed to soothe Jill. She straightened her back and let out a breath. "It's a clean break," he said. "We need an X-ray to rule out nerve and artery damage, but I wouldn't worry." He patted my sister's knee and then lowered her arm there, his way of saying, *Everyone breaks a bone, no big thing.* The nurse poked her orange head inside the door and said, "They're ready for you now."

The doctor said to Jill, "We'll get you x-rayed and then we can set it. I'll be right back."

Jill's face was puffed and pink in the cheeks and around her eyes. Her broken arm seemed to be releasing a poison into her blood. It was a process I didn't want to watch anymore. I asked her if she wanted anything and she said a Coke. I told her I'd go get it for her.

I walked down the hallway away from the waiting room. The clinic was not very large. An Exit sign and a Restroom sign glowed bright, one red, the other green, against the far wall. At the end was a lounge where a woman in purple scrubs sat at a table before a can of Diet Coke and a bag of Fritos and thumbed through a magazine. She was homely, heavyset; her hair bobbed to the base of her double chin. She smiled at me and followed me with her eyes as I slipped behind her to the Coke machine. I smiled back. She had a pleasant face, younger up close than far away, and her skin shined like a stick of warm butter. She looked as if she was good with children, a good nurse for a place like this. The Coke machine hummed and glowed, a soft light that illuminated the pink scalp beneath the crown of her thinning hair. I dropped my quarters and punched the button for a Coke. Nothing came. I tried Sprite, but that didn't come either. "The Coke man comes on Mondays," the woman said. She lifted her head and spoke to the side, to no one. "We drink a machine empty pretty fast around here. Try Orange." I pressed the Orange. The machine coughed and then dropped the can to the slot at the bottom. "It's cold at least," the woman said. I agreed. The can was so cold I could hardly hold it.

Another woman, also a nurse, walked into the lounge and said, "Okay, Maureen, enough suspense. Let's get a look at that rock." Maureen slipped her hand down the V-neck front of her scrub-top and hauled up a ring looped through a gold chain. The diamond was large, square, set high off the band and polished to a sparkle. The other woman wrapped her arms around Maureen's neck and squeezed. "I'm so happy for you," she said. When the nurse lifted her head, our eyes met, and I saw the glaze of tears in the corner of her eyes. She turned to Maureen and said, "So, how'd he do it?"

"Fink went the whole-nine," Maureen said. "Took me to Cody's for dinner. Everyone was inside dancing and the terrace was empty. So Fink led me out there. The whole city was lit up. He got down on one knee. Kissed my hand. When we went back inside, there was a bottle of champagne waiting at our table. He had it all schemed."

"Got down on one knee?" the other woman said. "Very romantic."

"I paid him back in kind," Maureen said. The two women giggled. The other nurse pressed her palm against the top of her chest and Maureen squeezed the ring in her hand. When they noticed me, they hushed up. I scooted past and back into the hallway. The innuendo surprised me because I knew what it meant and because Maureen had said it without any sense of shame. Even her face, when I turned and looked back at it from the hallway, was more proud than embarrassed. And why not? She was engaged and Fink sounded like a good man, unembarrassed by her. I thought of her and Fink having sex. Maureen's body seemed soft, easy to snuggle down inside, more erotic in the privacy of the dark than the cheerleader in the waiting room. What I knew of sex I'd learned from Showtime, but the thought of Maureen having sex seemed more comforting. An act basic and right, something everyone deserved to do. My father said he often felt more married to Kay than to my mother. Didn't they deserve to touch each other? My mother wouldn't touch him. It made sense to me that my mother didn't have much desire for sex, not because she was my mother, but because, unless she touched someone, she couldn't tell one body apart from another. Men checked her out all the time, especially in the mall. She looked younger than she was and her height kept her thin. Some men stared at her. Every now and then one would grow bold enough to approach her. She'd always waved them away, never interested, their good looks meaningless to her. I had talked myself into understanding the way things were between my father and Kay by believing that for my mother my father's body was nothing more than a mass of skin that took up half her bed. Now all that was turned on its head. I had broken my sister's arm and a sexless-looking woman was making jokes about sex.

The hallway wound around the back of the clinic where the windows faced the parking lot. The sun concentrated on the windshields of the cars and the yellow stripes, the glare bright enough to hurt my eyes and produce little dark shapes that floated across my vision. I figure I'd burnt a few rods and cones and was that much closer to blindness. I closed my eyes as I walked the hallway, moving slowly at first and then more boldly, as I did when I walked with my eyes closed in the woods alongside our property. I could feel the windows to my right but the rest of the hallway felt empty, blank. There was nothing, no one was moving back there, the exam room doors were all shut and quiet. I heard footsteps far off, way around the corner. I said, "Rowdy," and heard my voice echo off the long linoleum floor. The voice that bounced back at me sounded twisted and distorted, as if it belonged to someone else. It was my voice though. To the empty hallway I said, "I broke Jill's arm." I said, "Dad and Kay are having sex." I said, "They're fucking." The word bounced back hard and cold and I felt the hardness of the act performed above our garage, or in the car, or in some hotel near the city: my father and Kay grating against each other on the spread of some old tired bed, the curtains yellow and half-drawn and smelling of cigarettes, the two of them like junkies hiding out to shoot up.

I hoped the cheerleader had just turned her ankle, that she was not pregnant.

I kept my eyes closed until I knocked against the door at the end of the hall. The door cracked open against my weight and a dry breeze rushed against my face, sucked inside by the building. When I turned back to the hallway, I saw that the last exam room had its lights on and that people were milling back and forth before the window. The doctor's white coat filled most of the rectangular window, and he was flanked by a sheriff's deputy on either side, both wearing wide-brimmed hats and starched khaki shirts stretched tight over their bullet-proof vests, guns packed tight inside shining, patent-leather holsters. I might have just passed by had it not been for the guns. I leaned into the window and my breath fogged the glass. The doctor slipped behind the deputies and circled the bed to the other side. In the far corner of the room, a man in a khaki shirt and a brown necktie scribbled notes on a leather-bound pad. When the two deputies moved apart I saw the boy lying on the bed. Two big square gauze pads had been taped over his eyes and cheeks, and the doctor was carefully inserting wads of cotton into his mouth. The towel of teeth was spread on the counter. I wondered if the doctor joked with the boy about getting rich off the tooth fairy like he had with my sister about *E. T.*

The boy was in bad shape. His parents sat in the chairs against the wall, his father's head bowed between his knees, his mother's face clear and stern. She held a leather purse in her lap. She was the one who saw me. I watched her mouth move and then the doctor look up at me. I knew I shouldn't have been standing there, but I wanted to see the boy. I knew the man in the tie was not just a deputy, but something more, someone higher up. I wanted to hear how he figured things out, the way he pieced stories together and drew a conclusion, the same way a doctor listened to your lungs and stuck his fingers in your balls and thumped your stomach and could tell whether or not you needed an operation or medicine or nothing at all. I tried not to think about Jill just then, knowing that men like these could read guilt in a face. I didn't pull away though. I stood there until the detective noticed me and waved me away with the back of his hand. I took a step back and as I did, one of the deputies turned and looked through the window. His face was pink and large, his mustache almost white. He made no expression. I felt my stomach drop, my mouth fill with cotton. I hurried back down the hallway toward my sister's room.

• • •

Jill's X-ray hung against the light board. The space between the two halves of her broken bone was a black absence. My mother sat right where I had left her, in the chair near the wall. I popped the top of the soda and handed it to Jill. "Thanks," she said.

"It was all they had left," I said.

"It's fine," she said. "I like Orange."

"Took you awhile," my mother said.

"I walked around a bit."

"See anything interesting?"

"Not much," I said.

I sat down against the other wall so I could look out the open door. Our room was close to the waiting room, just inside the double doors that separated the admitted from the waiting. There was a low murmur, part television, part conversation between the triage nurse and the new arrivals. Every few minutes a nurse opened the double doors and called a name and then led the patient down the hallway. She bounced on the balls of her feet as she walked, in a half jog. The patients hurried to keep up. I heard someone vomit in the waiting room, and a minute later a tired woman with white hair in a bun walked past the door pushing a mop submerged inside a wheeled bucket. Then I heard footsteps coming down the hallway from the other direction—more than one pair, slow and heavy. The father of the beaten boy walked with his chin against his chest. He sobbed toward the floor. At first I thought he held his own hands together behind his back, but then I saw the chrome cuffs around his wrists. He walked on his toes, in tennis shoes, each step so gently placed it made no sound on the linoleum. The only sound came from the deputies behind him as their block heels and steel toes clopped against the floor. The deputies walked shoulder to shoulder behind the man, their faces shaded by the brims of their hats. Their jaws hung heavy in strange sympathy. One rested the heel of his hand over the handle of his holstered gun; the other silenced the radio receiver attached to his shoulder with his palm. Neither touched the man.

My mother turned her face toward the door. "Who's that?"

"Just the security guard," I said.

"I heard two," she said.

"Two guards," I said.

The man made me nervous, his slow and careful steps down the hallway, his silence that seemed to believe that if he could slip noiselessly out the door he might lessen the injury he inflicted. I, too, believed I could filter evil with silence and in the process I had done something even more terrible. Even if I confessed right then, I would still have known about my father and Kay and kept it from my mother. I would still have broken my sister's arm. Time could lessen the sting of it, perhaps, but not the fact. The fact would always remain, fixed and immutable in my sister's medical chart, filed away on a shelf where it could always be retrieved. It would never be not true.

The doctor returned and withdrew Jill's chart from the slot by the door and gave me a serious and accusing look. He had removed Snoopy from his stethoscope and his forehead still bore the creases from its crinkling. "Sorry I took so long," he said. "We're busy today."

"It's no problem," my mother said.

He said, "Okay then, let's get this bone set and make you a brother bonker."

"What's a brother bonker?" Jill said.

"You've never had a cast before? The best part about them is using them to bonk your brother."

Jill giggled. "He deserves it."

My mother turned her face to me, that reflexive act of accusation. In reflex, I turned away.

The doctor wrapped my sister's elbow in a towel. He filled a bucket with water and hung it from the crease of Jill's elbow. He slid her fingers into a mesh glove suspended from a pulley, the fingers of the glove like Chinese handcuffs that tightened around her hand as the bucket weighted her arm. "This will take a bit. You feel okay?" Jill looked at him and nodded.

He shifted the bucket once more and drew his hands away slowly. "That's it," he said. "It's going to hurt, but nothing like if we reset it in one blow. I'm going to see another patient. Sit tight awhile. Let it work."

"Okay," Jill said.

"Stay put," he said to me. His face said, *I mean it.*

"You have a restroom?" my mother said.

"Just down the hall," the doctor said. "Women on the left. May I show you there?"

"I can get there," my mother said. She rose and turned to me and said, "I'll be right back. Sit with your sister until I return."

"Okay," I said.

"In that chair, Rowdy," my mother said. "Right there. You so much as move around the room and you'll get it." My mother almost never disciplined me—that task had for years been given to my father and to Kay. After she left, I said to Jill, "Did you tell her?"

"No," Jill said. "I didn't say a word. I probably should have, but I didn't."

"I'll tell her myself when she gets back, if you want me to."

"Then you'll have to tell her about Dad and Kay."

"How do you know there is anything to tell?"

"You're so stupid, Rowdy," she said. "You think that by now you would give it up. But you don't. You think you can keep all these secrets. Everyone knows, Rowdy. Mom knows. It would have been better if you had just told her."

"Mom knows?"

"How could she not? She's not as dumb as you. No one is as dumb as you." Jill laid her head back against the pillow and rocked her head back and forth. I could tell the pain in her arm was intense, enough that it upset her stomach. She lifted the soda to her lips and took the tiniest of sips. Enough to taste, nothing more.

I walked to the side of her bed, opposite the broken arm. I stood close. She looked up at me with distrustful eyes. "I'm sorry I did what I did," I said. "I'm sorry about your arm. You can hit me if you want. As hard as you can in the stomach. I won't tighten up."

"Maybe later," she said. "When the cast is hard."

"I'm sorry I kept everything from you."

"Is Dad going to leave with Kay?" Jill said. "Is that what you're telling me?"

"It was supposed to be better by now. It was supposed to be over and everything back to normal. Now I don't know what's going to happen." Jill was the first one to speak of the possibility of someone leaving. I had thought about it for months, but I'd hoped that by staying quiet, I could keep it put away. It occurred to me my mother *did* know about my father and Kay and had probably known for a long time. But to acknowledge what she knew would mean something would have to be done about it. And what was there to be done? She could leave, but where could she go? Into an apartment co-op for the disabled or some apartment where she had nothing to do but listen to books faster than the prisoners could record them? She would never go for that. My father's adultery seemed better than that. A kept secret—even a secret we all knew—was better than the consequences of knowledge. I was not blind, but I understood its advantages. But by breaking Jill's arm, I'd made blindness impossible, even for my mother. "I better call Dad," I said. "Give him the heads-up."

"What if Mom comes back?"

"I'd rather get grounded. I don't care if I'm never let out again."

There was a pay phone in the waiting room, tucked back in the corner near the television. A mother held her baby's head against her chest. The baby's face was flushed red and her nose leaked snot all over her mother's shirt. The mother rocked her side to side, slowly, rhythmically. I slid a quarter into the phone and dialed my father's office at the Medical Center. The phone rang for a long time and then to my surprise he answered. "Jarrett lab," he said. "Lee."

"It's Rowdy. I wasn't sure if you would be there."

"I said I was coming here."

"I thought you'd be with Kay. I was about to try the Marriott."

"What do you need, son?" He sounded impatient with himself.

"We're in the clinic. Jill broke her arm." I covered the bottom of the receiver with my hand and turned my back to the waiting room.

"What?"

"It was an accident. She was about to figure out everything. Then she rode her bike down the bayou, hit a rock and flipped."

"Is she all right?"

"She broke her arm. That's the only thing. She's in some contraption now that's supposed to reset the bone. She'll wear a cast."

"You made her do it?"

"She knows everything," I said. "The gist of it, anyway. She says Mom knows, too."

"What did you tell Jill?"

"Nothing. Even when she figured it out, I played dumb. She figured it out on her own."

"I highly doubt that."

"It doesn't matter," I said. "I don't think Mom wants to know, so you're safe if you don't fuck up." The mother sitting near the phone jerked her head up and scowled. She cupped her hands around her baby's ears. "But she knows and so does Jill," I said, "so don't think you're fooling anyone anymore."

"Watch your mouth, son." He paused, angry, then swallowed his ire. His voice had lost its thunder. "I don't want to hear that kind of talk."

"We'll probably be here another hour or more," I said. "You can come if you want or you can sign Jill's cast later." I hung up before he could respond. It was melodramatic and immature to hang up on him, but it made me feel noble. I'd been responsible for his secrets long enough. That responsibility, I felt, was over.

• • •

My mother sat in the exam room with her arms crossed. Beside her sat the detective from the other room. His necktie was knotted tight against his large throat; his upper lip was thin and his hair was combed into tight black rows. Unlike the deputies, he didn't wear a bullet-proof vest beneath his shirt. He was nonetheless large, broad-shouldered, scary-looking. He held a notepad on his knee, which in the absence of guns and billy clubs, looked like a weapon all its own. He looked up at me when I walked through the door. "This is your son?" he said. "This Rowdy?"

"Is it?" my mother said.

"It's me."

The detective stood up from the chair and hiked up his pants around his waist. He closed the door and then reached into his pocket, withdrew his wallet, and opened it to his identification. A pair of chrome handcuffs hung from his belt. "I'm Detective Barber, Harris County Sheriff's Department." The ID card said, Child Abuse Unit. He said, "You and I might have something to talk about. You want to tell me how your sister broke her arm?"

"She fell off her bike," I said. "In the bayou behind our house. She hit a rock."

"Not everyone thinks it happened quite that way," he said. "Heard you may have caused it. Now where would an idea like that come from?"

"I don't know," I said. "It didn't happen that way." I looked at my sister. Her face was innocent. She hadn't said anything.

Detective Barber followed my face to my sister's and back to mine again. "Come on now, son. Tell the truth now. You don't want to have to come with me, do you? I just hauled one man out of here. I can haul you out, too. You can spend the night in juvie. You rather that?"

"No, sir." I looked at my mother. Her face pointed somewhere beyond my wrist, into the empty middle of the room. She dragged it up and focused on my chin. Her bottom lip slid up and then she tightened her mouth into a small point. She waited for me to speak.

"You're talking to me now, son," Detective Barber said. He pointed at his face. "You need to tell me if you broke your sister's arm."

"Not me. No sir. The bayou broke her arm, the ground. She fell. I was standing up on the bank. I can show you the rock. You can arrest it if you like."

"Let's go outside," he said. He withdrew the handcuffs and held them by the center chain between two fingers. They made a rattling sound that my mother turned her face toward. His hand was strong and he gripped my shoulder around the bone. He turned me and led me through the door. The edges of my mother's mouth pressed into a curl. She was in control. Detective Barber was doing exactly what she wanted.

As Detective Barber walked me down the hallway, I felt myself losing control of my own body. I would have fallen had he not held me up. The people sitting in the waiting room chairs looked up, shocked and fascinated seeing me with the detective, and by the flash of the handcuffs in his hand. The mother holding the baby nodded a little. I wanted to sit down, but when I tried the detective's hand tightened around my shoulder. He lifted me back up and pushed me through the front door of the clinic. His car was parked in the handicapped spot, a big brown Chevrolet with Texas exempt plates, two colored lights in the center of the grille. He opened the back door and said, "Have a seat." He pressed his hand to the top of my head to guide it inside.

The interior smelled of motor oil and cleanser and sweat. Between the front and the back was a metal grate, through which I could see the big radio attached to the bottom of the dashboard. I felt a pressure in the bottom of my belly and before I could stop it, urine filled the front of my pants. The detective smirked. He was used to perps who pissed themselves. He said, "Couldn't you have done that outside?"

"I'm sorry." I felt the piss soak through my jeans and collect on the vinyl seat beneath me. "I pushed her bike," I blurted, practically spitting on his shoes. "That's why she fell. I didn't mean to really hurt her. Our dad's sleeping with the woman who's lived with us since I was a baby. I found out and he told me not to tell my sister. Jill figured it out. So I pushed her."

Detective Barber leaned into the car, one arm propped on the open door, the other hand on his knee. I expected to go to juvie for the night. There was a kid in my class who had gone there once for stealing a car. Juvie was not a nice place; the kid had come back with a black eye and his lip stitched together. The detective said, "Your sister will be all right. But when I ask you a question, you tell me the truth the first time. You hear that?"

"Yes, sir."

"Lying to me only makes it worse. That man you saw arrested? That's what lies do. They make you violent. You know that now yourself?"

The detective made his living by prying the truth from people and because of that, he believed in the righteous power of the truth to set us free. The truth, though, did not set me free. The truth made me a criminal. I hated the truth and I hated protecting it. I said, "You should go on ahead and take me down to juvie. That would make things a lot easier."

He raised an eyebrow. "I don't think so. You should say you're sorry to that little girl in there first."

"She doesn't want to hear it."

"She will in time. You let your mother and daddy fight their own battles. That ain't no place for you."

"My mother's blind because of me," I said. "That's the real problem."

"You blinded your mother?"

"My body was too big coming out and she had high blood pressure and maybe some kind of infection. But it was still me coming out that did it."

"I don't know nothing about that." It wasn't one of the usual ways people hurt one another and he seemed not to have a place to figure it in. He stepped back from the car and told me to get out. I got out. He asked me if I wanted to go back inside, and I asked if it would be all right if I sat outside for a while. He said that would be fine. He told me he didn't expect to see me again. I apologized for wetting my pants in his car. He said, "That's why we have vinyl back there." He opened the door of his Chevy and sat down. The engine gunned up and sent a blast of air through the grille. He backed away and left me there alone.

I sat on the sidewalk for almost an hour, shifting positions every few minutes to keep my lap in the sun. As people drove up and parked and walked by me, their eyes were drawn to the dark stain in the center of my pants. I wondered if what I'd started would make things better or worse, and after a while, both options felt the same. Eventually my mother and my sister came out. Jill's hand, wrist, and arm were wrapped in a bright white cast, strapped against her chest in a sling. She stuck it out for me to see. The cast had made her into something new, a girl with a broken arm. My mother looked different, too, taller than before, anxious and alert, like a boxer waiting for the bell. She held on to Jill's good elbow and scanned the parking lot, turning one ear and then the other toward the cars. Her prosthetic eye glowed in the sunlight and seemed to see something beyond the darkness, beyond the parking lot. Jill followed my mother's face to my pants, and there was no sense anymore in turning away.

TESTIMONY

FOR THE LAST MONTHS OF HIS LIFE, my father lived in the room above the garage. The ceiling pitched all the way to the floor, and three tall windows overlooked the pines and the bayou behind the house. For furniture there was a double bed, an oak dresser, and a nightstand— any more wouldn't fit. The room had never seemed small to me when Kay lived there, but during my father's stay it felt very small, the bed hardly wider than a cot, the dresser cheap and shameful.

He didn't want us to see him in his condition, and, like the rest of us, he believed it was only temporary. A little time, maybe a week or two, and things would get better. Until then he'd just have to suffer through it— through the dizziness, the hallucinations, the clutching sensation he felt in his chest and stomach, as though he'd touched his tongue to a 9-volt battery, except all over his body. To distract himself, he cleaned out the garage below his room, killed the cockroaches beneath the stairs, and scrubbed the oil spots from the floor. In the evenings, if he felt well enough, he walked along the shoulder of the bayou, sometimes all the way to the neighborhood pool, not yet open but cleaned up and ready to open, the surface glowing blue, the lifeguard stands perched over the water.

But it didn't help. Back in his room he saw things that weren't there. Towers of newspapers stacked up to the ceiling. The baseboards swarmed with ants. The only way he could stop the hallucinations was to sit on the edge of the bed and concentrate on the floor, on the fractured colors cast over the stains in the carpet by the glass lamp on the nightstand. He unfocused his eyes until he couldn't separate one color from another, until the entire floor dissolved into a great spinning kaleidoscope, without center and without edges. Then he lay back and closed his eyes and stayed that way until morning. I avoided going up there and he had stopped coming downstairs for dinner.

. . .

What happened to him might be explained by a single substance in the brain: gamma-aminobutyric acid. GABA for short. It floats in the synapse between two nerve cells, that ethereal gap over which every thought must leap. GABA blocks excessive stimulus and quells convulsions; its deficiency is connected primarily with epilepsy, though my father's research also applied to more exotic afflictions. Batten disease, for example. Children who have it progressively lose the ability to walk and talk, and die bedridden, seizing. My favorite was stiff-man syndrome, in which sudden noises or jarring movements triggered spasms that made it impossible to bend; patients walked like toy soldiers and broke bones by tipping over, unable to extend so much as a hand to break their fall. Whenever I didn't want to take out the trash, I'd pretend to be stricken with it. I'd walk with my arms out, bumping against the can, unable to bend or cinch closed the sack. My father would crinkle his mustache, as though he regretted ever telling me about stiff-man. "You wouldn't think it was so funny if you had it, Rowdy," he'd say. "Taking out the trash would feel like a privilege." Compassion for the suffering didn't make him say this; he never saw a patient in his life. He just didn't like me using his work against him. Kay didn't like me walking that way because she thought I was making fun of my mother. She sometimes walked with her hands out.

. . .

Not much was known about GABA when my father started working on it, in 1975, when he was a graduate student at the Texas Medical Center. When I was younger and we still lived together, my father sometimes talked about his life before my mother, and wandering the building that housed his lab, I saw enough graduate students to understand how ascetic this life could be: your twenties, an entire decade of wildness, lost to sixteen-hour days in a linoleum room, the man to your right and left unshowered and unshaved after nearly a week, dinners of ramen noodles right out of the Styrofoam cup while the sequencer was running. Though it is not this way anymore, I could count on the fingers of one hand the number of women I saw on his floor. Everyone knew their names.

All parents, I'm certain, try to connect with their children by telling stories about when they themselves were young. My father's story was a cautionary tale, told to scare me, though about what, exactly, it's hard to say. Too much education? Each morning he withdrew a mouse from its cage, stroking its head and scratching the fur behind its neck. Calm mice were easier to anesthetize. He laid the mouse on the table and opened its skull with a scalpel, then attached to the brain two tiny cannulas, one to deliver drugs, the other to monitor the brain's response. The mouse was lowered into a glass box, where it lived for five days, convulsing beneath the wires, sometimes hard enough to bleed into the sawdust. On the sixth day my father withdrew the cannulas and placed the mouse beneath an upended glass beaker with a cube of dry ice. The mouse tried to climb the side of the beaker above the smoke, but the smoke filled the glass and soon there was no more air to breathe and it lay down and suffocated. Then my father decapitated it with a miniature guillotine, a device I've since seen in bagel shops. He extracted the brain, sliced it into thin strips, and floated the strips onto slides. He examined the slides and passed them to his adviser, humped over the bench around the corner. My father was the only graduate student in his lab, his friends from his first-year classes were in larger labs, his neighbors in his apartment complex were all medical students, always smoking and fondling their pagers. He had a black-and-white television perched on a milk crate, and a blind long-eared rabbit named Puka he'd rescued from euthanasia in a pharmacology lab. Puka lived in a refrigerator box in the bedroom, but at night my father would let him hop around the floor while he ate dinner and watched TV. The rabbit explored the baseboards and electrical outlets with his nose until he found his way to my father's legs and rubbed his soft head against his ankles. Puka calmed him. Made him feel locatable.

• • •

In the spring, Francis Crick came to Houston to give a lecture at Rice University, just across the street from the Medical Center. My father had lived in Houston for five years and had never been to Rice before. It took a Nobel laureate to lure him out. He descended the back stairs and entered the world through a fire exit, ignoring the alarm as he weaved his way through the hospitals and across Main Street. The trees at Rice surprised him, the enormous rectangles of grass filled with blue jeans and bare feet and short skirts, hats so elaborate they couldn't be taken in with a single glance. He squinted at the buildings surrounding the central quad. He looked at his watch and again at the pathways. He didn't know which way to go. When he looked up he saw a woman coming toward him. Her brown hair hung past her shoulders and her purple socks rose and rose. She was the tallest woman he'd ever seen. She later said that at first glance she thought he was James Watson, whose picture she had seen in *Time*. (In her recollection, it was Watson, not Crick, who was giving the lecture.) She was twenty years old, a junior, and had stepped away from her friends to get a better look at him. He who knew no one, who had pressed the wrinkles from his shirt with the heel of his hand, who even when he was outside the lab smelled mice and so was certain he smelled of them, who stood like a wind-tilted sign at the crossroads of a university campus that wasn't his. Him.

. . .

My father always stuck to the facts: the *who, what, when,* and *where.* He left me to fill in the *why* on my own. For example, he told me that my mother used to wait for him in the oaks and azalea hedges that bordered the Rice campus. I knew it as the misty netherworld that divides the university from the city; when I was in high school, three women were attacked there after dark, their assailant never identified. My father said he'd pull his car to the curb and stare into the black leaves, seeing nothing, and then, as though materializing in the dark, she'd be knocking on the windows. She never asked him to come to her dorm, or introduced him to her suite mates. When I asked him why not, he shrugged; he didn't have an answer. My best guess? He didn't want to tell me that my mother was slumming and didn't want her friends to know. Or her parents either, who were wealthy, with Texas pedigrees dating back to Moses and expectations about the kind of man she would date and eventually marry, almost none of which he met.

In his apartment he laid his twin mattress on the floor so that he and my mother could lie down together. When they turned out the lights, Puka charged the sides of his box, something he had never done before. As though he understood his own waning importance in the equation. My mother and father—not yet my mother and my father, but soon—lay braced in the silence, waiting for the sound of Puka's feet sliding over the cardboard, and the box snapped against his pointed skull. My mother laughed in his ear. "He's like a baby," and eventually my father lifted Puka from the box and draped the rabbit's long ears over his arm and stroked it back to sleep. "Come on now, Puka," he said. "Let's all get some rest." The light from the parking lot came through the cracks in the blinds. Puka charging the box was something both my parents mentioned, but not this next part: My mother lying with her arms folded behind her head, her breasts stretched nearly flat, her belly and chest a creamy orange, watching my father cradle Puka. The rabbit's ears draped over his arm were a curiosity she would share with no one. My father suspected she smiled not at him but at the pleasures of her rebellion. That part comes from me.

My father was certain that one night she'd walk into the trees and be gone from him for good, their time together a brief intrusion of company and sex into his loneliness. He collected souvenirs of their time together. When they went for ice cream, he pocketed her spoons, and in his lab examined them beneath the microscope, the twiggy cells of her saliva, the residue of her lips and tongue—her invisible everywhere, embedded in his open spaces, in his ears and navel and the folds of his elbow. It was a feeling he'd have again just fourteen months later, when my mother, still unused to blindness, her stomach still scarred with bedsores from the months she spent lying on it, kissed his neck and said she wanted to try. "Are you sure?" he asked, having waited for this moment since the beginning of July, but now nervous that after all that had happened she would never want him again, not like she did before. My mother said she was sure. She named what her lips touched; she kissed his ear and said, "This is your ear." It was an act of reclamation, the world perceived through touch and sound, and it started with his body. He felt her saliva cool beneath the ceiling fan, the nodes of his body emerging beneath her mouth. Other people are afraid to imagine scenes like this, but not me. This isn't the bad part of the story.

Later that night she woke up gasping. She said she'd been dreaming she was in a large room filled with babies; I was one of them, but she couldn't tell which. He smoothed her hair and said, "I'm right beside you. Reach out and I'm here." When he woke up again his hair was in her fist, as though she had anchored herself to him before drifting back to sleep. Before I was born he worried that an anomaly had somehow entered my genetic map, a single crooked or broken chromosome that could sprout a thousand potential horrors and change his life forever. Now his life *was* changed forever, and here he was, breathing in her hot exhaust, his heart full, more suited to it than he ever thought.

. . .

Two days after I was born, my father sat in a chair beside her hospital bed while a nurse shaved away my mother's eyelashes and eyebrows and flushed her bowels with an enema. Then she was wheeled down to surgery and strapped to a table that flipped upside down to encourage her retinas to float back into place, an experimental procedure in 1976. The ophthalmologists hoped to restore some of her sight, but told my father not to expect too much. He hadn't slept since they arrived at the hospital. He'd spent his nights walking the corridors, pacing his way up one hallway and down another, passing doorways open onto the bored, the sick, and the dying. He watched a nurse unfold a blue sheet, flap it once in the air, and allow it to settle over a shriveled, yellow corpse. By the time my mother was in surgery, he was consumed with the fear that she wouldn't survive the operation. I would be taken from him and given to my grandparents. She was their daughter. He was her husband, technically, but he hardly knew her. They'd been married for only three months, their last-minute wedding in Galveston unannounced in the *Chronicle* or the *River Oaks Examiner,* unattended by anyone but my parents and grandparents. As though by lacking witnesses, it never officially happened. And, if needed, could be undone.

My father showed the nursery attendant his wristband and his badge from the Baylor College of Medicine, and persuaded her to let him take me out. She made him promise to stay on the maternity floor, but when the nurse turned from the window he stepped into an elevator and rode it down to the lobby and did not stop until he had left the Medical Center and had crossed Main Street and was standing in the trees at Rice. If my mother had disappeared here, perhaps he could, too. It was midmorning, the slab of summer clouds cracked open to let the sun burn through. Sweat dripped from the back of his neck and slid down his spine, a narrow stream damming at his waist. I was wrapped in a blue blanket, my face bright pink inside his hand. He was thinking about what he was going to do, not what he was doing. When a few hours had passed he would slip back to the parking garage, tuck me into the gully behind the passenger seat and head toward the freeway, as swift and consuming as a river. We would join it, and we would be gone. Legally, he reasoned, he would only be running away, not kidnapping me. My birth certificate had not yet been printed. Legally, I did not yet exist.

He watched two women and a man descend a short flight of steps, each carrying a Styrofoam cup and bag of potato chips. At the top of the stairs he found the cafeteria open, nearly empty. A lone woman stood behind the counter, her gray hair tied in a bun and covered in a net. She was scraping a tray of hash browns into the garbage. He asked her for milk.

"For you or for the baby?" she said.

"For him."

"Whole milk. How old is he?"

"Two days. Almost. In a few hours."

"Two days! He's the newest thing in the world. Where's his mother?"

"Across the street. We're taking a walk."

"He's too young to be out." She leaned her forearms on the glass casing and examined my father's red face. He held up his wristband. "Okay, I see," she said. "He's yours. Go sit down. I'll bring it to you."

He sat at the table nearest the register and watched the woman pour the milk into a pan on the stove. On the griddle she toasted bread and slapped down slices of yellow cheese, and when she carried the tray to the table the milk was in a bowl and beside it was a grilled-cheese sandwich and a Coke in a glass bottle. "You look like you could use a little something yourself," she said.

He looked at the milk, then at me. "You don't have an eyedropper behind your counter, do you?"

"He's no hamster," she said. She sat down beside us and stirred the milk with the spoon. She lifted the spoon from the bowl and let half of it run out before touching it to my lips. The milk pooled on my tongue and I swallowed. "Just little tiny bits," she said. She passed my father the spoon, and he mimicked what she had shown him, one spoonful after another. When the milk pooled in my mouth and did not go down the woman showed him how to burp me, holding me face down until a thin stream of milk whitened her knee. Then she braced me against her shoulder and told my father to eat. The sandwich was the first thing he'd eaten since my birth that hadn't dropped from the coiled grip of a vending machine. The cheese melted over the sides of the bread and the bread was yellow with butter. It filled the spaces between his teeth, and he felt his legs and back settle into the chair. In his head we were in Dallas, or farther, close to Oklahoma on an open grassland road. The sandwich brought him back. He noticed the fine plucked hairs between the woman's eyebrows, her silver fingernails. He thought of my mother's eyebrows smeared across the nurse's towel.

When he was finished he wiped his mouth and took a long swig from the Coke, and said, "How much do I owe you?"

"Nothing. It's bread and cheese." She handed me back to him. "He'll need a better meal before too long. He needs his mother."

"We'll go back soon," he said.

"You should go now. Who knows what kinds of germs we're sitting in." He stood up. "Okay. We're ready."

"Hurry," she said. "Even half a day is a lot of life when you're two days old."

"We're going," he said. And we went.

· · ·

Downstairs, my mother sat at the kitchen table, listening to books-on-tape from the Texas Lighthouse Ministries. The tapes arrived in little metal boxes, army-green and plain, strong enough to withstand a grenade. Titles were in Braille, on the face and down the spine. I understood some Braille but not a lot. I did better when there were words to follow, to reassure me that what I was feeling was a space between words and not my finger straying from the line. My hands alone were never certain. I fingered the line of dots and caught fractions of the titles—a "B" here, a "mis" there—and tried to guess my way to the rest. "*Broken Promises?*" I asked, rattling the case near my mother's ear. "*Birthday Mishaps?*" I wanted her to tell me if I was right, but she wouldn't. Her books were her secret.

· · ·

Crowds made my mother nervous. She didn't like the sensation of strangers, her inability to discern which touches were accidental and which were violating. Whenever we went to AstroWorld or Christmas shopping in the Galleria, she walked between my father and Kay, her arm looped through both their elbows. They talked and laughed, and Jill and I followed behind, or else ran ahead. Occasionally one of them would do a kick or a shuffle step, like they were dancing the Cotton-Eyed Joe. Upstairs in Kay's narrow bed, his bare thigh pressed against hers, it felt to my father that my mother was still between them. They talked across her even when the space between their bodies was a negative distance. They tried to talk of other things. Kay had seen a television show about a town in Switzerland that could only be reached by train. "I'd love a vacation that did not include cars," she said. My father talked about seeing the Rockies or the Pacific coast by rail, whole days spent in the glass car watching the mountains or the coastlines. Jill and I could walk around if we liked, and at night our compartment would turn into a sleeping berth. "Like traveling in a movie."

"Cory would go batty," Kay said. She couldn't stop herself. "The old Cory, anyway. This new one, who knows?" She looked at my father sadly. My mother was her closest friend. But she did not look away, nor did my father. They both needed the attention. The need for human contact is a matter of survival; my father had abstained from it before and could not bear to do so again. It was sadness that had brought him to this point, and when his sadness returned so did his desire. He pressed his forehead to Kay's, locked his eyes with hers, and entered into sorrow as though entering the woods beyond our yard, touching the stalk of every tree. My mother's nose against the car window, her hand on his chest, her eyelashes, grown back long and wispy, fluttering against his neck, his stomach, his everywhere. Her beautiful oblivion obliterated by the awful present, the inescapable now.

• • •

I was still keeping the secret about him and Kay the day my father showed me a bunch of photographs of the brain. We were sitting in the car in the park where Jill and I played soccer in the fall, baseball in the spring. It was January and the park was abandoned; we were the only car in the lot, the fields all brown, water frozen in the culverts. Our breaths condensed on the windshield and front windows. The triangular window in the corner was totally fogged over. I felt we were doing something illegal; any minute a cop would come arrest us. Every conversation during those months felt that way. My father passed me a manila envelope and told me to look inside. The pictures were printed on thin, rolled paper that in the cold car suctioned to the heat and pressure of my fingers. Like many scientists, my father believed his work possessed the secrets of the universe. "The brain *is* the universe," he used to say. "All there is, is all we can process." There were about a dozen photographs in the envelope, all black-and-white, all with different lobes highlighted. He pointed to one highlighted area and said it was the temporal lobe. What I was seeing lit up was dopamine. "You know what dopamine is?"

"For pain," I said.

"That's right. Pain is how your brain says, 'change the course.'" He often explained his science like it had something to do with NASA. "What's interesting is that this dopamine release is triggered by desire. You see what I'm orbiting here?" I shook my head. He said, "Desire keeps us healthy. That tent in your shorts when you wake up in the morning is nothing to be ashamed of. It's your body's way of saying, 'all systems go.'" I said that made more sense, even though I was still confused. It was a confusing time in general. Houston was colder than I had ever seen it, the freeways so icy school was closed, and after this, my father would drop me off at home and drive somewhere to meet Kay. Everything he said was a code for me to decipher and guard. The pictures were his way of telling me what was happening with Kay was simply biological, his body making him do things his heart resisted. Once my mother came around, he would find his release another way.

. . .

My father pushed Stop on my mother's cassette player. "Can we talk about this?" he said. Kay had been gone a week. My mother's hands were set diagonally, right over left. He sat down and crinkled his lip, sucking his mustache into his nose. From the kitchen sink where I stood washing that night's dishes I could see his eyes working over her face for a sign of her attention. He had once attended a conference session on the neuro-mechanisms of human facial expressions. Lifting of the inner parts of the eyebrows, for example, was the mark of anguish; depressing the triangularis, at the corners of the lips, betrays distaste. The conference was in Las Vegas, and after the session ended my father had gone into the casino and won fifteen hundred dollars at a poker table. He came home with presents for all of us—T-shirts for Jill and me, twin bracelets for my mother and Kay. "How'd you do it?" we asked him. Reading minds, he said.

But my mother's silence was practiced. Her silence was a weapon. My father said, "Come on, Cordelia. Enough of this Madame Tussaud routine." He separated her cassette player from her headphones, and moved it to the far side of the table. He lifted the little metal plug at end of her headphones and spoke into it. "Hello," he said. "I'm not leaving until you talk to me. I'm going to sit right here." After I finished with the dishes I went and sat on the couch where I could look across the kitchen to the table and watch them, his eyes fixed on her, her eyes fixed on nothing. I watched a repeat of *Unsolved Mysteries*, and after that I watched the news, and after that I watched Leno. I waited up to see if anyone would tell me to go to bed, and because I believed what was happening at the table was something I needed to stay awake for. An event that might require a witness. But nothing happened. My mother didn't speak and my father didn't move. When Leno ended I looked over and saw my father's eyes were closed. I touched his shoulder and said, "I'm going to bed."

His eyes popped open. He hadn't meant to fall asleep. He looked at my mother and let out a long breath, deflating his chest. "I should, too, I guess." He'd been sleeping on the couch the last few nights, and, I could tell, not sleeping very well. The skin above his cheeks was sunken and crinkled; the whites of his eyes were full of blood. The window behind him was fogged. He brought his fist to his mouth and coughed into it.

"You okay?" I asked.

"Not feeling too hot," he said. He stood up from the table and stared down at my mother's head. Her scalp was a white line beneath the part in her hair. He studied it with his right elbow half-bent. "I'm just tired," he said, shaking his head. Instead of going to the couch, he went out the back door and climbed the stairs.

• • •

On Wednesday nights he attended a Marriage Recovery class at Pine Creek Community Church, a few miles north of us on the farm-to-market highway. The church was a square brick building flanked on both sides by aluminum trailer classrooms, sagging white boxcars set on blocks. The class met in the trailer at the end, the faux-wood wall paneling bowed beneath the window air-conditioner and spackled with posters of the Ten Commandments, gleaming bronze sunsets, a family smiling so widely they appeared ready to die from happiness. The trailers are still there, though Pine Creek is a larger church now, and surrounded on all sides by subdivisions where there once were only trees. My father had once described religion as a mass seizure, a kind of low-grade epilepsy. Temporal lobe epileptics were famous for their religious visions—Jesus emerging in a slice of burnt toast, the Virgin in beveled glass. Such visions were caused by an overactive bundle of nerves behind the ears, nothing more. He went to the class because Steven and Betty Stevenson, our neighbors, swore up and down that Reverend Gene Bunting had saved their marriage. He was willing to try anything.

Mildew had crept through the carpet, and the floor bounced every time someone stood or shuffled a chair. Sitting there my father could feel in his legs the movements of the others surrounding him. He could feel their discomfort. There were six other couples, fourteen people in all if my mother went with him, which she did only once, on the first night. He asked her to take a ride, there was a place he wanted to take her, and she stood up. A miracle, we thought; she was finally coming out of it. My father rubbed his hands together. His keys jingled when he took them out of his pocket. "We'll be back," he called from the back door. His voice was light, and he waved goodbye.

That night, Reverend Bunting paced the circle in the center of the chairs. His copper hair was combed sideways, and his long nose pulled his chin and lips to a point. He said, "Good marriages fail because couples lose sight of their beginnings." He bounced his weight into the floor, and held up an index finger: this was rule number one. "You used to spend all your time looking at each other's face, and now you don't do that anymore. You think you know all there is." He shook his head. "The first thing we're going to do is remember that there's more still to discover. Go on and turn your chairs so you're face to face. Look into each other's eyes and remember the moment you met. How everything felt mysterious. Go on now."

My mother sat unmoved, her eyes fluttering beneath her lids. My father thought about that day at Rice, her purple socks rising, but it was incomplete. He was lost and my mother was a stranger: what did he know then? The entire span of time between that first day and the day of my birth felt like an island slowly separating from the coast of his life. A shore he could see but could not cross over to. The day he really met her—the day he first saw the shape and direction of his life—was the day he stole me from the hospital. After we returned from Rice, after he'd convinced the nurse and my grandparents and the police he'd just needed air and meant me no harm, after I'd been fed and changed and allowed to sleep, he took me in to see her. Both her eyes were patched and beneath the patches her eyelids were sewn shut. Sandbags had been packed around her temples. She would spend six weeks this way, much of it on her stomach, kept dreaming by a steady drip of dopamine from a suspended plastic sack. He fingered the cannulas on the back of her hand. He kissed her forehead, the tip of her nose. When she exhaled swiftly, waking, he said,

"I'm here. I brought someone to see you." He slid me into her arms. She reached up and touched his chin, the still-hairless strip between his lip and nose. "You're holding your breath, Lee," she said. "I can hear it. It's okay to breathe."

His body was sitting in a folding chair in a trailer at Pine Creek Community Church, but my father was back in that hospital room. He was sitting in the green vinyl chair by the window, looking at my mother, smelling her witch hazel. He lingered there for one more second, one more drip of dopamine, and then he looked at my mother, again, in the chair across from him, strands of gray in her hair, one eye stolen and replaced with a fake. Her hands were cupped over her knees. He wanted to tell her Reverend Bunting was wrong: we have no one beginning; in life we begin again and again, and we can begin again this time as well. He reached for her hand, but she pulled it back. Her prosthetic eye stared out, fixed and indifferent. Her shoulders shook, and a tiny spasm advanced up her neck. It took him a moment to realize she was laughing, and a moment more to understand why. "Look deep," Reverend Bunting said. "Jesus tells us, *If thine eye be single, thy whole body shall be full of light.*"

· · ·

He stopped coming downstairs and I lost sight of him. Jill and I blamed him for Kay being gone. Even though we knew better, we blamed him for our mother's silence, too. Adultery, as I have learned, has a way of rearranging cause and effect. Jill and I would hear his car pull up the driveway and would stiffen our backs and cross our arms and get ready to ignore him if he came inside. He didn't come inside, and after a time I stopped expecting him to. Then I stopped thinking about him altogether. There's a blank spot in my memory. I remember his car cooling in the garage and mail coming for him, but I don't remember actually seeing him. Once I got to wondering where he was and went into the garage. The door of the stairs was closed, a tight bead of light creeping out from beneath the jamb. I touched the knob but didn't knock. The garage, with the door down, was pitch-black and hot as an oven. I stood in the dark and listened until I heard him cough and the ceiling creak and a rush of water fill the walls around me. Then I went back inside.

· · ·

A pulse orbited the crown of his skull, plunged into his temples and eyes, and worked back up to his forehead. It was April, the bayou was full of geese, but upstairs he could not shiver himself warm. He coughed up phlegm that looked as though it had come from his stomach, yellow and brown, except that it had come from his lungs. He clutched his stomach and rocked back and forth. He stared at the doorframe of the bathroom, and though he tried to resist, he came to see Kay standing there, undressing, slithering from her jeans and unhooking her bra with a flick of her wrist. Her silhouette hovered in the bathroom's yellow light. He could see her earrings lying separated from their backs on the dresser, her flimsy watch on the nightstand. In the mattress he could feel the indentations where she had set her knees.

Other times it felt as though he left his body. He followed my mother into the woods. The lawn and patio came right to the edge of the trees where little sunlight could penetrate and the brush was lavish, wisteria climbing the dead pines, pitcher plants blooming in the open spots. Jill and I over the years had made most of the paths ourselves. The ground was spongy and shifted beneath his feet, as though this specter of his fever had a weight to exert against the earth. My mother moved ahead of him, to the left and right, through the threads of sun. He hurried to catch her, but couldn't. She stopped moving and turned her head so that her face was illuminated. She did not squint—blindness had made squinting unnecessary—so the skin around her eyes was uncreased, as youthful as a child's. He wanted her to see him, for his shadow to register on the slim corner of her retina still capable of receiving light. For the shadow to add up to him. He wanted to call out that phrase from a long time ago, *Reach out and I'm here*, but his voice could not make a sound. Calling out from his bed, thirsty but too sick to walk to the sink, no one could hear him.

My mother was the closest to him, just inside the door at the bottom of the stairs. But her cassette player was turned up too loud.

• • •

From the road, it looked as though we were all together. My father's car was in the garage beside the van, the lights on upstairs and down. Had Family Services come to our door they would have seen our house in order, my mother home, our beds made, the four of us at home during breakfast and dinner. They would not have recognized Jill and me as orphans, though that's essentially what we had become. No one cooked anything, so Jill and I took turns. I got up early to make breakfast, usually eggs and toast, and coffee, which Jill and I drank black, standing up, at the counter. Some days I'd set a cup in front of my mother before going to school, just in case, and when I came home in the afternoon, it would be there untouched, cold as mud. I took the mug away and washed it out. My mother did not react, did not smile or refold her hands, but I sensed she was pleased with herself.

Jill made the lunches, ham slices and Kraft singles, squeezing the mustard into a smile the way Kay used to do. Working a knife was hard with her cast. At lunch I'd peel back the bread to peek at the smile before devouring it. It looked up at me, flat and even-keeled, same as it had for years. I often found myself thinking about it in the minutes before class let out for lunch—its steady gaze evidence that we could take care of ourselves. It was the tiniest of reassurances, but I depended on it. I was thankful to Jill for remembering it.

I didn't have my license yet, but I was tall and looked old enough. When my mother's disability benefits check came at the beginning of each month, I drove the van to the bank and cashed it. I used half the money for two weeks of groceries and stashed the other half in my closet so I could go back in the middle of the month. Jill came with me and we did our best to consider our diets. We bought low-fat lunchmeats and yogurts, low-sodium crackers, whole-wheat bread, artificially sweetened iced tea, fresh and canned vegetables, only one package of cookies. One week Jill put back the cookies in favor of a paperback *Easy Eats* cookbook, a thousand uses for a can of cream of mushroom soup and a bag of tater tots. She said she thought we could make most of the recipes, so I agreed to get it, and after that we ate pretty well.

We didn't have enough left over to pay the mortgage or the utilities, so I never did. I left the bills in a stack near the telephone, one month on top of the other. I considered asking my father about them, but I'd grown proud of my ability to avoid him and didn't want the streak to end. The utilities never shut off and no one came to tell us to leave the house. Every time I flushed the toilet and water returned to the tank, I felt filled with relief. Every light lighting was a tiny miracle.

• • •

My father returned to the Marriage Recovery class. He was still weak and moved slowly, and some nights he could do little more than watch the mosquitoes swarm around the light beyond the window, but the fever was gone. My mother didn't go with him, and in the trailer he sat beside an empty chair. In May, when Reverend Bunting shut the door and windows and turned on the air-conditioner, a woman came to the class without her husband. Her name was Leita. She said she had been there the entire time; she said she remembered my mother. "Tall," she recalled. "Something weird with her face." My father didn't remember her or her husband. While the other couples did their encounter exercises, my father and Leita practiced on each other. They faced each other in the folding chairs and pretended they were each other's other. Leita complimented my father's haircut, his good job; she praised his idea about spending a week water-skiing at Lake Conroe rather than with her brother's family on Padre Island. "I'm sorry I have such unrealistic expectations, Wendell," she said. "I don't need children to be happy. I put too much pressure on you."

Her hair scooped in at her chin, rounding her face. Her neck filled the collar of her yellow blouse and she folded her arms across the rolls of her stomach, as though to hide them. My father imagined her pacing her bathroom, her pants still on the hook behind the door, the pregnancy test lying on the sink. He squeezed her hands. "I still love you, Leita," he said. "You're still beautiful to me. Our children will be, too." He didn't know what else to say. Leita quit twisting her watchband around her wrist. He felt the floor stop vibrating.

When his turn came, my father apologized for sleeping with Kay. "It wasn't something I set out to do," he said. "It just happened."

Leita patted his knee. "You'll have to do better than that, honey."

"I was sad. It's like you're not even there."

"Where do you think I am?"

"I wish I knew. I wish you'd tell me. While we're at it, what the hell are you listening to all day?" He held both of Leita's hands and squeezed them tight. "I'm sorry."

He walked her to her car after class. She opened her door and set her purse on the driver's seat. She turned to him and said, "Thanks for play-ing along. It makes it easier."

"Thank you, too."

"It isn't a good sign. Them not being here."

"No."

"I don't know what I'll do if I lose Wendell."

For just a second, for just a single fall and lift of his eyelids, my father remembered the trees at Rice, running away from the cafeteria with me tucked into his arm, the sun a searchlight against his neck. The amber parking lights lit the moisture between Leita's eyebrows and beneath her nose. The night was warm and thick, like a blanket. "I guess it's fortunate," she said, but then, quickly, "Never mind. Dumb thought." She looked off, toward the church, and my father shifted his weight from right to left, his arms half-raised. Leita stepped forward, slowly allowing her breasts to mold against his chest. Her stomach pressed against his. She rested her head in the dimple of skin below his shoulder. He touched the back of her neck, the fringes of her hair crisp with hairspray. He laid his cheek against the top of her head. He felt his heart race as his palm floated over the clasp of her bra. Leita heaved and sighed. "You asshole," she said. He didn't know who she was talking to.

"I'm sorry," he said. "I really am."

· · ·

My father's life ended on the last Saturday in May. The last day of the Marriage Recovery class. Members arrived at the church in shorts and white T-shirts. Some of the men wore old undershirts, the cotton stretched as thin as tissue paper, bushes of chest hair visible underneath. Others wore shirts with logos, the Houston Oilers or Spuds McKenzie; it didn't matter so long as it was white underneath. Reverend Bunting led the class from the Fellowship Hall to the parking lot. An inflatable pool had been set up in the far corner of the lot, close to where the asphalt met the pines. The pool was the same shape and shade of blue as a kiddie pool, the kind of thing you fill with a garden hose on the lawn, only larger, a good twelve feet around with a rim four feet off the ground. Reverend Bunting slipped off his shoes and ascended the pyramid-shaped ladder, a giant stepladder, and came down the other side into the water. The water lapped against his waist. Pine needles had collected in drifts against the parking blocks, and the sun was reflected in the oil spots. Reverend Bunting said, "When Jesus came to the Jordan to be baptized, John the Baptist was hesitant. But Jesus said, *Let it be so now; it is proper for us to do this to fulfill all righteousness.* John consented and Jesus walked into the river and was baptized. At the moment he came up from the water, the heavens opened and the Spirit of God descended like a dove and lighted upon him, and a voice said, *This is my Son, whom I love; with him I am well pleased.*"

Reverend Bunting opened his hands and raised his arms above his shoulders. From where my father stood, the Reverend's legs appeared disjoined from his body. "Come forth in this spirit, as God's child," Reverend Bunting said. "With you he is well pleased."

The first couple—both brown-haired, both in their forties, both with tan-lines dividing their biceps and thighs—climbed the steps and entered the water holding hands. Reverend Bunting crossed their hands over their chests. He placed one hand atop the woman's hands and another on her back and said, "I baptize you in the name of the Father and the Son and the Holy Spirit." She fell backward and came up, her hair washed over her face and ears, water dripping from her nose. Reverend Bunting did the same to the man, and when he came up, he hugged his wife and kissed her lips. Then they climbed out of the water and dried off with towels stacked on a chair beside the pool. The next couple went up.

My father and Leita were without spouses and went last. Leita went ahead of him. When she came up from the water, her breasts were visible through her T-shirt and bra, the layers of cotton suctioned around her pointed nipples. My father looked once, then looked away. Leita passed him and squeezed his hand.

He climbed the steps to the water. The surface was warmed by the sunlight, but around his feet the water was cold. Stray hairs floated over the surface, riding the wrinkles of sunlight. My father crossed his arms over his chest and Reverend Bunting said, "God bless you, Lee. Cordelia, too. Don't give up." Then Reverend Bunting's large hands moved him under the water. The water filled the spaces inside his ears, and in his nose, and between his lips. He held his eyes open and stared up at Reverend Bunting's head and the liquefied sky and the sun, and he felt for that moment weightless. His feet left the bottom and his body rose up. The pulse in his head returned, except this time different from before. Rather than move around his head, the pulse happened everywhere at once; every neuron fired, all one hundred billion at the same instant, his entire brain sending and receiving the same thought simultaneously, the current passing through him unimpeded by GABA, by any other substance or thought. He was paralyzed, unable to move his hands or mouth. Unable to blink. All he could hear was the rapid percussion of his heart against his ribs. It drummed faster than he could count, and then he felt it slow, and then he felt it stop. He looked up and saw a face staring down at him. The eyes looking into his were clear, as though seen through air instead of water, and in them he felt seen: the ligaments joining muscle to bone, his thinning blood starved for oxygen. The eyes looked deeper, into his memory, so that looking up through the water he saw himself standing in the bathroom, watching my mother shower through the glass door, haunting her like a ghost beyond the perimeter of her perception. He saw the power he felt when she slipped her wrist through his elbow and leaned her ear toward his mouth and listened to him describe the world, the trees and buildings, the faces of people. How that power was, ultimately, the source of his love, and now, how my mother had taken that power back.

Reverend Bunting pulled him up and he gulped a mouthful of water. He wanted this substance inside him. Reverend Bunting slapped his wet back and said, "Go now and leave your life of sin." My father refused the towel and stood barefoot on the asphalt. Reverend Bunting pulled the drain plug and water flooded the parking lot.

• • •

My father once tried to explain to me how memory works: Electric pulses carry thoughts down the axon of the nerve cell. At the end of the axon the pulse fans out into the terminal branches, like a river delta, and eventually arrives at the synapse. Electricity is converted into chemicals, which drift across the synapse to the dendrites, the receiving branches of the next neuron. GABA polices the chemical signal. Receptor proteins on the dendrites collect the neurotransmitters, convert them back into electricity, and the process begins again. Each neuron may have as many as ten thousand dendrites, and so can receive signals from ten thousand other cells. A thought inside the brain moves in all directions, loosed from linearity, everywhere at once. Chemicals fluctuate in the synapses; even the receptor proteins traffic in and out. Occasionally some of the receptor proteins stick to the dendrites, strengthening the synapse and the transmissions between the neurons. The next thought passing through leaves a piece of itself behind. That piece is a memory. A memory is a fragment. Combined with others, it forms an incomplete whole. The illusion of a whole.

• • •

He swears the face did not belong to Reverend Bunting. He swears it wasn't a hallucination, either. He swears it belonged to Jesus. Jesus visited the parking lot of the Pine Creek Community Church on the last Saturday in May. Jesus drowned my father in an inflatable pool, killed him dead, and brought to the surface a different man, a believer. This is the story my father tells. It is his testimony.

After the legal affairs with my mother were settled and our house was sold, my father left his lab at the Texas Medical Center and took a job teaching biology and chemistry and a class called "creation science" at Victory Bible College in East Texas, not far from the Louisiana border. Deeper into the pines than we ever lived. He is encouraged, along with his colleagues, to share his testimony with his students. He tells about Pine Creek Church, the way the floor bounced, Reverend Bunting's vise-grip hands, the pool, the sky, the face—it's all there. How ironic, he says, that after two decades spent searching for truth in a microscope, he found it in a kiddie pool outside a trailer. He doesn't mention Leita's breasts soaking through her T-shirt, or the day he stole me from the hospital, or make any mention of Kay at all. When he remembers my mother it is only to tell how he came to a moment of crisis and how Jesus led him through it. "I committed adultery," he says. "I had an affair and it destroyed my family." He always says it that way—"I committed adultery"—as though adultery is a singular act that can be committed. As though he plotted his course into it the way a diver peers over the edge of a platform and plots a course to the water. As though adultery is the kind of thing that can be done and then left behind. As though he was the only one who did shameful things.

Sometimes, in the course of sharing his testimony, a bold student will raise his hand and ask for more. "Who did you commit adultery with?" he'll want to know. "Where is your wife now? Doesn't her blindness connect to Paul's blindness on the road to Damascus, after *he* saw Jesus?" My father will agree that they connect, but then he'll look around the room, his students nineteen and twenty, from small towns along the Sabine River. The women touch their stomachs, dreaming of babies, and between classes, in their dorms and in the cafeteria, he hears them talk about what's wrong with America: the silencing of prayer in school, the judicial assault on marriage, the crusade against the unborn. He knows there are things they'd rather not hear. "Speaking of sin is like speaking of Satan," he'll say. "We should only say enough to know what to avoid." He won't say any more and his students don't ask him to. They're content to let his story end there.

If I don't remember, who will?

A testimony is a story that relies upon an awful past. At the very least the arrangement of past events in an awful way. If Jesus is to rescue us from ourselves, and heal our necrotic hearts, we must leave behind who we were. Burn every bridge between now and then. In Christ's mercy our sins are forgotten, but so is the person who committed them. In Christ's mercy my father tries to forget that for fifteen years he was happy—that despite my mother's blindness, and her silences, and every bold plan that drifted away, he had all he wanted and hadn't wanted any more. Every time my mother laid her hand against his chest he felt located in the world. It was the kind of touch Jesus could never give, and had my mother given it again, Jesus wouldn't have stood a chance. My father would have spat the name of God from his mouth. Shaken the dust of Jesus from his feet.

. . .

He arrived home that afternoon still wearing his baptismal clothes, his T-shirt wrinkled from the water, his shorts clinging to his thighs. He swung open the back door and did not pause to consider my mother at the table. He gripped the back of her chair and spun it around. Its plastic feet screeched across the tile. He cuffed her wrists with his hands and pulled her to her feet. Her cassette player slipped from the table and landed on the floor. The tape spilled out and slid beneath the table. Neither of them spoke; they struggled in silence, my father pulling her forward, my mother pulling herself back. Finally, gritting his teeth and huffing, he was able to move her across the kitchen to the couch where Jill and I were watching TV. Sun came through the windows and glared out the screen. I had muted it when I saw him coming toward us. The only sound was of their feet sliding across the tile, my mother's stiff ankles cracking. He sat her down beside me on the couch. Jill was on my other side, her cast propped up on a cushion, faded from its original white to a dull gray and graffitied with autographs. "Just sit here for a minute. Please, Cory. Just give me a minute."

He disappeared down the hallway and came back carrying a stack of towels and a plastic basin filled with water. He set it down before Jill and knelt and lifted her foot and sank it into the water. His hands were shaking. "What are you doing?" Jill asked.

"Washing your feet," he said. He looked up at my mother. "I've been arrogant. I didn't understand it before today, but now I do. I'm going to make some changes."

"This feels funny," Jill said. "I don't like it."

"It's okay," he said. "Jesus did it to the Disciples, at the Last Supper."

My mother didn't say anything. She slapped her bare foot on the tile.

"I'm not saying this is a miracle," he said. He stared down at the water, grayed by my sister's feet. His scalp through his hair was pink with sun. "Just a start. So you know I mean it." He slid the basin over and I felt his hand lift my foot. His fingers were wet and clammy and pressed oddly into my arch. It felt like I had stepped on a snail. He sank my foot into the water, rubbed the skin between my toes and my cracked heel. Our eyes met, my discomfort with his grief-stricken stare. I looked away.

My mother stood up. My father said, "Cory, wait."

She turned and—at last—she spoke to him. "For what? You're not doing that to me."

"I need to. I need you to see how sorry I am. I understand things differently now."

"For Christ's sake, stop apologizing," she said. "I'm so sick of hearing it." She started to walk out and then she turned back. She set her hand on the top of his head and said, "You need to be forgiven? Okay, I forgive you in the name of the Father, Son, and Holy Ghost. All better now?" She stood there, looking down, impatient for a response. *Hmm?* she said. My father grinned. It was what he wanted to hear, but not the way he wanted to hear it. Kneeling on the floor, my father tried to envision the path his future would take, the calls he would make, the little apartment he would rent, the pots and pans he'd need to cook himself dinner. He felt his past returning to him, just not the past he wanted. He looked up at my mother. She stood with her back to the windows. The afternoon sun poured in, hazy and dispersed through the pines. It liquefied the glass and the floor and illuminated the air around her head, the flaming wayward hairs, the transparent fuzz on her neck and ears. Her face, her chin and mouth and nose, the curved outline of her body eclipsed in shadow, already gone, her corona a burning edge. He felt himself dissolving in it.

THE END OF THE STRAIGHT
AND NARROW

MY SISTER JILL SAT ON THE FLOOR in front of the television, charting the storm on her hurricane-tracking map. Glenda had made it past Cancún and was projected to hit Galveston Island sometime tomorrow. The weatherman paced back and forth in front of the satellite grid, the swirl of the hurricane like a cataract in the Gulf of Mexico. His outline was rimmed with a faint green light and each time he swept his hands across the map he showed us his wet pits. Watching him made Jill jumpy. She wrote fast, as though afraid of missing the one bit of data that would foretell our fortunes. With a blue pen she marked Glenda's wind speed, with a green she did barometric pressure, and with a red she dotted and lined the points along the hurricane's projected path. In the margins she noted that the north and east sides of hurricanes were stronger than the south and west, and that storm surge can rise at a rate of a quarter-inch per minute. She marked Pinar del Río, Cuba, where a photographer captured an image of a young boy clutching the upper branches of a tree as floodwaters climbed the trunk, and Puerto Morelos, Mexico, where a wrinkled brown arm was seen reaching through the bars of a window. A line like an open parenthesis cut the center of the map, from the tip of the Yucatán all the way to the lowercase "k" inside the square she had marked as Kay's house. Our house wasn't marked at all.

The Houston street guide sat on the floor beside her, Kay's street in Baytown brightened with a highlighter. Jill cradled her left arm in her lap, an unbroken habit from the months she wore a cast. The cast had been off for almost a month, but her arm wasn't used to being back in the world. She stroked the knob of her wrist bone, rolling the skin beneath her fingertips. Since I had caused the break, seeing her do this reminded me to be nice to her. I sat on the couch behind her, bouncing my knee beside her head. "Hurricanes are the size of Delaware," I said. "If one neighborhood gets it, they all do." I meant this to sound reassuring. A hurricane hadn't threatened Houston in a decade, and that time not a single drop of rain fell on our house. I thought Glenda would fizzle out in the Gulf, or at worst take a last-minute turn and hit either Corpus Christi or Lake Charles. We'd get rain, maybe a little hail, but not much else.

"*Icebergs* are the size of Delaware, Rowdy," she said. "Hurricanes are more like Missouri." Without looking up, she drew a red circle in the isthmus of hair that crawled down the length of my foot. The bottoms of my feet, and my toes and heels, were stained green from mowing lawns, my job that summer. "Stop that bouncing. It's shaking my pen."

I stopped. "I'm just saying that a sturdy house down there is as safe as we are here," I said. "She's no worse off." Kay lived with her mother now, down in Baytown. I missed her, but Jill missed her differently than I did. She wrote Kay letters, sometimes two a day, asking if she was Kay's true daughter. Wondering if she'd been given our last name in the hope of giving her a better life. "We have the same texture in our chins," she wrote. "Our faces are almost twins." Kay's letters were short responses: *Mama's feeling okay today. We took a walk down to the water. Take care, sweetie.* Jill looked more like our father than anyone, but the fact that he had slept with Kay fueled her suspicions.

"I played Glenda once," my mother said. The sound of her voice made both Jill and I jump. "It's just me," she said. She was standing in the doorway.

"Sorry," I said.

"I played Glenda the Good Witch. In *The Wizard of Oz.* I wanted to be Dorothy, but I was too damn tall. It didn't look right on stage, all of us lined up together. I was taller than the Tin Man and the Scarecrow. How big is this storm?"

Jill looked at me and I shrugged. We couldn't remember the last time she had interrupted a conversation. Or started one, either. Jill said, "Category Four. It might weaken some during the night."

"I hope she stays strong," my mother said. Her prosthetic eye shimmered beneath the bulb suspended from the ceiling fan. "Glenda's a big girl's name. Good for her."

. . .

That afternoon my father came downstairs from his room above the garage and said the Lord had spoken to his heart. Glenda would bring about unusual destruction, and we needed to prepare. I helped him nail plywood to the back windows and apply construction adhesive to the rafters in the attic, and after that, lash and secure the pines nearest the house. Pines were shallow-rooted and during hurricanes could turn into missiles. He recited Psalm 23 while we worked, *The Lord is my shepherd*, and a passage he said came from Nehemiah—*Thou art a forgiving God, gracious and compassionate, slow to anger, abounding in love*. Ever since he'd gotten saved he'd been reciting the Bible as though he was drilling himself in a complicated language he needed to navigate a foreign country, verse after verse, thee after thou. He spoke in cadence with his hammer, each comma a ringing blow. By the time the windows were boarded, I was saying the verse along with him, caught up in its rhythm.

When the last wire was staked, he stood beside the pine and gripped the trunk and shook it with his teeth clenched. Needles showered the lawn. "Let's pray that holds." He knelt on the grass and said, "Let's pray right now."

"I'll watch from here," I said.

"You don't have to talk, Rowdy. Just kneel." I knelt and he took my hand. His palms were roughened from the work, but thin, the phalanges pressing against his skin as though wearing through an old cloth. He'd lost a surprising amount of weight over the last months. His bent head exposed the delta of veins in his neck that joined his jaw with his heart. He closed his eyes and spoke in a low, mumbling voice. Across the street Mrs. Stevenson was giving her retriever Kirby a bath with the hose. "Hold still!" she yelled. "If you want to come inside, you got to get clean." During heavy thunderstorms Jill and I used to climb to Kay's room and watch the bayou fill, and within minutes we'd see Kirby's snout and ears floating back and forth, his dog paddle efficient and silent. The cottonmouths in the bayou never bothered him, and once the rain slowed, Mrs. Stevenson would cross our yard in her bright green raincoat and yell for Kirby to come out of there. Kirby spent most storms beneath the porch, but not this one. Glenda would be more than a big rain with a big girl's name. When my father said, "Amen," I said it with him.

• • •

Jill poured the milk down the drain, flipped on the disposal and ground up lettuce and leftover lasagna, fed the sink eggs one by one. She made Xs with masking tape on the inside of the windows and filled the bathtubs with water, along with every jar and pitcher she could find. Water we didn't drink could be used to flush the toilet. She gathered batteries and candles, clicked her flashlight on and off. My mother gave me her ATM card and asked me to get her cash, several hundred dollars, much more than I thought we'd need. The bank was only a mile down the road and required only one turn, but all the same I was glad to get away for a while. My mother was talking again, and my father was kneeling in the yard; I wasn't used to it. I'd had my license for a little less than six weeks. I steered with my wrist draped over the wheel, my hand dangling. I stuffed the cash into a bank envelope and kept out a twenty for myself. I used the money to buy a Coke and a Big Mac, which I ate in the car with the air running and the radio on. I pretended it was my last meal, chewing slowly, tasting the mayonnaise on the pickles, stoically facing my imminent end. "This is a mortal wound, doctor," I said, a line I stole from history class. "Tell mother, tell mother, I died for my country . . . useless . . . useless." The sky was gray, rimmed with green, and the wind had stopped. Cars drove past me with sheets of plywood on their roofs, others stuffed with pillows and sleeping bags. The hair on my arms and neck stood up. When I got home, I gave my mother the money with the bills folded in half, the ones on the outside to make it look like less. "Stay close, Rowdy," she said. She tucked the money inside the back pocket of her shorts. "I'll need you to get me out of here." I tried not to think of the roof ripping off, the four of us looking up into the hurricane's malicious eye, my mother reaching for my elbow, trusting my path. My instinct would be to run.

· · ·

Glenda arrived just after four a.m. When I opened my eyes my alarm clock was dark and my mother was standing in my room. "Get up," she said. She was long and lean, like a fencepost in the darkness. Lightning sparked beyond the windows, lighting her up, and rain hammered the roof. "You need to get away from the windows," she said. I followed her to the laundry room. She'd made a nest of pillows and blankets in front of the washer and dryer. Jill sat with her nightgown pulled over her knees, her flashlight like a lantern through the stretched cotton illuminating her skinny legs and arms and chin. I sat with my back to the dryer.

My father's dim silhouette was lit by the red glow of the battery-powered radio, which hung from a leather strap looped over the door-knob. I could see his right ear bent close to the speaker, and his eyes were closed. My mother sat with her shoulder against his. The radio dial glowed in her prosthetic eye. The reporter's voice was funereal and slow, probably coming from a fortified room without windows in the basement of the station. Most of my mother's books were recorded this way, in win-dowless rooms, by disheartened inmates at the state penitentiary in Huntsville. The times I found her headphones and tape player unattend-ed, I'd listen in and try to guess from the sound of the voice what the pris-oner was in for. Had he taken someone's arms and legs apart with a saw, or done something boring like stolen a car? I wondered if he liked what he read. It was no doubt a better job than the laundry or scrubbing the johns, but still a lonely way to spend a day. So was listening to the books, and that year my mother listened to hundreds of books, book after book after book, far too many to count. She leaned her head against the wash-er and closed her eyes. I listened to the air whistling through her teeth, and wondered if the nest of blankets, the enterprise of hiding in a laun-dry room, had come from a book.

Morning emerged beneath the door, a flickering gray light. The wind howled softly, and rain and thunder percussed through the walls, eroding the bricks and wood framing and plaster. I could hear creaking, and twice I thought I heard glass breaking, but my mother said I hadn't. I reached up and touched the door. It was moist. I wondered if the water had found a passageway inside, and how long it would be before it crept beneath the door.

Jill was shivering even though the laundry room was hot, the air close and wet with the condensation of our worry. My mother touched Jill's hair and pulled Jill's head into her lap. Jill resisted my mother's hand, not yet sure how to read the situation. "Quit listening to the rain," my moth-er said. "It will drive you nuts." She let out a long gust of air she'd been holding for some time, and said, "Once there was a girl who lived in a house in the woods. The walls were strong, the roof was strong, and the girl felt safe inside it. No one could hurt her there. But no one came to see her, and she was lonely. One day, a huge tidal wave flooded the woods and the house and washed the girl out through her bedroom window. She held on to a tree branch while the water carried her far away, past the woods, past the meadow, past the roads, all the way to the ocean. Pelicans caught fish for her and carried them to the tree branch, and after a week of floating she washed ashore on a squeaky white beach. Other girls were there, and boys too, all washed there from someplace far away. They were afraid. Some were away from home for the first time. But also for the first time they were not alone."

"Was that supposed to make me feel better?" Jill said. "Getting washed out my window?" She lifted her head, then settled it back down.

"Did it?" my mother asked.

"A little."

"It's a nice story, Cordelia," my father said. "Like Noah and the Ark."

"Tell it again," Jill said.

"Try making one up for yourself," my mother said. "We'll be here awhile."

· · ·

By late that afternoon Glenda was on her way to Nacogdoches. My father pressed his ear to the door, and when no sound returned he turned the knob and said it was safe to go out. The hallway was lit by a cool, gray light. The clouds were still panting moisture, a fine mist against the glass. We wandered the rooms, opening doors and peeking around corners, half expecting to find our bedrooms torn away from the house, doorways that once opened to bookshelves and desks now portals to the world. But each room was there, our unmade beds, the toys we were too big to play with, dolls with forgotten names. In the dining room a patio chair had come through the bay window. Its two side legs had pierced the glass; the other two and the seat dangled outside. The carpet was peppered with glass cinders and pine needles and mud. When I stepped on it the carpet held the shape of my foot. Water pooled in the indentations of my toes. "Step back, Rowdy," my father said. He wore shoes, I did not. He pushed the glass around with his toe. "We can clean this up," he said. "Maybe it's time to hardwood this room, and get a table." He looked at my mother and nodded and then rolled his eyes to the ceiling. He mouthed, "Thank you," so she couldn't hear.

"Not so bad," my mother said. She touched his shoulder, then his bicep, the slope of his thinning body. He winced, but didn't step away, and for a moment he leaned toward her, as though about to lean against her, to allow her to hold him up. He looked exhausted. "The worst is never as bad as we think," my mother said. She side-stepped, to put room between them, and then patted his back. "Things will be all right, Lee."

"I'll get the broom and clean this up," he said. He moved toward the garage.

My mother pinched my elbow and said, "Get your shoes. Wait until your father is sweeping and then go to the garage." She pressed the keys' toothed edge into my palm.

"Where are we going?"

"I'll tell you once we're on our way."

"What about the storm?"

"Hurricanes don't come back, and we'll be heading away from it. I'd drive myself if it wasn't for the mess on the roads."

"Without the mess you could make it?"

"Just get your shoes." Her eyes floated in their sockets, fluttering up beneath her lids. Even the prosthetic. She was preoccupied, daydreaming and strategizing. Planning her next move.

Jill had made a peanut-butter-and-saltine sandwich and sat on the floor in front of the television, waiting for it to flicker back to life. I watched her chew and lean on her good arm and felt I should say something to her, tap my foot on the tile and give her The Look, so she'd know, but my mother was already at the back door giving me The Look. Though she was blind, she had a way of putting her eyes where I would find them. I left Jill sitting there, though at the door I said, loud enough for her to hear, "Let me help you with that." My mother climbed into the passenger seat while I pulled the orange release handle dangling from the garage door opener. I hefted up the garage door, the closed-in air gasping out. I hurried to the driver's seat, certain we were doing something illegal, and shifted into reverse. Our gravel road, usually packed smooth, had been sculpted into a new topography: peaks pushed by spinning tires, lakes of oily water, a jay's water-logged chest rising from the puddle. I edged forward. The Stevensons' willow tree had tipped over onto its side, its branches like a tangled head of hair, the roots dripping mud back inside its hole. Kirby was barking, chained up to the gate. I checked the rearview mirror and saw Jill standing in the street. Her nightgown was pressed to her stomach, her stringy hair knotted. Her eyes were narrow—not The Look, but its own new thing. As though she had expected us to leave, and had come to the street not to wave us back, but to make sure we were really gone.

When we hit the freeway my mother said to head south. The road crossed over a floodplain fifteen feet above the ground, and water lay stagnant in pools below us, here and there catching the fractured sunlight from the weakly flaring horizon. We were the only car on the road. "Where are we going?" I asked.

"South."

"To where?"

"Till I tell you to turn."

"How do you know where you're going?"

"How do you know where *you're* going?" she said.

"I can see."

"You can see where you *are*. I wouldn't trust much beyond that." She reached over and squeezed my chin, the soft skin below the bone. Her index finger and thumb were cold; they felt more like tongs than fingers. "Look straight," she said.

It never occurred to me to stop the van and demand to know where she was taking me. Perhaps I feared her punishment, but really I think I was shocked she had asked me to drive in the first place. The little we'd spoken already added up to our longest conversation in over a year, and as the speedometer needle arched toward sixty, I thought of how easy it could be to ignore another person, and other people altogether. I couldn't remember when I'd stopped trying to get her to answer me, or when I'd started walking by her at the table as though she were a centerpiece. Isolation was a habit as easy to accept as any other. "What did you listen to all that time?" I asked. "On your headphones?"

"Nothing," she said. "Mostly."

"Tell me."

"I am," she said. "For a long time I read those old Midlands romances, the ones set in England. I liked the scenery, but *God* do they repeat themselves. The isolated heroine, the dashing rescuer, the confinement. I drank that cup of tea pretty dry. I switched to crime novels, which were only better until I got the hang of things. I did like the readers, though. Prison inmates really get into the crime stories. Some even do voices for the villains. But I could only listen to so many. Just before my eye came out, the librarian at the Lighthouse Ministries sent me an autobiography of a woman who has swum the English Channel more than two dozen times. Each crossing takes more than twenty hours, and once she swam it three times in a row without taking a break. Almost seventy straight hours. She lived in an apartment in London where she could hear people around her all the time, morning and night, and during the day she worked in the currency exchange where people were almost always yelling. The English Channel was her quiet place. I thought about that. In my life, someone's always talking. Even my books are talked. People say the same things over and over again. They do the same things, too."

"Now you're talking about Dad and Kay," I said.

"Say I am. I go radio silent and they get in bed together. Straight out of Oprah, or whatever show is big these days."

"Geraldo."

"Whomever. Next month it'll be someone else."

"Is that what you were doing all that time? Some kind of experiment?"

"No, Rowdy, that's not what I was doing. I was trying to think. And I got tired of stories. Dialogue and plots, skies flashing and people yearning. Save me. After that last book I started listening to tapes of water running. Oceans and rivers mostly. The librarian at the Lighthouse Ministries thought I was having trouble sleeping and sent me a tape called *White Noise*. It did the trick. For the first time in who knows how long, I could hear myself think. A long time. Take the next exit, please."

"This one?"

"This one. Go east."

I followed the off-ramp around, easing off the gas as we descended from the elevated freeway to the feeder. My mother told me to go right at the stoplight, and I turned onto a road I had never driven, wondering what sort of radar she possessed, how she knew where we were. The road took us along the back side of a miniature golf park. The Dutch windmill lay on its side and the greens were all underwater. Across the street, semi-trailers were jackknifed into one another. The sky was wrinkled with humidity and red and purple light, thick enough to bend the trees and telephone poles. We passed a row of sagging, white-shingled houses. Their doors were open and people were moving through the blackened door-frames carrying buckets to the street. The next stoplight T-boned into an industrial park, the powerless light dangling from the wire like a wet shoe. "Good boy," my mother said. She touched my chin again. She had a plan and I was a part of it. "Good old Rowdy. I knew I could count on you."

. . .

Twenty minutes later, we crossed Buffalo Bayou and moved into downtown. The windows of the buildings returned the elongated reflection of the van, the sky a colorless backdrop. The water had receded, but the asphalt was smeared with a pulpy overflow. A newspaper vending machine had been knocked over and the papers spilled from the open mouth, sheets of yesterday's news floating in the humid air. I drove past Jones Hall and the George R. Brown and Texas Commerce buildings, then turned down Main and passed a long line of darkened bars. My mother said, "Go ahead and pull over. Read me some names."

"The Flying Cup," I said. "Sam's. The Tortilla Curtain."

"Any lights on?"

"No."

"What about across the street?"

"There's a place called Bar X. There's a man smoking in front of the door and the Budweiser sign is lit up. I guess that means they have a generator."

"Bar X," she said, nodding. "Sounds like the one. Swing around and park in front."

I could hear the ring and grind of chain saws, and a police car crawled by, the officer's worried face slowly scanning the sidewalk. A strobe was flashing on the next block. We got out of the van and my mother looped her arm through my elbow. She told me to look sharp. I didn't know what that meant, so I scowled at the bouncer. He looked tough, in a white Bar X T-shirt stretched over his big chest, but up close he had a young face, and on his left hand he wore a gold class ring, the stone a platter in the center. He smiled at us and held open the door without asking to see my ID. The room was a narrow rectangle, the bar to the left, tables to the right. It was in the middle of being renovated—a line of wood studs was bolted to the bricks on the table side, new, unpainted drywall in the back, a scuffle of boot prints all across the plywood floor. Behind the bar was a drawing of the sushi bar that would be coming, the windows shaded a pastel blue, a glass wall with water flowing down both sides. Below the picture was a slogan: Warning: Typhoon Approaching. I thought about

whispering the name to my mother, but I didn't. For now, we were in Bar
X. Bob Seeger's redneck rasp hissed out of the corner speakers, and the air-
conditioner box pegged through the wall recycled the smell of sweat and
beer. It blew a cold stream through the muggy heat, and the chairs were
all turned to catch some of it. Everyone inside looked like a refugee, people with nowhere else to go: the man with the glistening shaved head staring at the last swig of his beer; the booth of sun-leathered Mexican men
in long-sleeved plaid shirts, who kept their eyes on one another and on no
one else; a table surrounded by men all in wheelchairs, the regular chairs
in a cluster off to the side. The forgotten. The abandoned. The left-to-
their-own-devices.

I led my mother to the bar. The bartender had a short tuft of white on
his chin and glasses with that tint that never fully recedes, even in dim
lighting. He wore the same Bar X T-shirt as the bouncer, except that his
had "Eddie" embroidered in cursive above the pocket. My mother asked
for Drambuie. "Something different," she said. I ordered a Coke.

"Coke and what?" the bartender asked.

"Coke and ice," I said. I added, "I'm driving."

A man sat down beside her, on the other side of me. He had streaks of
gray in his hair and a thin upper lip, as though he used to have a mustache
but had shaved it off. When he sat, his stomach inflated his black T-shirt
like a balloon. He watched Eddie pour my mother's drink and then fill
my glass with the soda gun, and when the drinks were set on the bar he
touched my mother's hand and said, "Let me get it." He unfolded a ten
and set it on the bar. "For Lassie's Coke, too," he said.

"What a gentleman," my mother said.

"How'd you fare in the storm?" he asked.

"We're here," she said.

"I'm Ray." I didn't for a second believe that was his name. Ray was a
name made up on a dime, and he looked like he had something to hide.
Later, during my interview with the police, I mentioned him, but no one
at the bar knew him, and by then Bar X was Typhoon.

"I'm Kathleen," my mother said. She was playing the same game. She
turned her head so he could see her face, then touched his arm, rubbed
the hair near his elbow, spider-walked her fingers across his shoulder and
chin. "You look nice."

"How long has it been?" he asked. "You been blind?"

"A while. You'll never guess how it happened."

"Vietnam," he said. He pointed his finger, like a gun. "Agent Orange."

"Close. Plane crash. I had a boyfriend who flew Cessnas. Wheel blew on the landing and we flipped. The instrument panel shredded my eyes. I lived. He didn't." I was shocked by her story, but she said it so convincingly a part of me believed her. I wondered if the story I'd grown up with—the story of her retinas detaching while I moved through her—had been made up. A legend to keep me from back-talking or neglecting my homework, to make sure I didn't get my girlfriend pregnant, or get a girlfriend at all. It was an exciting possibility.

Before things got bad, my mother used to tell Jill and me stories all the time, different from the story she told in the laundry room that morning. They were mostly about places she'd gone as a girl. My grandfather was a hotshot in an oil company and had traveled a lot; my mother had been through most of Europe, and through a fair bit of Africa, too. She scared us into finishing our broccoli by telling about the time she slipped a plate of food outside her door in Cairo and watched a dozen filthy hands grab at the chunks of her rejected lamb. She bent the story around her purpose, inventing details on the spot. She had a photograph of herself sitting atop a camel with her back to a pyramid and a small flower vase carved from soapstone to prove she wasn't completely lying, but I didn't need them. I accepted the leaps as part of the experience. I liked how the stories got her talking, how she would wave her hands around, as though the memory was a fly buzzing in front of her she wanted to catch. And the moment a story was told, it would disappear. When we asked her to tell it to us again, she couldn't. If she tried, it came out a different way.

So I knew that even disappearing stories required plausibility: a real moment when you could have chosen a different path. A time you zagged instead of zigged. A single alteration of the truth can make all the difference. She told Ray she had studied art at Tulane, and after New Orleans she had taught painting in Mobile, and in Tampa after that, where she met the pilot, with whom she spent every summer on St. Thomas in the Virgin Islands in a house without glass in the windows where the water practically lapped against her door. "As close to my bed as we are to the john." She had truthfully studied art at Rice, had met my father as a junior, and had me the following summer. But in her story she was freed from us—freed from my violent birth—and had followed the circumference of the Gulf of Mexico with her eyes intact. In her story she could see. She painted the jasmine sticking through the iron fences along St. Charles Street, and when she opened her Caribbean door she watched the sailfish tack and jibe in the window-blue water beneath her feet. The plane crash was a means of reconciling her fantasy with reality, like the seal on an envelope. She was blind now, but had not always been. And now she was Ray's. He touched her fingers, her hair, reeling her to him. He never once looked my way.

My mother's Drambuie melted the ice and crept up the side of her glass. Ray's whiskey looked like water drained from a rusted pipe. I sipped my Coke, my one glass, sucking the syrup from the ice, down to the last tangy drop, not wanting to ask for a refill, to remind either of them that I was still there. I leaned closer to her, leaning almost against her but not, close enough to feel her heat escaping away from me, trying to gather it all in, every last word of the story I was nowhere a part of.

She was the one to kiss him. She leaned forward on the stool, almost falling into him, and at first I thought she was going to whisper something in his ear. She wrapped her arm around his neck and pressed her mouth to his. The way she closed the space between them made me think lips have an inherent sense of how to come together. When she pulled back Ray did a little nod, congratulating himself for getting this far, and then leaned toward her. His hand came around her back, his beat-up fingers with black streaks in the valleys of the knuckles, and slid up into her hair. My mother let out a little hum. After the year we'd come through, all those recriminating months lost to the kitchen table, I had no way of understanding why she was doing this or what she wanted from it. Revenge? It didn't feel like revenge, and it didn't feel like desire, either. Either way, it was terrible. It was terrible to see this man kissing my mother, and it was terrible to see her kissing him. I had been the one to discover my father's affair with Kay, but then I had seen only the aftermath— the two of them standing together in Kay's window above the garage— not the act itself. What's that line from *Macbeth*? *Horrors in the imagination are worse than fears of real things.* It's a lie. The sound of my mother's lips sucking Ray's was worse than anything I could have imagined.

Ray said, "I know a spot of water not far from here."

"Lake or ocean?" my mother asked.

"Which do you want?"

"Definitely ocean. The Gulf. Not the Bay."

"Okay," he said. "I'll show you."

They stood up, and Ray coiled his arm around her wrist. I said, "Hey, Mom. We should get home. Jill and Dad will be wondering what happened to us."

Ray said, "I'll bring her back later on." He slid his hand from her wrist to her upper-arm, the softer flesh above her elbow. "I'm sure you can find your way home." He started to move her toward the door.

"Let go of her," I said. I could tell she wanted to go with him, but I couldn't let her. How could I let her? "She can't go with you," I said. I tried to pry Ray's fingers from her, but he wouldn't let go. He squeezed her tighter, her flesh coming up between his fingers. My mother said, "Let go, Rowdy," but I wouldn't. I chopped at Ray's elbow, twice, as hard as I could. It was a childish action, the kind of move I used on Jill, but it was all I could think of. "Let go!" I shouted. Ray held on, and I had the quick, dread-filled thought I was going to have to punch him. I'd never punched anyone before, not a real punch. I made a fist and looked him in the face, but Ray was no novice when it came to trouble. Before I could even bend my elbow to raise my hand, I saw his fist come across my mother's body. It caught me just above my left eye. My head snapped back, and my shoulder hit the floor and a sharp pain shot through my neck. My hair landed in something sticky. The floor of the bar was wet and strings of blue and red swam in the puddles, flowing one way and then another, fringed with an erratic glow from the overhead lights. I was an inch from my mother's foot, from the ridges in her ankle, and the tendons plunging into her shoe, and beside it a nearly invisible hair folded into a figure eight, a little infinity. To see this part of her at such proximity, from this height, made her feel far away. The bulb above me widened and twisted out of focus. I reached for my mother's foot, but I couldn't grab it. She was moving away.

Eddie the bartender helped me up. He raked his fingers through the back of my hair and asked if I was okay. I said I was. The bouncer had Ray's arm in a twist behind his back. "Nice one, dickbrain. Punching a kid." Ray didn't argue, or resist. The bouncer hustled him toward the door, and through it.

"You two are out of here, too," Eddie said. I held my mother's hand at first, then, to be safe, I tucked her fingers inside my elbow. The bouncer waited while I unlocked the van and then opened the passenger door for my mother. Before I walked around to the driver's side, he stepped in front of me and said, "I never should have let you in. Eddie's on probation with the TABC. Something like this could cost him his bartender's license. I don't want to see that happen."

"I won't tell," I said.

"You won't tell a soul," he said. "Not a goddamn soul. If anyone asks, you were never here." He wiggled his meaty fingers in my face, the amethyst in his ring catching the glow of the neon Budweiser sign. "Get going."

My mother sat with her arms crossed, her bottom lip between her teeth. "I didn't need your help, Rowdy. You didn't hear me ask for it, did you?"

"He wasn't as nice-looking as he sounded," I said. I held my eye with the heel of my hand, my palm absorbing the throb from my head. "He was going to take you with him. Who knows where you would have ended up."

"I was willing to see where the road took me," she said.

"Mom," I said.

"I don't need looking after. God, you're as bad as everyone else. Find a payphone and I'll call a cab. You can go on home."

"I'm not dropping you off," I said. "I'll take you where you want to go. Want to find another bar?'

"No," she said. She settled back into the seat. "That was just a thought I had on the way. Another way to skin the cat."

"Where to now?" I closed the bad eye and started the engine.

"South," she said. "Just keep heading south."

• • •

South took us through the broken jigsaw of the city, past the darkened, rain-stained churches along Main and the museums surrounding Rice. Then the Medical Center, then the Astrodome. Everything was caked in the hurricane's silty residue, regurgitated slime from the gutters smeared against the curbs and across the grass. Overflowed ditches had receded some, a little, the water line just below the shoulder, two black runways on the periphery of the headlights. I couldn't see much. I turned to avoid a mound of cardboard, two shredded car tires. At one point I thought I saw a dog's legs rising from the water in the ditch beside the shoulder of the road, but I couldn't be sure. Though in the recesses of dark that lay beyond the headlights I was certain something was moving, I couldn't see anything. No McDonald's, no gas stations, no billboards. My mother almost *could* have driven herself; my range of vision was only slightly better than nothing. But with each hesitant revolution of the odometer, each mile that clicked by, I came to approve a little more of the debris. I thought about how every human effort to maintain cleanliness and orderliness—our trash collection services, our underground sewage systems, our landfills out past the edge of town—was nothing more than a way to hide the consequences of living, the fact that we all eat and drink and then piss and shit. Eventually the system had to break down; everything we had siphoned out of sight over the years would come gurgling back. Now the breakdown had come and we were making our way through it. It wouldn't drown us. It was a strange comfort, but my eye was still throbbing and I still didn't know where we were headed, so I took my comfort where I could find it.

The freeway on-ramp was blocked. A sign said all lanes were northbound, away from the water. I stopped the van about six feet from the blockade and stared at the orange-and-white stripes. This was my chance to turn back without my mother suspecting, to ease up onto the freeway and head north in the southbound lane, toward home. But I thought about her story, and a part of me wanted to see the water now. My mother asked, "What's the matter?"

"Nothing," I said. "All the streetlights are out. I'm just making sure the coast is clear." I lifted my foot from the brake and steered around the blockade.

I never went above thirty. It took us almost an hour to reach the bridge to Galveston Island when, all at once, the freeway was without a floor. I held my breath while we rose and plunged and glided back to solid ground. I steered through town and came to the Seawall. Beyond it was the Gulf, the kitchen of the hurricane; I could see the whitened fringe where the water worked the sand, but beyond that, nothing. A hot, black blowing wind. I could hear waves crash against the breakwater, loud as thunder. "We're at the water," I said. "The end of the road."

"Not yet," she said. "Keep going. We're not all the way there yet."

I realized, finally, where she was taking me. Galveston Island is a seahorse with its tail unfurled, the northern island in the thin archipelago shadowing the Texas coast. My grandparents owned a cottage on the southern tip, their vacation home since the days when Galveston was still a fashionable place to take a vacation, before the rich traveled by plane between their properties. Past the Seawall the road along the coast was two lanes, with not much shoulder. The power was out, of course, so the houses remained invisible. Now and then I saw a mailbox in the head-lights, the trunk and tires of a parked car. Palm fronds lay across the asphalt, and sand was smeared everywhere across the road. The water had come this far. The tires pressed into the sand and crunched the palms. The tracks we made were the only evidence that we'd come this way.

The cottage sat nearly at the end of the road, facing the water, a half mile from Hooper's store, where we went for sodas and snacks during the summer. The house was a solid, square box, coffee-brown with white-washed trim and a balcony all the way around, like a ring around Saturn. The building stood atop wooden pillars of such circumference that for years Jill and I measured our growth by how close we came to joining hands around them. The storm shutters had been closed up and locked—Mr. Hooper's son was a caretaker for the dozen or so homes within walking distance of the store. The pillars were water-stained nearly to the floor of the house, but otherwise it looked in reasonable shape.

I parked beneath the back stairs and wearily climbed to the entrance. My mother produced a key and threaded it into the lock. The air smelled like an armpit, hot and moldy. The living room was almost pitch-black, the night sealed out by the shutters. My hands told me that plastic tarps draped the furniture and that the refrigerator was empty. I knew that beyond the living room were the bedrooms and the bathrooms, but my lids were spasming and I felt nauseous and I couldn't bear to go back there. I undraped the sofa and collapsed on it, my elbow peaked across my face to shield me from a light that wasn't there. I heard my mother open-ing the cupboard doors, the silverware sliding in the drawer. I heard a clicking, metal on wood, and a minute or two later she called me to the table saying dinner was ready.

Dinner included one bag of unshelled pistachios, a sleeve of Breton crackers, two jars of D.L. Jardine's Texas martini olives, four soft Oreos that turned to dust in my mouth, three cans of soured tonic, and a bottle of red wine, I didn't know what kind. Each taste was new in my mouth, unimpeded by vision. I was hungry and ate fast. My mother chewed slowly, snapping her crackers in half.

"So," she said. "How do you like sitting around in the dark?"

"It makes me tired. But I'm getting used to it."

"You do get used to it," she said. "It becomes your friend. I hardly think about seeing anymore."

"What about colors and lines? Can't you still see those?"

"Sometimes. But lines aren't lines like you're used to. I don't have any reference. They're more like separations."

I'd never apologized for blinding her throughout all the years I'd lived with the knowledge that I was the cause. We almost never talked about what she could see and what she couldn't. I said, "I'm sorry I wrecked your eyes. That you're this way because of me."

"Oh, Rowdy," she said. "Hush up about that. I'm not any way because of you. It wasn't your fault."

"But it was, in a way at least."

"No," she said. "You were just there when it happened. Sometimes that's enough to be guilty, but not for you. You need to stop feeling guilty about it, okay? Being blind is not the last word of my story."

"Okay."

"Promise," she said. "Say, 'I do not feel guilty for my mother being blind. I did not cause it. It was not my fault.'"

"I do not feel guilty for my mother being blind. I did not cause it. It was not my fault," I said. It was a conversation we'd never had, not once, and having it made me feel strangely better. Maybe it was having come through the storm, or my secret pride at having fended off Ray, but whatever it was I felt that latent tightening of my bones whenever I was around her begin to ease. It was as though a fever had broken, the mercury just beginning to ride back down, the shivers turning to sweats. I was sweating. It was hot in there.

"Good," she said. "If anything, I've come to prefer it. It keeps my thinking cap on. It's everyone leading me around I've grown so tired of."

I'd had two glasses of wine and felt courageous. "What's going to happen with Dad?"

"Your father's found the Lord. That should see him through. He feels better when he has something to believe in."

"I'm talking about what will happen with you and him."

"So am I."

"So, that's it? It's a done deal?"

"Oh, Rowdy. It's been a heck of a day. We'll have better weather tomorrow. Things will make better sense."

Things already did. We'd come all this way, through a hurricane, and had ended up at a place I liked. The cottage was roomy, built-to-last, hardly used throughout most of the year. If Glenda couldn't knock it down, nothing could. With the windows open the breeze blew right through, cooling down the entire house, and nights smelled of ocean: salt percolating through the floor and glass into the lampshades and pillows and bed linens; at the end of a day in the summer my skin smelled of sunshine. I could see my mother living here, her mottled view of the sea speckled with drying seaweed, and fish, sand crabs making their way from the sand to the sea each night. She could follow the handrails of the planked walkway down to the beach and stand in the tide and find her way back all on her own. Hooper's would deliver, and in the spring and summer and early fall there would be people around her, music and kids playing tag in the tide. Jill and I would come see her on weekends, with our friends, drink Cokes from a big cooler packed with ice, put off going back on Sunday.

My mother and I drank that entire bottle of wine, and that night I got drunk for the first time in my life. I lay down on the couch with my head spinning, and soon I was dreaming, about bonfires in the sand, oysters on the half shell, and the wind, the wind—gulps of open, unimpeded air. I may have dreamt this, too, but sometime during the night I felt my mother's hands against my face. Her callused tips traced the outline of my eyebrows and nose, my earlobes and chin, the crown of my head. I felt her lips, or what I dreamt were her lips, in the same places, here, and here, taking me in, one last time. Had this happened at home, I might have sat up frightened, but here I didn't. I didn't feel aroused either, nothing like that; I didn't know what was happening, nor did I wake up knowing it had happened. I have merely a vague memory of it taking place. I cling to its possibility.

• • •

The weather was better in the morning. The sun worked through the tight slits of the storm shutters, illuminating in fractured glimpses the room where I had passed the night: the tarp-covered furniture, the dusty fireplace, the old Zenith the size of a fireplace. A note on the table, in my mother's scribbled, blind-woman's handwriting said, *Got a ride into town for real food. Meet up later.* But when I stepped out onto the balcony she stood at the bottom of the planked walkway leading from the cottage to the beach, wearing a navy-blue bathing suit she must've dug out of the bedroom drawer. Clouds speckled the sky as though stones in a shallow lake, sturdy enough to support human weight. The tide came right to the edge of the walkway, returning to shore what Glenda had stolen the day before, Igloo coolers and collapsible chairs, buckets and shovels, cans of motor oil and shredded Lone Star flags, encrusted in yellow-brown foam. I walked barefoot down to where she stood. "Up early," I said.

"Not early enough it seems," she said. "You sleep okay?"

"Hot. Hard to breathe in there. But okay."

"Good." She reached her hand out to me and I took it. She felt her way up my arm to my face. "I appreciate you making the trip down here."

"No problem," I said. "Did you go to the store?"

"Not yet."

"Want me to go for us?"

"Sure," she said. "That would be fine." She stared out at the horizon dotted with oil platforms, tankers delayed by the storm now heading for the mouth of the Channel, gliding on the edge of the earth. The sun was on her face. She took a deep breath and held it, and allowed it to leak out through her nose. "Take the money from my purse. Buy whatever you're hungry for. I'm going for a swim."

"In this water? It's full of disease."

"I'm here, Rowdy. I'm swimming. Go get something to eat."

I watched her wade in, the brown and frothy surf around her ankles, then her knees, then her neck. She arched her back and dove forward, disappearing beneath the surface before coming up and starting to swim. She stroked forward for a moment and then lifted her head and turned toward the shore and waved. Not so that I could see where she was, but to tell me to go on, get going. I climbed the walkway back to the cottage, trusting her to find her own way back.

· · ·

She didn't do it that time. She didn't keep swimming until she was too far out. She didn't do that with me there. But a few weeks later, she did.

Or at least we think she did. Mr. Hooper went to the cottage to deliver her groceries and found the doors and windows open, a towel hanging over the balcony railing, my mother nowhere in sight. By then it was after Labor Day and the beaches, especially at that end of the island, were almost empty and no one who was there reported seeing her. Nor did anyone see her walking along the road. A six-foot-one blind woman would have been hard to miss. No one reported any strange cars on the road, no taxis either. The only thing missing from the cottage was the bathing suit she wore that morning. Her clothes were folded in a corner of the closet, and her purse was on the table, everything in it except for some of the cash. She had eighty-seven dollars left, another dollar and a half of change floating around the bottom. So swimming is our best guess, though if it was an accident, if she simply got pointed in the wrong direction, swimming out when she thought she was swimming in, she should have washed ashore somewhere. But that never happened.

Why did she do it? All of this happened a long time ago, in another time, when the world was just beginning to understand depression. Even my father, the neuroscientist, who knew almost everything about epilepsy, knew almost nothing about it. My grandparents used to joke that his research was a few inches too high; he should have studied the eye instead of the brain and found a cure for blindness. Now we see he studied the right thing all along, just not in the right way. But that was the case for all of us when it came to my mother; we all studied the wrong thing. We chalked up everything to blindness—every silence, every sadness, every hour lost to the kitchen table. Despite all the years we lived with her, despite every filial obligation of childhood, of marriage and friendship, despite the habituation of time, none of us wanted to look past her blindness for an explanation. As though she could be explained. The real question is why do people do anything? Why do people jump out of airplanes? What good does that do in the world? What stroke of ennoblement or charity is accomplished by challenging the force that holds Earth in line with the sun and the moon? And when it comes to people taking themselves away—despite the hordes who have done so and the myriad ways in which they have made their exits—is there ever a satisfying explanation? Is it ever, in the end, explainable?

What I do know is that she had been telling the story of her disappearing all along: the girl washed out her window, the swimmer crossing the

English Channel, the floating house in the Caribbean. She was moving herself to another shore, she was saying, and it was all right. She'd been going for a long time—long before my father ever set his hand on Kay's back—edging her way farther and farther out, testing to see if she could fade into the woods behind our house, or could slip away from us in a crowded mall, or sit so still we'd forget she was there.

· · ·

We were already forgetting. That morning, while I stood watching my mother swim, Jill was pedaling her bike down our street. My father was pacing the kitchen, talking on the phone and didn't notice her go. In her backpack she carried three bottles of water, a peanut-butter sandwich, a candy bar, a sandwich baggie filled with change. She had studied the maps. She stayed on the freeway feeder roads, following the path my mother and I had taken the day before, into the city, weaving through the downtown grid just past three that afternoon, using the toilet in the lobby of a Holiday Inn, and again in a Ramada in Pasadena, riding east to Deer Park and across the corner of La Porte before standing up on her pedals to climb the Fred Hartman Bridge, her tires bouncing over the grating, pointing her chin over the railing to see the Ship Channel slide by in sandy streaks beneath her. On the other side was Baytown. The Exxon refinery torched holes in the clouds. Jill's legs and throat burned, and her distal pulse pounded in her wrist, but she knew she was close. An hour later, more than fifty miles from our house and twelve hours gone, she peddled the short rise up Kay's mother's driveway, its cracking cinderblock walls stained with algae, the grass burnt to straw from the summer and now drowned in Glenda's rain. She could see Kay in the living room, thumbing through the newspaper, figuring out a way to go back to nursing school. She didn't knock. She waited without moving, controlling her breath and the overwhelming need to holler, waiting for Kay to turn her head and see her straddling her bike in the driveway, to come open the front door for her. Only when Kay said her name did she throw down her bike and backpack and run, locking Kay's neck inside her arms, sobbing and swearing, *I'm not going back. I'm not going back.*

When my mother did not come back, my father did not force Jill to, either. She started school in Baytown in September, told her classmates Kay was her mother, and no one ever questioned it. By the next summer my father was in East Texas, in a little town called Pineland, teaching at Victory Bible College and telling his students and colleagues how he met Jesus and left behind his adulterous life. I was allowed to stay in the Stevensons' guest bedroom while I finished out my senior year. The couple who bought our house tore out most of the remaining pines and rolled out fresh sod, pressure-washed the algae from the bricks, planted all sorts of color in the beds. They worked outside on the weekends while I mowed the Stevensons' lawn. They waved to me, but never invited me over. Jill says she can no longer remember how our house used to look when we lived there, but I can. Having watched our house change a little each week, I can reconstruct everything they took away. I can walk to the very brick on the side of the garage where I etched my name with a pocket knife, even though it's been sanded smooth. I remember what Jill, and my father, and Kay, forget. I put back what they take out. Since I'm the keeper of these stories, I decide how they are told, who speaks and who doesn't. I get to say how this all turns out.

. . .

Go back to the place where a decision was made, that lighthouse in your nostalgia. The time you zagged instead of zigged. Head southeast instead of northwest. Follow the circumference of your existence away from the state you know, into Louisiana, or Mississippi, or Florida, to a strip of white sand sloped by the wind and the waves. Behind you the dunes are poked through with maiden cane, and behind them is the narrow highway leading straight back to the town at the bottom of your map. Watch the horizon's bent edge until you see my mother swimming toward you, at first far off, like a gull flapping over the tide, then nearer, her loping stroke irregular but steady, one hand and then the other. Remember how she prepared for this, a year of starving herself of conversation and contact and the need to see something different, her courage drawn from a woman swimming back and forth across the English Channel. The surf retracts and surges, pushing my mother to her feet, and she walks out of the water naked, her bathing suit disintegrated miles ago, her skin a wrinkled sack too heavy for her bones. Her first steps on dry land are the first steps toward her new life, the final and farthest corner of my family's diaspora rather than its exploded core. She is unassisted, unlooked-after, and unafraid. See her. And forgive me for everything I've left out, for everything I didn't see, for standing there that morning with my hand planed across my eyes, watching her swim out until she was a bedazzled speck at the limit of my vision, a flaw in my retina, just before she reached into that place I could not see, and one last time, for the last time, disappeared.

ACKNOWLEDGMENTS

THE STORIES IN THIS COLLECTION have appeared, often in different form, in the following publications: "Moonland on Fire": *Mid-American Review* (Spring 2007); "Landslide": *Best Christian Short Stories*, edited by Bret Lott (Nashville: Westbow Press, 2006); "Deep in the Heart" (as "Flesh and Blood"): *Black Warrior Review* (Spring 2004); "The Eyes to See" (as "Enucleation"): *Alaska Quarterly Review* (Fall/Winter 2007); "Sweet Texas Angel": *Shenandoah* (Spring 2006); "Consequences of Knowledge" (as "Look Here Boy"): *Northwest Review* (Spring 2005); "Testimony" (as "The Newest Thing in the World"): *Image* (Summer 2007); and "The End of the Straight and Narrow": *Ascent* (Spring 2007). Thanks to the editors of these publications, especially Michael Czyzniejewski, Bret Lott, R. T. Smith, John Witte, Greg Wolfe, and W. Scott Olsen. Thanks also to Kathryn Lang, George Ann Ratchford, and Keith Gregory at SMU Press. This book wouldn't have happened without Kathryn's advocacy, intelligence, and perspicacious attention.

For steering my initial research, I'm grateful to Dr. Julia Kleinschmidt at the University of Utah Moran Eye Center and Chris Unander and Suki May-Miller at the Utah Division of Services for the Blind and Visually Impaired. Schalee Lodge courageously guided me through her world of sudden vision loss, prosthetic eyes, and three-dimensional painting. Dr. Aaron Rowland showed me around his lab and explained the basics of pharmacology and neuroscience. I am also thankful for our time together in the Utah mountains, and to Jenny Rowland for being a part of the action from the beginning.

I owe extra helpings of gratitude to Sam Pickering, Mary Kenagy-Mitchell, Alyson Hagy (long live the Blue Ox!), and especially Melanie Rae Thon. And to my legion of family and friends: the McGlynns, the

Thompsons, the Sagers, Jon and Mindy Armstrong, Stephen Tuttle, Nicole Walker, David Durden, Rich and Jess Sarkisian, Joanne Johnson, Karen Hoffmann, Garth Bond, Faith Barrett, Tim Spurgin, and Gretchen Revie.

Finally, something more than gratitude is owed to my sons, Galen and Hayden, whose unexpected arrivals changed everything, and to Katherine, whose faith and love is never ceasing. *My cup overflows.*

DAVID McGLYNN'S fiction and creative non-fiction have appeared in *Alaska Quarterly Review, Image, Mid-American Review, Shenandoah,* and other literary journals. He received his M.F.A. and Ph.D. from the University of Utah. He teaches at Lawrence University in Appleton, Wisconsin, where he lives with his wife and sons.